Hair
of the
Dog

A MELANIE TRAVIS MYSTERY

by
Laurien Berenson

k

KENSINGTON BOOKS
http://www.kensingtonbooks.com

KENSINGTON BOOKS are published by

Kensington Publishing Corp.
850 Third Avenue
New York, NY 10022

First Kensington Hardcover Printing: November, 1997
First Kensington Paperback Printing: November, 1998
10 9 8 7 6 5 4 3 2

Printed in the United States of America

*Any author would be lucky to have an editor
as kind, as caring, and as supportive
as John Scognamiglio.*

This one's for you, John.

❦❀ *One* ❀❧

At my Aunt Peg's house, there's often a pot of chicken simmering on the stove. Visitors, however, shouldn't get their hopes up. At least not two-legged ones. The chicken is for the dogs. Peg breeds Standard Poodles and has about a dozen, all of whom eat like royalty. Humans have to fend for themselves.

Which was why I was so surprised when she called one morning in late June and told me she wanted to throw a party. "Maybe a backyard barbecue," she said. "Something simple."

Simple? I wasn't sure Aunt Peg understood the meaning of the concept. The summer before, she'd finagled me into helping find her missing stud dog by insisting that it would be simple. Then last fall, she'd initiated me into the joys of dog ownership by assuring me that that, too, would be simple. Is it any wonder I didn't rush to volunteer my services?

No matter. Aunt Peg merely assumed I'd help out and went on making plans. She's nearing sixty, and in all those years I doubt that anyone has ever said no to her and gotten away with it.

Peg lives in a big old farmhouse on several acres of land that even I had to admit would make the perfect setting for an outdoor party. Her husband, Max, had died the year before, and if you didn't count the dog shows she attended several weekends a month to exhibit her Poodles, she'd done almost no socializing since. Even though I knew it would end up costing me, it was nice to hear her talk about inviting friends over.

"I was thinking fifty people or so," she said blithely. "There are three shows in the area that weekend, and everybody will be around. I'm sure we'll draw a crowd."

I didn't doubt it. Dog people travel a fair amount in their pursuit of the biggest wins and the best judges, and with a trio of important shows in the neighborhood, exhibitors from all over would be converging in Connecticut for the Fourth of July weekend.

"You'll bring Davey, of course," she told me. "And Sam."

Davey was my son, five years old and very full of himself. He'd started morning day camp at the beginning of the week and I was due to pick him up in an hour.

Sam Driver was a friend. Actually he was a good bit more than that, but I still hadn't figured out how to refer to our relationship in polite conversation. Calling him my boyfriend seemed to imply that I was still a girl, which, at thirty-one, I most assuredly was not. Significant other was definitely too unwieldy. Lover got to the heart of the matter, but seemed a little blunt. Not that Aunt Peg would have minded. She's a great fan of Sam's, and a strong believer in speaking one's mind on any and all occasions.

"Faith isn't invited," she told me firmly. "There will simply be too much going on."

"Right," I agreed.

Faith was Davey's and my Standard Poodle. A gift from Aunt Peg, she was fourteen months old and a true adolescent: rambunctious, willful, and growing what, to my mind, was entirely too much hair. Otherwise known as a Poodle show coat.

All forty-five pounds of her was lying draped across my lap as I spoke on the phone. I glanced down and Faith thumped her black tail obligingly. Intelligent as Poodles are, I imagine she knew we were talking about her.

"Chicken and ribs," Aunt Peg was saying. "Mounds of them. Nobody eats dog show food if they can help it. People will be starving by the time they get to us. Then ice cream and brownies for dessert. That sounds easy enough, doesn't it?"

Listening to Aunt Peg chatter on, I almost believed that the party might come together without a hitch. Of course that was before either of us knew that before the weekend was over, one of the guests would be dead.

"Will there be presents?" asked Davey. "And games and goody bags?"

I'd just finished dressing him in a perfectly presentable outfit, and with only minutes to go until we left for Aunt

Peg's, I was hoping he wouldn't find any dirt to attach himself to. With his sandy curls and chubby cheeks, Davey has the innocent look of a Botticelli cherub. He also has the energy, and potential for damage, of a small tornado.

We were in the kitchen, where I was mixing Faith's food. "Sorry, sport, not this time. This is a grown-up party, with eating and drinking, and people to talk to."

"That doesn't sound like much fun." At his age, my son's idea of fun was anything involving cars, loud noises, or fast action—preferably a combination of the three. "Will there be other kids?"

"Not many."

Even that was probably an overstatement. Most of the people Aunt Peg had invited were exhibitors and judges, who would come straight from the Farmington dog show. Aunt Peg had never had children of her own, and while she enjoyed Davey, I knew she held the opinion that one child in the vicinity was often more than enough.

"Sam will be there," I said, setting the dog food bowl down on the floor. "That's someone you know."

Faith sauntered over to have a look at the offering. She was full grown now physically, if not mentally, and the top of her head was nearly level with my waist. A Standard Poodle, she was the largest of the three varieties: strong, solid, and fully capable of retrieving game, as her ancestors had been bred to do. Not that there was much call for that in the suburbs.

"Go on," I said. "Eat."

Faith sent me a look. If I'd been in the habit of ascribing human traits to dogs, I'd have sworn she rolled her eyes.

"She doesn't like it," Davey chortled. "She wants pizza."

"She does not," I said firmly. I nudged the bowl closer to Faith's muzzle with my toe. Grudgingly she took a mouthful of the food and rolled it around her tongue.

She'd always been a finicky eater, and there wasn't an ounce of fat on her. When she'd turned a year old, Aunt Peg had clipped her into the continental trim, which is a modern descendant of a traditional German hunting clip and is required in the show ring. Since the trim mandates a large mane of hair on the front half of the body, and a hindquarter that is shaved mostly down to the skin, it was easy to see just how lean she was. Luckily for me, Faith was taking six months off from showing to grow into her new trim, so her weight had yet to become an issue.

I put the dog food in the refrigerator and patted the top of the Poodle's crate. Obligingly, Faith strolled in, circled once, and lay down. When she was a puppy, we'd used the crate as an aid in housebreaking and to keep her from chewing when we weren't home. Now that she was older and knew how to behave, I usually left the door open. Faith had come to think of the crate as her den, and was perfectly content to nap there while we were gone.

Davey and I live in North Stamford in a snug cape on a small lot. The street was developed in the fifties, and looks it. What we gained in function, we unfortunately sacrificed in charm. Aunt Peg is one town away in Greenwich. Her house is set back from the road in the midst of a meadow studded with wildflowers. A veranda wraps around three sides of the house, and the roof is gabled. A small kennel building out back holds the Poodles Peg is conditioning for the show ring. Though she has neighbors, none of their houses are visible. It's a far cry from my road, where in the summer, with the windows open, I can smell what the people next door are having for dinner.

Davey and I had been at Aunt Peg's earlier in the day to help with the preparations, but now, when we arrived for the second time, the party was already in progress. Cars and vans, most filled with crates and grooming equipment, already lined both sides of the back country road. Since the show site was an hour away, I knew that those who'd stayed through Best in Show had yet to arrive. Bearing in mind what Peg had said about everyone being hungry, I hoped she'd ordered enough food.

As soon as we got out of the car, Davey ran on ahead. Following the sound of voices and the smell of barbecued chicken, he raced around the back of the house. In pursuit of brownies, no doubt.

At six-thirty, it was still fully light. As I followed my son to Peg's backyard, where throngs of people had already begun to congregate around the tables that held food and drinks, I could see perfectly well where I was going. So when I bumped into Sam Driver from behind, and managed to insinuate my body along his, I couldn't exactly say it was an accident.

"Not now," he whispered without turning around. "Melanie will be here any minute. I'll meet you later."

"Hmmph," I muttered, wrapping my arms around him and snuggling my face between his shoulder blades. "How did you know it was me?"

Sam turned, grinning. He was holding a cold bottle of beer in each hand. "It might have had something to do with that three-foot streak of energy that preceded you. Here, one of these is yours."

I popped the top and took a long, icy swallow. It tasted so good going down that I could feel the tingle in my toes. Or maybe that was Sam's doing. It's been a year and he still has that effect on me.

Sam is tall, and built along lean lines; the kind of man who jogs but wouldn't dream of lifting weights. He has sun-streaked hair the color of wheat and eyes as blue as the Caribbean. There have been other men who have made my motor race, but none who have accomplished it with Sam's casual, graceful ease.

"Speaking of the streak," I said. "Which way did he go?"

Sam pointed toward the back door. "I think he was heading for the kitchen. Does he know something we don't?"

"Brownies, stashed inside for later. You know Aunt Peg's sweet tooth."

"There you are!" called a loud voice. "It's about time!"

"Speak of the devil," I muttered.

Sam grasped a bit of skin in a place where I wished there hadn't been any excess, and pinched a gentle reprimand. Next time I'd volunteer him to come early and help set up.

"Hi, Aunt Peg," I said, turning to greet her. "How's everything going?"

"So far, so good. We've really pulled a crowd. Scuttlebutt has it that Austin Beamish's Golden is going to win Best, but no one's arrived yet to confirm that."

Golden was shorthand for Golden Retriever; Best was Best in Show. At its highest levels, the world of dog shows is actually a rather small place. Everybody knows everybody else, from the judges to the exhibitors to the top professional handlers. They've all long since scoped out the strengths and weaknesses of one another's dogs, and they all know which judges tend to prefer what traits. I wasn't surprised that results were being predicted before they'd had a chance to happen; I'd seen other exhibitors do the same weeks in advance of a show on the basis of a judging schedule alone.

Peg lifted the lid of the large cooler beneath the picnic table. She's a tall woman, and had to bend way down to reach. Her gray hair, worn pulled back in a bun for as long as I could remember, had recently been cut and now fell in waves to just below her ears. She tucked back a strand that tumbled forward, and she frowned at the nearly empty cooler.

"Sam, there's another case of beer in the refrigerator in the garage. Do you suppose . . . ?"

"Of course. Be right back." Before he'd even finished speaking, Sam was already heading off to do her bidding. Aunt Peg tends to have that effect on people.

"This is quite a gathering," I said, looking around. I'd been going to the dog shows with Aunt Peg for a year now. Some of her guests I knew, and many others looked familiar. "How many people did you say you were expecting?"

"Too many." Peg sighed, but she didn't look entirely displeased. "At least I had the foresight to call the caterer yesterday and tell him to double the order."

There was a small commotion as a new group of people arrived, two middle-aged men with a strikingly attractive woman walking between them. Aunt Peg followed the direction of my gaze. "Good. If they've arrived, that means the show's over and we'll be able to find out who won."

"Who are they?"

"The couple is Vivian and Ron Pullman. They live in Katonah and show some very good Chows. Their dog won the Non-Sporting group today. The man who came in with them is Austin Beamish."

"The one whose Golden Retriever was supposed to win Best in Show?"

"Quite right. With Ron's Chow winning a group as well, they'd have been competing against each other. Still, everyone looks perfectly chummy." Aunt Peg grinned slyly. "I wonder if that means they both lost. Come on over, and I'll introduce you."

I followed in Aunt Peg's wake as she went to greet her new guests. From a distance, I'd wondered briefly which of the two men was Vivian's husband. Now, as we drew closer, she laughed at something somebody said and twined her arm around the waist of the good-looking man standing to her right. Ron Pullman had long legs and wide, linebacker's shoulders. He was casually dressed in khakis and a button-down shirt with the cuffs rolled back, but his clothes fit his large frame impeccably.

Vivian wasn't a small woman, but beside her husband, she looked petite. Her tawny hair curled in artful disarray and her luminous skin was flawless. She was younger than Ron by at least ten years. That, and the expression in his eyes when he looked at her, were enough to make me wonder if she was a second wife.

"Ron, Viv, Austin!" Peg held out her arms wide. "I'm so glad you could make it."

All three smiled, but it was Austin Beamish who stepped forward and smoothly planted a kiss on Aunt Peg's cheek. He wasn't a physically impressive man, shorter than Peg by at least an inch and bald save for a fringe of rust-colored hair around the base of his skull. It didn't seem to matter. The best show dogs all have presence, and Austin Beamish had it too. Ron struck me as someone who might have played football in college; Austin looked much too intelligent to ever allow himself to be blindsided by a tackle.

"Thank you for having us. This looks wonderful." The merest trace of a southern drawl coated Vivian's smooth-as-honey voice. She lifted her nose to the wind and sniffed delicately. "Do I smell ribs?"

"You can take the girl out of the country . . ." Ron teased. "Her mouth's been watering since we got off the Merritt Parkway."

"In a minute, you can help yourselves," said Peg. "But first—"

"Don't even ask," Austin broke in good-naturedly. "Robert Janney's Peke skunked us both. I don't suppose you have a neon sign around here where we could post the news?"

"Don't worry, if you told the group at the gate, it's probably traveled around the whole yard already." Peg motioned me forward and performed the introductions, and we shook hands all around.

Vivian's grasp was surprisingly firm, and Austin added to his by throwing an arm around my shoulder and giving me a squeeze.

"You mustn't mind him," said Ron. "He's like that with all the girls."

"If you've got it, flaunt it," said Austin.

"Oh?" I lifted a brow. "What have you got?"

Austin roared with laughter. "Everything I need," he said firmly. "And then some."

"Don't get him started," said Viv. "At least not while I still have an empty stomach." Linking her arms through both men's, Viv led them toward two big grills, where an abundant supply of ribs and chicken were basting in barbecue sauce.

Now that she mentioned it, my own stomach was feeling pretty empty. I saw that Davey had settled himself in an Adirondack chair. He had a plate holding two ears of buttered corn and a generous mound of baked beans balanced on the big wooden arm. I told myself that it was better than brownies and was about to go get some food myself, when Aunt Peg muttered something under her breath.

Peg was raised in genteel times. Coming from her, "Damn!" meant business.

A new group of guests who'd just arrived from the show was strolling around the side of the house. Among them was Barry Turk, a Poodle handler with low professional standards and even less moral character. I'd visited his kennel when I was searching for Aunt Peg's missing Poodle and found it to be dark, cramped, and filled with dogs that barked incessantly. Turk's prices were right, however, and he did his share of winning in the ring, so he never seemed to lack for clients.

"Don't tell me you invited him," I said, surprised. Turk was not one of Aunt Peg's favorite people.

"I most certainly did not. Obviously he tagged along with everybody else."

Turk hung back for a moment as the group he was with moved on. I saw why when a slender woman, stylishly dressed, hurried around the house and caught up with him. Turk reached out and took her hand.

"Oh, Lord," said Peg, sounding as though she were truly hoping for divine intervention.

"She looks familiar." I frowned, trying to place the woman.

"That's Alicia Devane. You've probably seen her at the shows. She and Barry have been living together since last fall."

I gazed at Alicia with new interest. She was attractive in a quiet sort of way, her dark hair bobbed to just below chin length, her features even and unremarkable. All in all, she looked perfectly normal. That being the case, I wondered what she was doing with a jerk like Barry Turk.

I would have asked Aunt Peg, but it was clear her attention was elsewhere. She was standing on her toes, her gaze searching avidly through the assembled crowds. Considering that Peg's height already placed her above most of the guests, I took this to mean that it was a matter of some urgency.

"What's the matter?" I asked.

"Maybe nothing," she said, sounding relieved. "I don't see Bill. Maybe he's not here."

"Bill?"

"Bill Devane. Alicia's husband."

I told you it wasn't going to be simple.

❧* Two *❧

"Alicia's *husband?* I thought you just told me she was living with Barry."

"She is. She left Bill to move in with Barry, which tends to make things very awkward, if you see what I mean."

I did.

"Bill gave her a divorce, but it was clear he didn't want to. They haven't spoken since, but I've always had the impression that he would still take her back if only she would ask him to."

I found myself looking around at the guests as well, though I hadn't a clue what Alicia's ex-husband looked like. "Did you invite Bill Devane?"

"Use your eyes, Melanie. It looks like I invited just about everybody who was at the dog show. Bill's a sporting dog judge. I believe he had rather a large assignment today. With any luck, all that judging wore him out and he went home."

"Sporting dogs?" I thought for a moment. "Didn't you

say Austin Beamish was showing a Golden Retriever? Maybe he would know."

"Quite right." Peg deftly caught Austin's eye and gave a discreet wave. He excused himself from the people he was talking to and headed our way. He was carrying a plate filled with fried chicken and potato salad. The aroma made my stomach rumble.

"Wonderful party, Peg. But I see I've forgotten my manners. Are you looking for someone to escort you through the buffet line?"

"Maybe later," said Peg, understandably distracted. "I was wondering if you'd seen Bill Devane?"

"Earlier at the show, yes, of course. He was the judge that gave Midas the group. We spoke briefly afterward, and he mentioned that he had another assignment tomorrow. I believe he was heading home. Were you expecting him?"

"No, not necessarily. It's just that Barry Turk's arrived—"

"And he has Alicia with him. I see your problem." Austin nodded. "I think you'll be all right as far as Bill is concerned. However, if Barry and Ron should get together . . ."

"Dear Lord." Aunt Peg groaned. "I'd forgotten all about that."

"What?" I asked.

"Ron Pullman had a specials dog with Barry last winter," said Peg. "It was rather a nice Chow, and he did quite a bit of winning with it."

A specials dog is one that has already accumulated the points necessary to be awarded the title of champion.

Most dogs are retired once they've "finished," but specials dogs are those beautiful and talented individuals that continue to be campaigned, chasing the elusive glory of the group wins and the top prize, Best in Show.

Class dogs—those looking to win points toward their championships—were the backbone of a professional handler's business, but specials dogs were their tickets to fame and fortune.

"Yes?" I prompted. Clearly, there was more to the story than that.

"Last April, Ron snatched the dog away. There was never any explanation given, at least not one that the rest of us heard. It wouldn't have been so bad if he'd retired Leo, but he didn't. Ron gave the dog to Crawford, who's won even more with him."

Crawford Langley was another professional handler. I'd known him for a year now, our relationship evolving slowly into friendship over time. Crawford was an old hand at the dog show game. Skillful and experienced, he'd made his mark in a time when dedication to hard work was considered a more valuable trait than the ability to cut corners without getting caught.

Over the winter, Crawford had been specialing a Dalmatian belonging to one of the members of Aunt Peg's kennel club. When that dog had gone home in the spring, there'd been talk that Crawford was thinking of retiring, but once again he'd managed to bounce back, coming up with yet another good dog.

Now that I knew where Crawford's Chow special had come from, I was beginning to understand the problem.

In dog show circles, it's considered the ultimate insult to take a dog away from one handler and give it to another. It implies that the first handler's skills aren't good enough, that for the amount of money being spent, better results could be had elsewhere. It was bad enough when a handler lost a class dog, but specials had high visibility. Turk had not only been fired, he'd had to endure the insult publicly.

"That's not all," said Austin. "Ever since Ron moved the dog, Turk has been bad-mouthing him to anyone who'll listen. He claims there's a bill still outstanding that Ron refuses to pay."

"Is that true?" I asked.

"Probably not," said Peg. "But Barry Turk isn't the sort of man to let the truth distract him when he thinks a lie would work to his advantage."

"Ron's been livid over the whole business," said Austin. "At least at the shows Turk's had the good sense to avoid him. If they meet here tonight, we'll see some fireworks."

"Terrific," I said, biting back a laugh. "Is there anyone else we're hoping Barry Turk doesn't run into?"

Aunt Peg snorted indelicately. "You might as well add me to the list. Everything about that man rubs me the wrong way. He's showing a Standard Poodle bitch for Rona Peters that's due in season any time now, and Rona wants the bitch bred to my dog, Joker. I'll have to deal with him when the time comes, but until then . . ."

"Say no more," Austin said gallantly. "If you like, I'd be happy to ask him to leave."

"Thank you for the offer." Peg was still frowning. "I'd

rather not cause a scene. If we're lucky, Alicia will keep Barry in line and they won't stay long."

Austin went back to his friends and Peg and I headed over to the picnic tables, where the caterers had set out a sumptuous spread. Earlier, the day had been warm and muggy, but now the night air was cooling rapidly. A quarter moon was on the rise and the odor of wood smoke hung in the air. Crickets trilled in the meadow, a backdrop to the pleasant hum of conversation. For the moment, the party seemed capable of running itself. Before the next potential crisis erupted, I was going to grab my chance and eat.

Behind the tables that held the food were two long barbecue grills. One was being tended by a young man with the name of the catering company stenciled across the front of his T-shirt. An older man I hadn't seen before stood beside the other. He had a full head of gray hair, sharply defined features, and wore a jacket and tie beneath his apron. Holding a drink in one hand, he wielded his tongs efficiently with the other. He didn't look like part of the catering crew, but he did look as though he were having a wonderful time.

"Douglas!" cried Peg. "There you are. I wondered where you'd gotten to."

"Always happy to help out." The man smiled cheerfully. "It seems there was a bit of an emergency. Ice melting out in the truck or some such. I volunteered to fill in until things got sorted out."

"Melanie, I'd like you to meet a friend of mine, Douglas Brannigan. Douglas, this is my niece, Melanie."

"Nice to meet you," I said, extending a hand without thinking.

Douglas never lost a beat. He simply extended the tongs to meet my fingers. I took them and we shook. I like a man with a sense of humor. Besides, that gave me a chance to lick the barbecue sauce off my fingertips. The way things were going, that might be the closest I'd get to food all night.

"It's my pleasure," said Douglas. His voice was deep and gravelly. "I've heard so much about you."

"You have?" I glanced at Peg, who did her best to look innocent.

"And your son too. Davey, right? I believe I gave him a drumstick a few minutes ago."

"Thank you," I said uncertainly. I was sure we'd never met before, so why would Aunt Peg have been talking about me to him? Figuring he'd come to the party from the dog show along with everyone else, I asked, "What kind of dogs do you have?"

"I don't have any, actually. Although in this crowd, I'm finding that a dangerous thing to admit. Your aunt is trying to interest me in a Poodle."

Nothing new there. Aunt Peg thought everyone ought to have a Poodle, preferably Standard. It was a bias she came by naturally.

"So far I'm holding out, though," Douglas continued. "At my age, I'm too old to get started with something like that."

"Pish," said Peg. "You're not old. You're just stubborn."

Douglas laughed heartily, and I looked back and forth between them. Peg's cheeks were flushed becomingly and a smile lit her features. Belatedly, I realized that it wasn't only her hair that was different. My aunt, who lived in blue jeans, was wearing a silk shirtwaist dress—and lipstick. I'd thought she'd dressed up in honor of the party, but maybe not . . .

"How long have you two known each other?" I asked, directing the question to Douglas. Peg tends to shade the truth when it suits her purposes. She's very good at telling me only what she wants me to know.

"Just about a month," he said, lifting a side of ribs and deftly basting it with sauce. "We met in Greenwich. Bumped right into each other."

Peg nodded. "What Douglas is too much of a gentleman to tell you is that I ran into his car with mine. You know how hard it is to get a parking space on Greenwich Avenue. I saw one opening up and didn't stop to look and see if anyone else wanted it too."

Like maybe someone who might have had the right of way? I wondered. Aunt Peg was a very impatient driver with a rather heavy foot on the gas pedal. Woe to anyone who got between her and where she thought she was going.

"I hope nobody was hurt?"

"Only a ding and a couple of scratches," said Douglas. "It didn't seem worth bothering the insurance companies over."

"So he suggested we work out an equitable solution over a cup of coffee," Aunt Peg continued. "I thought that was an excellent idea."

They looked at each other and smiled.

"Here you go. I'll take that!" Another young man wearing a shirt bearing the caterer's logo came hurrying over to the grill.

"You're certain you have everything under control?"

Reluctantly Douglas handed over the tongs and pulled off his apron. "I'd be happy to stay on if you need me."

"Thanks, we're all set now."

"Perfect timing," said Aunt Peg. "Let's go eat."

As we went to get plates, I glanced around the area. Since our arrival, I'd been keeping tabs on Davey from afar. He enjoyed the freedom, and there didn't seem to be too many ways he could get himself into trouble in Peg's backyard. Now I realized, however, that at least five minutes had passed since he'd last flashed through my field of vision.

When Peg and Douglas picked up napkins and silverware, I held back. "Have either of you seen Davey recently?"

Aunt Peg shook her head.

"I think I saw him go inside the house," said Douglas. "Maybe he's still there."

He'd been inside earlier looking for dessert, but by now several large trays of brownies had been brought out. Davey might have been looking for a bathroom. Then again, knowing my son, he was probably exploring.

Left to his own devices, Davey's imagination was boundless. I could picture him turning on Aunt Peg's computer and deleting the files that didn't feature games, or adding to the general excitement by turning loose the half dozen Standard Poodles Peg had crated in her house for the duration of the party.

"I think I'd better go find him."

"Off you go, then," Aunt Peg said heartlessly. Easy for her to say, she was already filling her plate.

From the vantage point of the back steps, I took one last look around the yard. Davey was nowhere in sight.

I walked through a small mud room and into the kitchen, ascertaining quickly that it was empty too. Davey liked to play hide-and-seek; finding him might take some time.

But when I simply stood still and listened, I realized I'd worried for nothing. The television in the family room was on, and unless I missed my guess, whoever was watching had tuned to Nickelodeon. A moment later I found Davey there, curled up on the couch, with a plate of brownies within easy reach.

"Hey, sport, what are you doing in here? The party's outside."

"Some party," Davey sniffed. "No toys, no games. It's no fun at all."

Looking at it as a five-year-old might, I could see his point. I sat down beside him. "Are there any good shows on TV?"

"Lots." At home, Davey's television time was restricted. I could see he sensed we were about to strike a bargain.

"Enough to entertain you for another hour or so?"

"I'll say!"

We agreed that I'd bring him a glass of milk and check back when it got dark.

All right, so I'm not the best mother in the world. I'm not the worst either. There's a lot to be said for teaching a child the art of negotiation early in life. It's a skill that will come in handy as he matures.

I was in the kitchen, head deep in Aunt Peg's refrigerator as I searched for milk, when the back door opened and shut behind me.

"Nice view," said Barry Turk. As I'd bent forward from the waist and had my back to him, it wasn't hard to figure out what he was talking about. His tone was oily and insinuating. That was probably his version of flattery.

I straightened, and shut the refrigerator door. "Hi, Barry."

"If I'd known the kitchen was the place to be, I'd have found my way in here sooner."

I sighed. Barry wasn't bad-looking in an overdone, overly macho sort of way. He had dark, curly hair that he wore short on top and longer in the back, and a body that looked as though it made frequent visits to the gym. The problem was, his emotional maturity seemed to have peaked in high school.

He was known for being smooth and glib, and taking plenty of time to schmooze with the judges. A lack of self-confidence had never been Barry's problem, and he did well enough in the ring. But like his sex appeal, his talent with dogs was all just surface flash, with nothing decent and honest to back it up.

"Can I help you with something?" I asked.

"Nah, I was just on my way to the john." He took a step closer. "I haven't seen much of you at the shows lately. I always notice when there's a pretty lady around."

Yeah, right. I wondered if he rehearsed those lines in front of the mirror. More to the point, I wondered if he'd used them on Alicia.

"Faith turned a year old and she's growing coat," I explained, hoping it would move him along.

It didn't. Instead, he took another step closer.

"The bathroom's that way," I said pointedly.

"That's all right. I'm not in a hurry."

By then I had my back against the counter. If Barry took one more step, I was going to give him the shove he deserved.

"Everything all right in here?" The door opened again and Sam let himself in. "You've been gone so long, Peg sent me to look for you." His gaze lingered on Barry, and there was nothing friendly about it.

"Everything's fine," I said firmly. "I was just getting Davey a glass of milk."

"And I was on my way out," said Barry, beating a retreat.

Sam watched him leave, then turned back to me. "I hear you haven't had a chance to eat yet. If you're hungry now, I thought I'd join you."

"You're a man after my own heart."

"I should hope so."

We found the milk, poured Davey a glass, then went outside and pigged out on ribs and corn on the cob. I didn't see Barry again for the rest of the evening, and luckily for Aunt Peg, he didn't cause any problems. She told me later that he and Alicia hadn't stayed long.

Considering it was Saturday night, the party broke up early. The rest of the world takes Sundays off. Not dog show people. Most of the judges and exhibitors would be at the Wallkill dog show the next day.

I stayed home from the show myself and went to the beach with Davey. I hadn't given the competition the slightest thought when Sam called mid-morning Monday.

"Barry Turk won the group yesterday with his Poodle," he said. "He beat Ron Pullman's Chow."

"That must have made him happy."

"Probably so, but not for long. When he got home last night, somebody shot him."

⤃* Three *⤀

"Shot him?" I gasped in disbelief. "What do you mean, somebody shot him? Is he dead?"

"That's what I heard from Crawford. He'd spoken to Bill Devane, who'd been called by Alicia from the hospital. Apparently she was pretty hysterical."

"I don't blame her," I said, feeling somewhat queasy myself. I carried the phone over to the kitchen table and sat down.

If Davey'd been home, Faith would have been with him. Since he was at camp, the big black Poodle was in the kitchen, keeping me company. Faith has an unerring instinct for sensing my mood. She came over, sat down beside me, and rested her head in my lap, offering what comfort she could. I ran my fingers into her neck hair and scratched behind her ear.

"Did Crawford say how it happened?"

"He had only sketchy details. Apparently they'd been in the mood to celebrate, so they stopped and had dinner on the way home from the show."

"They who?"

"Barry and Alicia and Beth. She's Barry's assistant. You've probably seen her at the shows."

"Right." I'd met Beth Wycowski the summer before. A young woman who really liked animals, she'd struck me as eager to learn and ambitious to move up.

At the time, Alicia hadn't been in the picture. I'd once been told that the Chinese symbol for discord was two women under one roof. I wondered how smoothly things had been running at Barry's kennel lately.

"According to Crawford, Barry was high as a kite over beating Ron's Chow, Leo, in the group."

"I can imagine. Aunt Peg was just telling me at the barbecue that Barry used to show that dog himself, and I can certainly picture him holding a grudge."

"Me too," said Sam. "Anyway, the three of them arrived home after dark. They were all riding together in the van, along with the string of dogs they'd taken to the show. Alicia got out at the house, then Barry pulled over and parked beside the kennel. He hopped out and turned on the outside lights. That's when he was shot, as soon as the lights came on."

"Then what happened?" I was caught up in the story as though it were an item on the news. It hadn't really sunk in yet that it had happened to someone I knew.

"Alicia ran outside and stayed with him. Beth went in the kennel and called 911. An ambulance came and took him to the hospital, but he was already dead by the time they got there."

Faith nudged her body closer. I'd slumped so far down in my chair that she could reach up and lick me on the chin. "Do they have any idea who did it?"

"None that Crawford mentioned. The police are involved, of course, but I don't know if they have any leads. I'll let you know if I find out anything else."

I disconnected with Sam and immediately called Aunt Peg. For once I had news she didn't already know.

"Dead?" she cried. "How can Barry Turk be dead? Good Lord, all I did was give one simple party. Don't tell me he died of food poisoning."

"He didn't. Somebody shot him."

"That's a relief." There was silence as Aunt Peg reconsidered what she'd said. "You know what I mean."

"Yes," I agreed mildly.

"This is unbelievable," said Peg. "How could he have been shot? If memory serves correctly, Barry lives up near Poughkeepsie, hardly what you'd call the inner city. What was somebody doing running around there with a gun?"

"Looking for Barry, apparently. It didn't sound like an accident. He was shot when he returned home from the Wallkill show."

Aunt Peg harrumphed loudly into the phone. "I heard that his Poodle beat Ron's good Chow."

"Don't tell me you think the two things are connected."

"I'm willing to consider the possibility."

"Come on," I scoffed. Dog show people tend to take winning very seriously but, as far as I was concerned, the notion that the two events might have been connected strained credibility. "So Barry beat the Chow. It was one time, under one judge. That's hardly a motive for murder. Like you say to me when I lose with Faith, there's always another dog show coming along next week."

"True. But I still wouldn't strike Ron Pullman off the list."

"Really? Which list is that?"

"I'm just thinking aloud," Aunt Peg said innocently. "What about Bill Devane?"

Good old Aunt Peg. Curious, yes. Subtle, no. Now we were checking alibis. I decided to humor her.

"According to Crawford, he was the first person Alicia contacted. Presumably he was home to get the call. Where does he live?"

"Just a minute, let me look in my judges' book."

Left hanging on the line, I used the time to walk over to the cabinet and get out a peanut butter biscuit for Faith. She stood up and cocked her head inquiringly.

"Sit," I said firmly.

Faith wagged her tail and settled her haunches on the ground. Lots of people will tell you that you should never teach a dog basic obedience while it's still showing in the breed classes. The requirements for the two sports are very different—for example, while sitting on command is integral to an obedience performance, you never want your dog to sit while it's being judged in the breed ring.

Like all Poodles, however, Faith is very intelligent. She doesn't seem to be having any trouble figuring out the difference between the two routines. Besides, now that she was older and bigger, it seemed like a good idea for her to understand that I was the one in charge. Lord knew, Davey was still having trouble with that concept.

"Bill lives in Patterson," said Aunt Peg, coming back on the phone. "Melanie, are you there?"

"Right here. Patterson isn't that far from Poughkeepsie.

Of course, we don't know how long it was after Barry was shot that Alicia made the call."

Peg and I both considered that.

"I wonder if the police have any ideas?" she mused.

"Sam didn't know. He's going to keep me posted."

"I might make a few calls myself," Aunt Peg said, surprising nobody in the vicinity. "You know how people love to talk."

I considered it a sign of maturity on my part that I didn't utter the remark that comment called for.

The call ended moments later. Aunt Peg didn't exactly give me the bum's rush, but now that she'd gotten what little information I had, I could tell she was eager to find someone who could fill in the details. It was just as well as it was almost time for me to go pick up Davey.

He goes to Graceland Summer Camp, which is held at the same facility where he attended preschool when he was younger. The summer before, I'd worked at the camp as a part-time counselor to pick up some extra money. Now, however, with my child support payments from Davey's father finally back on schedule after a lengthy hiatus, I was enjoying having some time off.

Winters, I work in the Stamford public school system as a special education teacher. The job takes a lot out of me. By the end of June, when school gets out, I'm always ready for a break. And not having to work all summer too? The prospect seemed positively luxurious.

I dug a tennis ball and a Frisbee out of the closet and loaded Faith into the Volvo. Like most dogs, she loves to ride in cars. She knows better than to bark at passing attractions, but that doesn't stop her from having an opinion. The third time the pom-pom on the end of her tail whacked me across the face, I banished her to the back-seat.

At Graceland, we joined the line of cars that snaked down the long driveway, inching slowly forward to the pickup zone. Faith had her nose pressed against the window and was whining softly under her breath. She loves kids, and I knew she was dying to get out and play.

Finally I relented and put down the window. Tail wagging happily, Faith climbed up and hung her front legs out over the door. It says in our breed standard that Poodles are supposed to be elegant and dignified, but I was quite sure that the people who put that thing together had never met Faith.

Enthusiastic, irrepressible, certainly. Maybe even charming. But elegant and dignified? Not on a bet.

With the puffs on her legs, the big coat of mane hair, the tiny colored rubber bands that gathered her topknot hair into ponytails to hold it out of the way, and the ear hair that was wrapped and similarly banded, even I had to admit my dog was quite a sight. Certainly enough of the mothers stared. The children, being more accepting of something different, seemed to find her entertaining. Faith managed to lick at least a dozen faces before she finally found her own child.

From the way Davey and Faith greeted each other, rolling end over end in a tangle of legs and hair on the backseat, you'd have thought they'd been separated for months rather than a matter of hours. There are times when I'm doing the seemingly never-ending job of looking after Faith's coat, and I think back to the day Aunt Peg dropped her off and wonder whatever made me take on such a responsibility. Then there are moments like these, when I realize how quickly and completely the Poodle had become a part of our family, and I know how truly lucky we were to find such a wonderful companion.

The three of us spent the rest of the afternoon at the park. I threw the Frisbee with Davey and the tennis ball for Faith; and when the two of them entertained each other, I sat in the shade and thought about Barry Turk. I hadn't known him well, and I hadn't much liked what I had known. I couldn't mourn his passing, but I could feel a sense of regret for a life needlessly cut short. Even Barry Turk deserved better than that.

I found myself wondering what would become of Barry's operation. Would Beth try to carry on by herself, or would she find another position elsewhere? The dogs could, of course, be sent to other handlers. But what about Alicia? Where would she go?

As things turned out, I got a chance to ask her. Aunt Peg called Friday morning and requested a favor.

"Sure," I said without thinking, then immediately regretted it. With Aunt Peg, it's much wiser to ask questions first. "What?"

"Davey's at camp, right? I need you to drive up to Poughkeepsie and pick up a Standard Poodle for me. I think I mentioned her at the barbecue. She's booked to be bred to Joker and apparently she's just come in season. Her owner lives in Maryland, so I told Rona I'd take care of things."

Joker was Aunt Peg's new stud dog, a youngster she was bringing along slowly. I knew she was eager for him to be bred to some nice bitches.

"I figure it will take you an hour to get there and an

hour to get back," she was saying. "You don't need to pick up Davey until one. There should be plenty of time."

That was the danger in letting Aunt Peg know too much about my schedule. Wherever she saw empty blocks of time, she couldn't resist trying to fill them up for me.

"Why don't *you* go get her?" I asked reasonably.

"I'm not the one whose Poodle is sitting home growing coat," Aunt Peg replied tartly. "Tory's entered this weekend in New Jersey. She needs a bath, and a blow-dry, not to mention scissoring. I'll be busy all day."

Preparing a Standard Poodle to be shown takes time, lots of it. First the dog must be clipped into the trim that's appropriate for its age. Puppies are clipped on the face, the feet, and the base of the tail. The rest of the hair on the body is carefully shaped—longer in front, shorter behind—to form a harmonious outline.

For an adult Poodle, there are two choices, continental or English saddle. Both trims involve leaving a long mane of hair in the front of the body, and removing the majority of the hair on the hindquarter. In the continental, the hair that remains in back is shaped into pom-poms. In English saddle, a short "pack" covers the back and loins, and there are pom-poms on the legs.

After clipping comes bathing, and with all that hair, a proper bath and blow-dry can easily take three to four hours. Dry and brushed through, the coat is ready to be scissored, which sets the trim into fresh lines. Aunt Peg was right, she would be busy.

All of which did nothing to explain why she couldn't pick up Rona Peters's bitch on Monday. If the Poodle had just come in season, timing wasn't critical yet. I didn't even bother to ask the question. Somehow I just knew

Aunt Peg would have a good answer. There are times when it's easier to give in before you've argued yourself blue in the face.

It's a pretty trip by car from Stamford to Poughkeepsie. Heading north, you start by driving through the horse country of New York's Westchester County and end in the farms of lower Duchess County. These days I'm driving a brand new Volvo station wagon, courtesy of my ex-husband. Having spent the last five years nursing my previous car well into old age and beyond, I was sorely tempted to push my foot down on the gas pedal and fly. Unfortunately, the Taconic Parkway is famous for its speed traps. Bearing that in mind, I traveled a sedate fifty-five and enjoyed the scenery.

With so much open land in the area, you'd have thought Barry Turk would have lived out in the country, but he didn't. His kennel was in a residential zone, house and outbuildings wedged together tightly on a half acre of land that had been meant to hold lawn and trees. I assumed his right to be there was grandfathered, but still, considering the amount of noise the dogs in his kennel generated, it was hard to understand why the neighbors didn't complain.

The last time I'd been at Turk's kennel, it had looked pretty run-down. The buildings had been in need of paint, and weeds had sprouted along the flagstone walk. Two scraggly bushes by the front door had sported more bare twigs than leaves.

Now as I pulled in and parked, however, I saw that the painting had been seen to, and a row of colorful impatiens had been planted along the driveway. The kennel runs were still too small for the dogs they housed, but the roof had been fixed. There was a new, hand-carved sign out front, announcing that I had arrived at Winmore Kennel. All in all, the place had an air of respectable, if modest, prosperity. It wasn't a stretch to imagine that it was Alicia's presence that had made the difference.

I got out of my car, then paused. The driveway was short but wide. A maroon Chevy van had been pulled up in front of the kennel building and was parked off to one side. I wondered if that was where it had been the night Barry was shot.

There were houses and trees in all directions, plenty of cover, lots of places for a gunman to hide. Two large floodlights were positioned just beneath the eaves of the building. Once Barry had turned those on, he would have been standing in a circle of light.

An easy target.

Even in the morning sunshine, the thought made me shiver. I turned and walked to the house. Rona's Poodle was undoubtedly in the kennel, but I wanted to offer my condolences to Alicia first.

I had to knock twice before the front door was drawn open. Alicia answered it wearing shorts and a ratty T-shirt. Her feet were bare and her eyes were red-rimmed. Up close, in the bright sunlight, she looked older than I'd guessed the week before.

"Yes?" she said, her voice soft and quivery.

I held out my hand and introduced myself. "I'm here to pick up a dog. I believe Peg Turnbull called about her?"

Alicia nodded. Even that small movement seemed to

require more strength than she had. "You need to see Beth. She's back in the kennel."

"I know. I just wanted to stop in and tell you how sorry I was about what happened to Barry."

"Thank you," Alicia whispered. She held up a hand to brace herself as she sagged against the door frame.

"Are you all right?" I asked. Dumb question. Anyone could see just by looking at her that Alicia Devane was nowhere near all right.

"I'll be—" She stopped and swallowed. She brought her other hand up and placed it, palm flat, against her stomach.

"Why don't you sit down? Here, let me help you."

She didn't protest as I took her arm, so I took that as acquiescence. The front door opened directly into the living room. Two chairs were piled high with newspapers and magazines, but there was a couch on the opposite wall. Slowly we made our way there. I'd thought she was slender, but Alicia felt frail, almost weightless, beneath my hands.

"Is there anything I can get you?" I asked. "Maybe some coffee?"

"Not coffee. Here." She patted the seat beside her. "Sit for a minute."

I was glad she'd asked. She certainly didn't look like she was in any shape to be left alone. For a full five minutes she didn't say a word, so we sat in silence. I'm not very good at offering comfort. I know women who are naturally empathetic. Not me. I never seem to know the right thing to say.

Then she finally spoke, and what she said was a surprise.

She sat up and her shoulders seemed to stiffen with resolve. "I know who you are. You're Peg Turnbull's niece, the one who figured out who killed Harry Flynn."

I grimaced slightly. There are other ways I'd rather be known.

"I need your help," said Alicia. "I want you to find the person who did this to Barry."

ᴗ❋ *Four* ❋ᴗ

"I can't," I said. The response was quick and automatic. "You need to talk to the police."

"I've already done that. They're questioning the neighbors and running tests on the bullets, looking for witnesses and physical evidence, when what they should be doing is talking to dog people. The dog show world was Barry's whole life, and the police don't have a clue how it works. You do. You solved those other crimes."

"That was—" I stopped, searching for the right word. "Kind of a fluke. I just happened to be there."

"And now you just happen to be here."

She had a point. I'd figured Aunt Peg had sent me to Turk's kennel because she was hoping I'd come back with some good gossip. Now I wondered if there'd been more to it than that.

Then again, I was the one who'd just been standing out in Alicia's driveway, trying to imagine where the shots might have been fired from.

"I'm a teacher," I said. "Not an investigator."

Alicia lifted her hands and let them drop, the gesture conveying her feelings of utter helplessness. I sympathized, but it didn't change my mind.

"The police will find the person who shot Barry. You just have to give them some time."

"All the time in the world won't help unless they start looking in the right direction."

"What do you mean?"

Alicia frowned. "The detective I spoke with seems to think that I might have had something to do with Barry's murder."

"Did you?"

I wanted to see her response, and I wasn't disappointed. Alicia looked positively shocked. "Of course not. Would I ask for your help if I had?"

Maybe, maybe not, I thought. A moment ago, Alicia had had me convinced she was totally helpless. Now her jaw was set with determination.

"You might be hoping I'll come up with another suspect to draw attention away from you."

"No. You don't understand . . ." Her voice drifted, then came back stronger as her fingers spread, once again, over her stomach. "It's not just me I'm worried about. My baby is going to grow up without a father. I need you to find out who did this to me. Who did this to us."

I stared at her for a moment, wondering if I'd misunderstood. "You're pregnant?"

"Yes." Alicia smiled for the first time since my arrival. "Three months. It doesn't show yet, but it won't be long."

"I had no idea."

"Almost no one does. Barry and I didn't exactly plan

this, it just happened. But you can see now why I have to know."

I wondered if it had been chance, or if Alicia knew how close to home she'd hit. I, too, had a child who was growing up without a father. But at least Davey knew Bob, and he knew that even though his father lived in Texas with a new wife, he still loved him very much. It wasn't nearly as much as I would have wanted for him, but it was more than Alicia's baby was going to have.

Before I'd sympathized. Now I empathized. The tug was stronger.

I settled back on the couch. "Will you answer some questions for me?"

"Of course," Alicia said quickly. "I'll tell you anything you want to know."

"Why do the police suspect you?"

"Partly because that's what they do. They always look at the person the victim was involved with first." She twirled a strand of hair around her index finger. The small, unconscious movement was innocent, almost childlike. "And partly because . . ."

"Yes?"

"Barry made out a new will about six months ago. I inherit everything. What there is of it." Alicia cast a derogatory glance around the room. "The house and the kennel are both mortgaged. As to the rest, I couldn't care less what happens to it."

I looked around too. Despite what appeared to be recent attempts to brighten up the decor, the furniture in the room was worn and shabby. The small glimpse I'd had into the kitchen had revealed brown linoleum and outdated appliances.

Alicia picked at the umber tweed upholstery on the couch and sighed loudly. "The only reason I was even here was because of Barry."

"Did you love him?"

"Of course I loved him. I left my marriage for him. Bill was much more stable. He was established. You know."

I nodded.

"But Barry was exciting. He had charisma. He made me feel alive."

I wondered if I dared suggest she'd been having a midlife crisis.

"Barry wasn't the easiest man in the world, but he had some wonderful qualities. He was caring and sweet, and he could be very romantic."

I opened my mouth, then shut it without saying a word.

"I know some people thought he could be brash, and maybe a little arrogant . . ."

And grating, pushy, and sexist.

". . . but that was just his way. His childhood was pretty rough. Barry had to learn how to stick up for himself. But he loved me," Alicia said firmly. "And he took very good care of me." Her lower lip began to quiver. "And now he's gone. What am I going to do?"

I took her hand and held it. "You're going to stay calm and healthy for the sake of your baby. The last thing you need is more stress."

"You'll help me, won't you?"

She looked so hopeful, I couldn't help but nod. "But I can't promise I'll find out anything."

"Promise me you'll try," she said, and I did.

* * *

I found Barry's assistant, Beth, out in the kennel. She was small but stocky, with sandy hair that was cropped short and a direct, unwavering gaze. Like Aunt Peg, she was blow-drying a Poodle in anticipation of the next day's show. She brushed through the damp coat with practiced ease, her movements brisk and efficient.

"Melanie, right?" she said when I entered. "Peg called and told me you were coming. Let me just finish this side, and I'll get the bitch for you."

"No hurry."

In order to achieve the plush, full look needed for showing, the coat had be perfectly straight. Left to air-dry, it would kink and crinkle. Beth had the Standard Poodle lying flat on his side on a rubber-topped grooming table. She was using a large, freestanding blow dryer that directed a strong, steady stream of hot air into the coat. She'd started in the back and was working her way forward. Since she was drying the part of the mane coat that covered the Poodle's shoulder, I figured another fifteen minutes would do it.

There was a desk by the window where Barry used to keep his accounts. Now the surface was clean. I dragged out its chair and sat down.

The dryer made a lot of noise. Beth had been watching a talk show on a small color TV that was sitting on top of a crate, and she'd turned the volume way up. The combination was enough to preclude any hope of conversation.

"Do you mind if I turn that off?" I asked when a commercial came on.

"Go right ahead. I wasn't really paying attention. I just leave it on for something to do."

With one source of noise removed, we were able to speak in almost normal tones. "I see you're getting ready for the shows," I said.

Beth nodded. "Two this weekend. We've got six dogs entered."

"All going?"

She hesitated before answering. "Only one owner bugged out on me," she said, sounding almost defiant. If Beth was feeling even a fraction of the grief Alicia'd felt, she was hiding it well. "I told each of them that this was a freebie. Just give me one weekend to show what I can do. The entry fees were already paid. They had nothing to lose by giving me a chance."

"Do you think you can handle the business by yourself?"

"I don't know. To tell you the truth, I'm not even sure I want to. I liked being Barry's assistant. All I had to do was work with the dogs, and that's what I'm good at. Being the one in charge is a whole different ball game."

I'd liked Beth the last time I met her, and I liked her now. She didn't seem to waste a lot of time bullshitting people.

"So how's business been lately? Was Barry having a good year?"

"Better than ever. He was getting some good dogs and having some good wins. He seemed to be calming down a bit personally, and that was good too." She grinned with all the wisdom of her twenty-two years. "Maybe he was maturing."

"I guess that means you think Alicia's coming was a good thing."

"Yeah, sure." Beth stared downward at a mat she was working free with her fingers. "She's okay."

"She wants me to do some asking around about Barry's murder." I noted that Beth didn't look surprised, and wondered how much the two women spoke. "Would you tell me what happened the night he was shot?"

"I'll tell you what I know. The same thing I already told the police. It isn't much."

I waited a moment while she gathered her thoughts. The brown Standard Poodle on the table was almost dry. His eyes were closed, his breathing deep and even. No doubt he'd slept through most of the procedure.

"We'd been at the show all day. Wallkill, you know?"

I nodded.

"We stayed through Best in Show, then had some dinner. By the time we got back here it was dark, probably a little after nine."

"Had you left any lights on?"

"No." Beth ran her fingers through the Poodle's chest hair, making sure it was fully dry. "It was light that morning when we left, and Barry hates wasting money. I'm sure everything was off."

I listened to her refer to Barry in the present tense and felt a small pang. "So the place looked just as you would have expected it to. Nothing unusual."

"I guess. I mean, like I said, it was dark. Besides, it had been a long day at the show. I wasn't really paying that much attention to how things looked."

"The three of you were in the van?" I prompted.

Beth nodded. "Barry and Alicia had the front two seats.

I was in the back. Which is another reason I wasn't paying attention. I couldn't really see out very well."

I wondered why she felt obliged to keep making excuses. Had being questioned by the police put her on the defensive, or did she actually have something to hide?

"Go on."

"Alicia was feeling really tired and asked if we could unload without her. Barry said okay. He stopped next to the house and she went inside."

"And you stayed in the van?"

"Right." Beth sounded annoyed, as if maybe she'd resented the special treatment Alicia had been given. "Barry pulled up next to the kennel, just like he always does. We had a bunch of big crates with us. The closer we are, the easier it is to unload. Then he got out and turned on the lights."

"Did he have to go into the kennel to do that?"

"No, there's a switch outside, right by the door. That's the one he used."

"And when he did that, you were still inside the van?"

"Yeah, I was gathering up my things. Besides, the sliding door sticks, so it's tough to open from the inside. I was waiting for Barry to let me out."

"You didn't climb up to the front?"

"What for? I wasn't in any hurry."

The drying process was finished. Beth prodded the Poodle, and he lifted his head. There were some supplies on a crate behind her. She reached over and picked up a knitting needle for making parts and a handful of small rubber bands. Working by rote, she began to section and band the long topknot hair.

"Then what happened?"

"I heard a noise, you know, like a car backfiring. I didn't think anything about it until I heard Alicia screaming. That's when I looked out and saw the blood."

She paused and swallowed heavily. I knew she was replaying the scene in her mind.

"And then?"

"Everything seemed to go crazy at once. Alicia came running out of the house. All the noise she was making set the dogs off and they began to bark. I thought I was going to go deaf. Finally, I got the door open and then I saw Barry lying in the driveway. He was on his stomach and there was blood everywhere. Whoever did it shot him in the back."

For a minute, neither of us said a word. I'd found a dead body once, so I knew how she was feeling.

"Do you know what kind of gun the killer used?" I asked finally. "Was it a rifle? A handgun?"

"One with bullets," Beth said, frowning. "That's all I know. I don't know much about guns."

Neither did I except, oddly enough, how it felt to have one pointed at me, which I'd found out the previous November. It wasn't an experience I cared to repeat, and I'd stayed as far away from firearms as possible ever since. But even with my limited knowledge I realized that a rifle would have given the shooter much greater range. No doubt the police would have the answer to that.

"What about clients?" I asked. "You said Barry'd been having a good year. Any exceptions to that? Anyone he'd been having trouble with lately?"

Beth shrugged. "Every operation has a few dissatisfied

customers. Some people are impossible to please. But nobody in particular comes to mind."

She wrapped the long hair on the Poodle's ears in colorful plastic wrap, then flipped the ends up and under, and banded them out of the way. The blow-dry was over. The dog stood up and shook. Beth cupped her hand around the Poodle's muzzle and hopped him down from the table.

"Be back in a minute," she said, disappearing through a door that led back to the pens where the dogs were kept. It seemed like less time than that before she returned. This time her hand was cupped around the muzzle of a rangy black bitch.

"This is Vanna," she said, releasing the Poodle. The bitch came over and sniffed my outstretched hand. "Tell Peg today's day four."

"Got it." That meant that this was Vanna's fourth day in season, which meant that she would probably be ready to breed in about a week. "Anything else?"

"No. She's a real sweetheart, I'm sorry to see her go. Barry'd already put six points on her and he hadn't shown her that much. If you talk to her owner, you could give me a plug. I'd love to get her back."

I slid my hand around the Poodle's muzzle as Beth had done. That way, I didn't have to use a collar that might make mats in her all-important neck hair. "You really think you can make a go of it on your own?"

"Who knows?" said Beth. "But I'm sure as hell going to try."

By the time I got back to Greenwich, it was almost twelve-thirty. My stomach was rumbling, but I didn't hold out any hope that Aunt Peg might feed me lunch. When she's doing out a dog, she never allows herself to be sidetracked by anything as mundane as mealtime. I found her back in the kennel, just as I knew I would.

Aunt Peg's kennel building consists of two large rooms. The one in back contains the pens that house the Poodles she's currently keeping in hair. The room in front is where she works.

Windows in two walls and a skylight above provide plenty of light, and a wall of shelves holds her grooming equipment, everything from pin brushes and shampoo to extra ear wraps and clipper blades. A bathtub mounted waist-high fills one corner of the room, and a glass-fronted trophy cabinet takes up another.

The rest of the wall space is covered with pictures, "win photos" from the shows the Cedar Crest Standard Poodles have attended over the last three decades. Aunt Peg tends to ignore the silverware, most of which needs polishing, but given the slightest encouragement, she's delighted to walk a visitor through the rows of pictures. They're a visual history of all that she and her husband had accomplished over the years, and she's justifiably proud of the results.

When I arrived, Aunt Peg had Tory on a grooming table in the middle of the room. The Poodle was dripping wet and Peg was blotting her coat with a succession of thick towels. I opened the kennel door a crack and peered inside.

Aunt Peg's favorite Poodle is a retired campaigner named Beau, who's almost always by her side. He's also a retired stud dog, and with Vanna in season, I could think of all sorts of reasons why the two of them shouldn't meet. At least not on my watch.

"Where's Beau?" I asked.

"Up at the house," said Peg, leaving Tory on the table to come and open the door. "And not the slightest bit happy about it. I knew you'd be along any minute. Come on in, let's have a look at you."

The second half of her comment was directed at Vanna. Being around Aunt Peg, I'd gotten used to that. She tends to include Poodles in the conversation as if they're extra family members.

"You're a big girl, aren't you?" Aunt Peg crooned as she ran her hands over the Poodle's sides. Vanna wagged her tail and did a little dance in place. In dog-speak, that meant they were already halfway to being friends. "Pretty face. Could use a better front. Maybe Joker can help with that."

Peg fished a dog biscuit out of a bin by the door, then led the way into the other room. Vanna followed happily in her wake. "Now then," she said when she returned. "How were things in Poughkeepsie?"

"Unsettled," I said, and told her about my visit.

Aunt Peg likes solving puzzles, and she's nosy too. It's a dangerous combination. She listened carefully to everything I said. If she hadn't had a wet Poodle on her hands, I got the impression she'd have been taking notes.

"Interesting," she said at the end. "I'd say that all worked out rather well."

No surprises there. "I told Alicia I'd ask a few questions," I said firmly. "That's all."

"A few questions here, a few questions there . . . Who knows what may turn up?"

Hoping to distract her, I changed the subject. "Sam's coming over tonight. I'm making lasagna, and after dinner the three of us are going down to listen to music in the park. Would you like to join us?"

"I can't," said Peg. "I've got a date."

"A date?" I repeated stupidly. Then I remembered. "With Douglas?"

"Of course with Douglas." Peg looked very pleased with herself.

It was time to go pick up Davey. I grinned as I headed to the door on my way out. After all the meddling I'd had to endure from Aunt Peg over my relationship with Sam, it was nice to have the shoe on the other foot for a change. "Don't do anything I wouldn't do."

Aunt Peg glanced pointedly down her nose. "Presumably that leaves me a great deal of latitude."

"Not *that* much," I warned her.

Aunt Peg likes to have the last word, and she's a master at it. "I'll see you tomorrow," she said as I opened the door.

"You will?"

"The Saddle River dog show. Where else do you expect to begin asking questions?"

The Saddle River show, of course.

Just like old times.

❧❊ *Five* ❊❧

Before last summer I'd barely even heard of dog shows, much less envisioned myself going to one. But once Aunt Peg got me started, I was hooked. At our first dog show, Davey and I had walked around in awe. The American Kennel Club recognizes one hundred and fifty breeds and varieties of dogs, and at most shows a majority of them are present. The dogs are immaculately groomed and skillfully presented. We didn't know which direction to look in first.

By this time I'd like to think that we're getting to be old hands, but that didn't stop me from feeling a small tingle of excitement as we drove onto the show ground. The day was warm and sunny, with a slight breeze and just enough humidity to frizz my hair around my shoulders. Perfect weather for showing a dog would have been a bit cooler, but it was certainly perfect for watching.

The grounds the Saddle River show had chosen were large and well laid out. As we drove to the parking area, I saw at least a dozen rings. They were positioned in two parallel rows, with a big green-and-white-striped tent covering the center expanse. At one end of the rings was another large tent, which the exhibitors used to either groom their dogs or just keep them crated in the shade until it was their turn to be shown.

I knew from experience that eventually we'd find Aunt Peg in the handlers' tent. Since we hadn't brought a dog to show, however, Davey and I had plenty of time to park the car and look around.

"Look!" cried Davey. "Those are my favorite."

I turned and saw that he was pointing at three Great Pyrenees, massive white dogs with broad heads and ample coat. Davey picks a new favorite at each show, and his choices have included everything from Old English Sheepdogs to Border Collies. The two things they all seem to have in common are large size and lots of hair. Luckily, Standard Poodles fill the bill on both counts.

"I thought Faith was your favorite," I mentioned.

"She is. I meant my favorite *here.*"

That was my son's idea of a subtle dig, as he'd voted to bring Faith with us. Aside from the fact that it was going to be hot, however, Aunt Peg had made it perfectly clear that no Standard Poodle of hers needed to be seen in public at the gawky age of fourteen months. Deferring to her better judgment, I'd left Faith snoozing happily at home with a cool bowl of water and a new marrow bone.

We passed the Great Pyrenees, then paused by the next ring, where sporting dogs were being judged. According to the schedule in the front of my catalogue, Golden Retrievers were about to start. Austin Beamish's dog, Midas, was entered in the Best of Breed class, and I decided to stick around and have a look.

The main purpose of the competition at dog shows is to acquire enough points to make a dog a champion. Points are won within each breed, and the classes are divided by sex. The classes that a nonchampion dog can be entered in are: Puppy, Novice, Bred-by-Exhibitor, American-Bred, and Open, with some shows adding a class for entrants between the ages of twelve and eighteen months. Most dogs are eligible for several classes, and owners may take their choice. Males are judged first, followed by the females.

After the individual classes within each sex have been judged, the class winners are brought back into the ring to contend for Winners Dog and Winners Bitch. Only these two winners are awarded points. The number of points given out at a show varies from breed to breed, and is dependent upon the number of competing dogs that have been defeated.

The fewest number of points awarded is one, the maximum, five. It takes fifteen points to make a champion, and included in those fifteen must be two "major" wins, that is, wins large enough to produce at least three points.

Even with a good dog, the process can be long and arduous. I'd shown Faith nearly a dozen times as a puppy. Pretty as she was, we hadn't acquired any points yet, although she had managed to win Reserve Winners Bitch twice.

Davey liked the looks of the Goldens and watched the class competition happily. He's not known for his patience, so I imagined I'd be paying for this goodwill sooner or later. The Open class winner was awarded Winners Dog, and the Open Bitch won her points as well. As the judge marked the results in his book, the steward stepped to the gate and called the champions into the ring.

There were only three, and in that competition, Austin's dog stood out immediately. The listing in the catalogue said Champion Glengarron Midas Touch, and the name suited him well. In the sunlight, Midas's coat shimmered like golden silk. His body was beautifully conditioned and he carried himself with pride. I don't know much about Golden Retrievers as a breed, but even I could see that this was a really good one.

The dog was handled in the ring by a pro named Tom Rossi, who clearly had the situation well under control. In no time at all, Midas was awarded the purple and gold ribbon for Best of Breed. I heard a smattering of applause from the other side of the ring and followed it to its source just in time to catch a glimpse of Austin before he turned and walked away.

Most winners like to hang around and bask in their dogs' reflected glory, but apparently not Austin. Maybe he had another dog being judged at the same time; or maybe a Best of Breed win, terrific as it seemed to me, wasn't that big a deal for him. From what Aunt Peg had said at the party, I gathered he set his sights on Best in Show and very often hit the mark.

All the breeds recognized by the A.K.C are divided into seven groups: Sporting, Hound, Working, Terrier, Toy, Non-Sporting, and Herding. Later in the day, Midas would go on to compete in the Sporting group against all the other BOB winners. If he won there, then it was on to the ultimate pinnacle—competing against the other six group winners for Best in Show. I guess when you aimed that high, Best of Breed might seem like just another stepping-stone along the way.

Davey and I did some more browsing around the rings, then made our way over to the handlers' tent. Most casual spectators at a dog show never bother with the grooming area. They figure the action is in the rings. And it is, up to a point. But for every dog that spends ten minutes in the ring being judged, someone has spent an hour under the grooming tent, getting it ready.

That's where people have time to talk and visit with one another. They look at puppies, compare equipment, and exchange all the latest gossip. What happens in the rings is important, certainly; but the interaction that goes on under the handlers' tent is what keeps the sport alive.

Poodle people bring a lot of stuff to a show. Even Aunt Peg, with only one dog, had a portable grooming table, a big metal crate, and a wooden tack box filled with brushes, combs, scissors, and hair spray. Inevitably she finds someplace interesting to set up, so I wasn't surprised to find her parked just down the aisle from Crawford Langley.

What did surprise me was to see Douglas Brannigan backing her station wagon out of the unloading zone beside the tent. At nine-thirty in the morning, no less. I stared at Aunt Peg. She gave me a saintly smile. Davey, luckily, was transfixed by a litter of Norwich Terrier puppies in an exercise pen beside the tent and didn't notice a thing.

"Good morning, Melanie," Aunt Peg said cheerfully. "You're here early."

"So is Douglas."

"So he is." Aunt Peg bent **down** and began unpacking

her tack box, pulling out slicker and pin brushes, a wide-tooth comb, and a spray bottle of water. "This is his first dog show. I hope he doesn't find it too long a day."

"I guess that depends." I hiked myself up and sat on the edge of the grooming table. "Did he get a good night's sleep last night?"

"Very," Peg said smugly. The woman had no shame.

"I can't believe it!"

"What?"

"You just met."

"Oh, pish," said Peg. "You're just sorry you wasted so much time with Sam."

All right, maybe she was partly right. Sam and I had taken things slowly in the beginning; my choice, not his. But with Davey's feelings needing to be taken into consideration too, I hadn't wanted to make any mistakes. Now, in hindsight, it seemed as though I'd worried for nothing. Which didn't mean I still didn't find Aunt Peg's actions to be slightly precipitous.

"Mom," Davey interrupted, coming up behind me. "Can I have a puppy?"

"No." I didn't even have to think to answer. Any mother of a five-year-old knows the feeling. "You already have a dog at home."

Davey gazed wistfully at the Norwiches. "Two would be nice."

"Two would be too much."

"Come and give me a hug," Peg said, and Davey did, his short arms circling her hips.

"Aunt Peg has lots of dogs," Davey mentioned. "She doesn't think they're too much."

I glanced meaningfully toward the parking area. Douglas was making his way toward us across the field. "Apparently Aunt Peg is more liberal than I am."

She untangled my son's arms, lifted him up, and set him down on top of the big metal crate. "Don't be such a prude, Melanie."

"I'm not," I said, just to set the facts straight.

"What's a prude?" asked Davey.

"It's someone who doesn't want anyone else to have any fun," said Peg.

"Like someone who won't let me have a puppy?"

"Precisely."

I looked at the two of them and resisted the temptation to bang their heads together. "I'm going for a walk," I said.

"I'm staying with Aunt Peg," Davey informed me. "She's not a prude."

Knowing Peg, she probably also had a box of cookies stashed in the bottom of her tack box.

I put Davey's bag on the crate beside him. It held crayons, a coloring book, and a selection of toy cars, enough to keep him busy for at least ten minutes.

"You'll keep an eye on him?" I asked. Considering my son's penchant for playing hide-and-seek, it wasn't the easiest job in the world.

"Of course," said Peg. "Douglas will help."

The man in question arrived at the setup as I was leaving. "What a perfectly lovely morning," he said, smiling broadly.

"Indeed," I muttered, feeling every bit the killjoy that I was.

It wasn't that I begrudged Peg her happiness, just that the idea of her in a relationship took some getting used to. Especially a relationship that had gotten that serious that quickly. Or then again, I thought, maybe it hadn't. Aunt Peg had always considered herself to be rather a free spirit. Maybe they were having casual sex.

Smiling at the thought, I strolled down the aisle to Crawford's setup. The first time I'd met the handler he'd reminded me of a show dog—sleek, self-possessed, and very well groomed. I knew he was gay, but Crawford handled that part of his life the same way he handled everything else, with reserve and a great deal of discretion.

He'd been part of the dog game for longer than I'd been alive, and had connections everywhere. Crawford always seemed to know where the next really good dog was coming from, and why the last one had gone home. Everybody's secrets were safe with him, and I'm sure it was a continuing source of annoyance that I was always asking him questions he didn't want to answer.

Crawford's setup was large and impressive. In addition to a double row of crates there were five grooming tables, three of them currently holding Standard Poodles. All had been brushed and had their topknots in. Now they awaited the finishing touches of hair spray and scissoring that would be done just before it was time to take them up to the ring.

In the meantime, Crawford was working on top of a toy-sized crate, putting matching bows in the hair of a tiny, impossibly white Maltese. Another man, whom I hadn't seen before, had a second Maltese on a table.

Specialized assistance is beyond my abilities, but with coaching, I'm good at helping out. Several times in the spring, Crawford had found himself shorthanded and I'd been pressed into service. Little by little, I was learning how to make myself useful.

I walked over to where he was working. "Need any help?"

"No, I got it." The Maltese stood like a statue as Crawford finished smoothing the hair into place. "I'll be heading up to ringside in a minute. What's new with you?"

That was his way of warning me that if I'd come to bug him about something, I had to talk fast.

"Alicia asked me to look into Barry's murder," I said.

"I figured the police would be handling that."

"They are. I just told her I'd ask around a little. Care to speculate who might have done it?"

Crawford's expression left little doubt as to his feelings about speculation. Finally he said, "Plenty of people had a problem with Barry Turk. That was just the kind of person he was. But someone who was mad enough to pull out a gun and shoot? That's way beyond anything I'd know about."

I was used to Crawford's evasiveness. Before he'd even finished speaking, I was ready to try another tack. "I heard that maybe the two of you weren't getting along so well."

He sent me a stern look. "What you heard was that Barry lost his specials dog and I ended up with him."

"That must have made him angry."

"I imagine it might have, but we never talked about it."

That surprised me. "You didn't?"

"No reason to. Barry never contacted me, and it's not as if I was about to call him."

Crawford picked up a comb and placed it in the pocket

of his sports coat. Next he lifted the small white Toy and tucked it carefully under his arm. If I was lucky, there was time for one more question.

"I heard Barry was saying that Ron still owed him money on a bill. Do you know anything about that?"

"As much as I needed to." His gaze narrowed. "Handlers have an unwritten rule. You don't take on someone else's dog until all the past accounts are squared away."

"Then Barry was lying?"

Crawford didn't answer. Instead, he looked past me and said, "Terry, you ready?"

"All set." The man working on the other Maltese appeared at my elbow. He looked to be in his late twenties, slender, tan, with crisply styled hair and chiseled features. He offered me an infectious grin and a broad wink.

I found myself returning the grin before we'd even been introduced.

"My new assistant, Terry Denunzio," said Crawford.

There wasn't the slightest bit of innuendo in his tone. It didn't matter. Looking at Terry, there didn't have to be.

"Lucky you," I said.

Crawford frowned slightly, but Terry only laughed. "You got it, hon."

It looked to me like Crawford wasn't going to be needing my help anymore. As the two of them headed over to the Maltese ring, I went back to check on Davey.

"I see you met Terry," said Peg.

I nodded, looking past her to where Douglas and Davey were reading the show catalogue together. Amazingly, they both looked content. A small miracle, and one I wasn't about to question.

"Have he and Crawford been together long?"

"About a month." Peg was beaming. Deep down, she has the soul of a matchmaker. "See what happens when you don't go to shows? You miss things. My first impression of Terry was that he was a little young, but he certainly seems to mean well. He may turn out to be the best thing that could have happened to Crawford."

"Good," I said. "Crawford deserves it."

I caught the look Aunt Peg sent me, and smiled ruefully. "And so do you."

"You see?" said Peg. "I knew you weren't as backward as you look."

On that cheery note, I was sent off in search of doughnuts. It seemed that Douglas had fixed a nutritious breakfast that morning, which hadn't included any of the sweets Peg considers to be the staples of her diet. Then in the rush to pack up and get to the show on time, she'd neglected to bring any along. By now she was well into sugar withdrawal.

The concession booths and food stands were strung out in a long row that started at the far end of the handlers' tent and looped around the field. Halfway there, I came upon a compact setup manned by a tall, stunning redhead: Alberta Kennedy, casually known as Bertie. Bertie was relatively new to professional handling. At a typical dog show she spent more time hustling for clients than she did in the ring. Hardworking and ambitious, she was determined to work her way to the top. Her handling skills were merely competent, but what she lacked in technique, she more than made up for in presence. It was a rare male judge who didn't immediately notice when Bertie walked into his ring.

Today she was wearing a turquoise silk dress that draped and clung in all the right places. Her long hair was cut in layers that curled around her face and her fingernails were painted pink. A quick scan of the crates in her setup revealed she'd brought eight dogs to the show. Not a bad-size string for someone who was just starting out.

I paused beside a grooming table, where she was busy scissoring a Bichon Frise into a perfectly sculpted puff of white hair. Bertie looked up and nodded but kept on working.

"I guess you heard about what happened to Barry," I said.

She shrugged, being careful not to let the motion travel down her arm and affect the precise line she was scissoring.

"Pretty shocking, huh?"

"You mean that somebody was murdered, or that it was Barry Turk?"

"Both."

Bertie finished the side she was working on, straightened, and leaned back to take a look. "I guess you didn't know Barry very well."

"No, I didn't. Did you?"

"Better than I wanted to, all things considered."

I remembered a show I'd been to in the spring, where Bertie had been helping Crawford, learning the ropes and piling up favors at the same time. He probably wasn't the only established handler she'd approached.

"Did you ever work for Barry?"

Bertie snorted. "Are you kidding? Just being in the ring with him was bad enough."

"Bad how?"

She glanced around the tent. "It wasn't just me. You can ask nearly any woman here."

"Ask them what?" I asked, feeling suitably dense.

"Barry Turk," she said. "The dog show world's poster boy for sexual harassment."

❧❋ Six ❋❧

After the encounter I'd had with Barry at Aunt Peg's party, maybe I shouldn't have been surprised, but I was.

"Bertie, what are you talking about?"

She reached around behind her, took a narrow show lead out of her tack box, and slid the loop over the Bichon's head. "I don't even think it was that much of a sex thing with Barry. It was ego, and power. Combined with the fact that he found himself irresistible and seemed to think everyone else did too. It's been going on for years."

"What's been going on for years? What did he do?"

"Make himself a real pain in the ass, mostly. You always knew you had to watch yourself when Barry was around because chances were he'd try something. A little squeeze maybe, or a suggestive comment whispered so that only you could hear. It was always just enough to throw you off balance, and I'm sure that's what he was after. When I'm in the ring, I need to be concentrating on my dog, not wondering whether Barry Turk is going to sidle over and rub up against me."

I could certainly understand that. In the limited amount of showing I'd done, I'd already learned how stressful it could be. Judges were expected to evaluate twenty-five dogs an hour. Add in the paperwork and technical details they had to see to, and it worked out to less than two minutes to form an opinion of each dog.

With that kind of pressure, a handler had to be on her toes—and keep her dog at its best—the entire time she was in the ring. A distraction like the one Turk had threatened her with could easily mean the difference between winning and losing.

"Are you sure it wasn't just you?"

Bertie frowned. She was slipping a supply of dried liver into her pocket to use as bait in the ring.

"I mean, look at you. I'm sure Barry wasn't the only one who was interested."

"No, but he was the only one who came after me in the ring." She ran her comb through the Bichon's tail, then flipped it back up over the dog's back. "And what I look like had nothing to do with it. Barry was like an experienced stud dog. He went after any female he saw."

"What did you do about it?" I asked curiously.

"Nothing," said Bertie. "Mostly I just tried to laugh it off. But there were other women he tried the same thing with, who got really upset. They talked about filing a complaint with the rep."

The rep was the A.K.C. representative, on hand at nearly all shows to ensure that rules were followed and things were running smoothly.

"And did they?"

Bertie shook her head. "You know how it is. Barry'd been around a while and he went out of his way to suck up to anyone who mattered, so he had enough friends in high places. The women were afraid they wouldn't be taken seriously, and that they'd only wind up making things tougher on themselves."

"Men have always counted on logic like that to protect them," I said angrily. "If women don't speak up, nothing ever changes."

"It did this time, didn't it?" Bertie picked up the Bichon, ready to head up to the ring. "Maybe we all just got lucky."

The food stand had doughnuts and brownies both. I bought enough to need a box to carry them in, then added tea for Peg, coffee for Douglas and me, and a carton of milk for Davey. When I returned to the setup, I was the most popular person in the area for at least five minutes.

There turned out to be a boy Davey's age in the next aisle, and while the two of them compared toys, I helped Aunt Peg finish getting Tory ready for the ring. It sounds more important than it was. All I did was cup her muzzle in my palm and hold her steady while Aunt Peg scissored her trim.

Although the lines of each dog's trim are set at home, the finish is always perfected just before the Poodle goes in the ring. The work is exacting and can take a fair amount of time. All show Poodles are trained to stand quietly on their tables, but in order to make the hair fall correctly—that is, exactly the way it will when the dog is in the ring being shown—the Poodle's head must be held in a very upright position. A dog at attention would stand that way willingly, one being groomed wouldn't bother.

It isn't the easiest pose to hold, especially since Tory tended to relax by leaning into me. Every time I was tempted to let down, however, Peg reached around and poked me with her scissors. I noticed she hadn't asked Douglas to come and stand with his hand up in the air. Instead, he sat comfortably in a folding chair and heaped her efforts with praise.

"Those lines are so precise," he said. "It must take years of practice to learn how to do that."

"It does," Peg agreed, never one to belittle her own achievements. "It's not learning how to use the scissors that's important, but developing your eye so that you can see the best trim for each dog. Look around the tent."

Douglas and I both did. As Standard Poodles were due to be judged soon, there were a number of them out of their crates and up on the tables.

"Every single dog you're seeing right now has a slightly different trim. Even though they're all in continental, the lines on each will vary to accentuate the dog's good points and camouflage his faults."

"Look here, for instance." Peg placed her hand on Tory's front leg just below the elbow. "This bitch is square, just like the standard calls for. Even so, judges tend to reward for an exaggerated look, and that means long legs and a short back."

Her fingers brushed the bottom of Tory's mane coat. "See how high I've scissored this line? That gives her the illusion of more leg. Luckily, she has a good front and I can get away with it."

When she pointed it out to me, I could see what she was talking about, although I never would have noticed it on my own. Douglas, however, just shook his head.

"Sorry, Peg," he said. "To me, they all look alike."

"Been there," I said, smiling.

When she was finished scissoring, Peg took down Tory's topknot, brushed through the long, thick hair, then replaced the rubber bands in a tighter formation that would set off her face and expression. Between brushing, scissoring, and spraying, I'd seen her spend nearly two hours getting a Standard Poodle ready to go in the ring. Then, when the judging was over, it could take half as long again to undo everything she'd just done. Peg, however, didn't seem the slightest bit perturbed by the effort it all took. She hummed softly under her breath as she worked her magic with comb and hair spray.

When judging time approached, we all accompanied her to the ring. Holding Davey's hand tightly in mine, I stood with Douglas at ringside and tried to explain how the competition worked.

It was easy for him to understand the individual examinations, where the judge ran his hands over each dog's body, making a mental image of the structure beneath the hair. And he was enough of an athlete himself to understand why so much time was devoted to assessing the dogs' movement. But in the end, he still couldn't detect the subtle differences that set a really good Poodle apart from one that was merely average.

"I can see I'm going to have to work on this," said Douglas, clapping with delight when the judge awarded Tory the purple ribbon for Winners Bitch. "Peg's entry certainly looked the best to me, and of course I'm delighted she won, but I really have no idea why."

"Tory's very sound," Davey said knowledgeably. "And she has nice feet too."

I stared down at my son. What he'd said was true, but how had he known that?

Peg left the ring briefly while Reserve Winners Bitch was judged. Douglas started toward her, but Davey and I both held back.

"We'll see her after," I said. "She has to go right back in."

"Best of Breed, right?" Douglas guessed. "I may not know much about dog shows, but I have heard of that."

"Best of Variety," Davey corrected Douglas. "That's because they're Poodles."

This time I could only shake my head.

"What's the difference?" asked Douglas.

I couldn't help myself. I waited a beat just in case Davey wanted to go on and explain that too. He didn't, so I did.

"You're right in thinking that most dogs are judged for Best of Breed. But some, like Poodles and Cockers and Dachshunds for example, have separate varieties within the breed. Poodles come in three sizes: Toy, Mini, and Standard, so they're divided by size. Cockers are divided by color. And Dachshunds are divided by the kind of coat they have, either smooth, longhair, or wire-hair."

"Stop." Douglas held up a hand. "You're making me dizzy. Just tell me one thing. Did Peg accomplish what she set out to do today?"

"Yes."

"Good. That's all I need to know."

Not only did Tory win the points, she also beat the Winners Dog for Best of Winners. Then there was a twenty-minute wait before Peg could have Tory's picture taken with the judge. Douglas wandered off to check out the concession stands and took Davey with him. I could definitely get used to having that man around.

Afterward, Peg and I strolled back to the grooming tent in a celebratory mood, passing Crawford's setup on the way in. He and Terry were taking a lunch break, and they'd been joined by Ron and Viv Pullman. The Pullmans had apparently watched Crawford handle their Chow to Best of Breed, and were eager to discuss Leo's chances of winning the Non-Sporting group.

"Who won in Standards?" Crawford asked as soon as he saw us.

"Pogo," said Peg, hopping Tory back up onto her table.

"Good," Crawford replied.

It never ceases to amaze me how exhibitors manage to keep track of all their competition. They know one another's dogs by show name, by call name, and by handler as well. Pogo was a young Standard Poodle who'd been doing well in the variety but wasn't yet much of a factor in the group. One name, and Crawford immediately knew where he stood.

"Pogo." Viv frowned slightly. "I don't believe I've seen that dog. Is he new?"

"Jack Stacey just started specialing him this spring." Ron's arm was looped around his wife's shoulders, and he gave her an affectionate squeeze. "Leo's been beating him pretty easily."

"Pogo's not a bad dog." Crawford was ever the diplomat. "Just young. Next year he'll be more of a threat."

"Who cares about next year?" Terry plucked a cherry tomato out of his salad and popped it in his mouth. "Today we're winning Best in Show."

"Don't say that!" Ron cried. "You'll jinx us."

"Maybe he'll bring us luck," said Viv.

Crawford, as usual, declined to comment.

"Did you hear Melanie's news?" asked Terry.

Viv and Ron both turned to look at me, but all I could do was shrug. I had no idea what he was talking about either.

"She's going to figure out who murdered Barry Turk!"

Oh, Lord.

"Really?" Ron didn't look impressed. I couldn't blame him a bit.

"You have big ears," I said to Terry.

"You bet I do." He placed his fingers behind his lobes and waggled them impishly. "And a big mouth too."

"We're working on correcting both," Crawford said sternly.

"But we're not succeeding," said Terry, mimicking the stern tone.

I had to laugh, in spite of myself. Viv did too.

Ron was silent for a moment, as if thinking something over. "I imagine you're aware that Barry used to handle Leo?"

I nodded.

"Does that make me a suspect in your investigation?"

Whoa, I thought. Everyone was taking this much too seriously. "I don't have any suspects. Or an investigation. Alicia requested that I ask a few questions and I told her I would. That's all there is to it."

Viv shook her head sadly. "I have to admit, I do feel sorry for her."

Abruptly Ron's arm slid down from around his wife's shoulders. "Why on earth would you say something like that?"

"Because it's true. Obviously she was in love with Barry. She left Bill for him."

"And got stuck with a man who refused to do the right thing by her," Peg chimed in.

"Do the right thing?" I repeated. "As in marry her? Is that what Alicia wanted?"

"Of course she did, hon," said Terry. "Anyone with eyes could see that. You straight people are so conventional."

"Alicia mentioned it to me a couple of times," said Viv. "We used to talk when Leo was there. She said she felt like she was living in limbo with Barry. She wanted a commitment. I don't think she ever gave him an ultimatum or anything, but it was pretty clear she was beginning to get fed up."

When I'd seen Alicia at her house, she'd offered to tell me anything, but she certainly hadn't told me that. I wondered if there were any other important facts she'd neglected to mention. I also wondered just how much of a temper Alicia had. It looked like there was more than one reason that the police had settled on her as their prime suspect.

"Barry and Alicia were already living together," I said. "Why wouldn't he marry her?"

"Because that's the kind of bastard he was," said Viv.

"Because he liked his freedom," guessed Terry.

"Because he was a fool," Ron said.

Crawford leaned into the group and spoke up for the first time. "Barry didn't marry Alicia because he didn't have to. He knew she'd stay with him regardless, and she did."

"I wonder if the baby would have made a difference," said Peg.

"Baby?" Viv turned and stared. "What baby?"

Terry grinned with delight. "I guess we won't be keeping that cat in the bag any longer."

"Alicia is *pregnant?*"

"Apparently so," Ron told his wife.

"Three months. She told me about it yesterday. How did you find out?" I asked Terry.

"Who had to find out? It was perfectly obvious to anyone who was paying attention. Poor Alicia, for a while she had morning sickness something awful. And if you've ever been in a Portosan at a show, you know nobody visits them unless they absolutely have to. When I saw Alicia heading that way two and three times in a morning, it was pretty easy to figure out."

"Portosans? Is that what you're all standing over here talking about?" Austin Beamish's voice wasn't loud, but it carried with authority. He strolled up to join the group. "And here I thought it would be something interesting."

"We know the only thing that interests you," said Ron. I wondered if I was imagining the edge to his voice. "And that's who's winning Best in Show this afternoon. Care to clue us in?"

"I wouldn't be so presumptuous as to speculate this early in the day." Austin's gaze swept around the group, settling on Peg, Viv, and me. "Ladies, may I say you're all looking extremely lovely?"

"I don't see why not," Peg responded lightly, but I could tell she was flattered.

"Now, now," said Douglas, coming to join us with

Davey in tow. "Enough of that. Get your own girl, Austin."

"I would, but all the best ones seem to be taken."

"Pish," said Peg. "Surely you don't expect us to believe you're looking for sympathy?"

"I doubt it," Ron said dryly. "More likely he's come over to size up the competition."

"You've seen through me again." Austin peered around the setup until he found Leo's crate. "And how's your boy today?"

"Very well, thank you," Crawford shifted his weight ever so slightly, blocking Austin's view. "I trust Midas is the same?"

"Always. Luckily for me, that dog never seems to have a bad day."

"I'm glad to hear that." Crawford was obviously unimpressed by Austin's attempts to psych him out. "Tell Tom I hope I have the chance to give him a run for his money later. Terry? We've got Affenpinschers in twenty minutes."

"Yes sir!" Snapping to attention, Terry cleared away the remains of their lunch.

Ron and Viv wandered off; and Douglas and Austin continued a conversation about municipal bonds that they'd apparently started at Peg's party. While Aunt Peg took Tory's topknot down and spritzed her coat with a conditioner that would dilute the hair spray, I reached for my catalogue and looked up the group schedule. Non-Sporting was first, at two o'clock.

"Go get some lunch," said Peg. "And bring back plenty for me. I'm starving."

Was there ever a time when she wasn't? Peg tends to

argue the point, but I don't think it's any coincidence that in the year we'd been going to dog shows together, I've put on five pounds. As if that isn't bad enough, but it seems to have attached itself to all the least becoming places. When Aunt Peg puts on an extra pound or two, I think it lands in her feet.

With a selection consisting of greasy hamburgers or generic hot dogs, lunch was hardly a gastronomic treat. After we ate, I took Davey for a walk around the back parking lot, where the exhibitors park the vans and motor homes they use to transport their strings of dogs to the shows. Davey is into big rigs, so the knowledge that he'll eventually have a chance to investigate the trucks up close is usually enough to ensure his good behavior for the rest of the day.

We got back to the rings just in time to join Aunt Peg and Douglas in watching Crawford and Leo in the Non-Sporting group. The breed winners entered the ring and lined up in size order, which placed the Standard Poodle and Dalmatian toward the front, and the slower-moving dogs, like the Bulldog and Boston Terrier at the rear. Leo, with his relatively short legs and stilted gait, was right in the middle.

"That was easy," I said barely twenty minutes later as the judge awarded the blue ribbon to the Chow.

"Crawford makes it look easy," said Peg. "Believe me, it isn't. Not only that, but Ron Pullman's been involved with Chows nearly for twenty years, so you might say that dog is the culmination of two decades of dedication to the breed."

Aunt Peg likes to lecture. In another life, I think she must have been a teacher. Or maybe a mother.

She and Douglas went off to get her car, and Davey and I went back to the handlers' tent to help load up. After that was done, we'd leave as well. Sam was coming over again that evening, and I wanted to go home and get ready.

Davey ran on ahead to Peg's setup. As I was waiting outside the tent, a familiar-looking maroon van pulled up to the loading zone and Beth got out. I waved and she smiled slightly.

"Leaving already?" I asked. The professional handlers were usually the first to arrive and the last to leave.

"No point in staying," Beth said. "It's not as if I have any dogs in the groups."

Oh.

"How about your class dogs? Did they do well?"

"I got one point. On a Tibetan Spaniel. Wow."

"Better than nothing."

Beth grimaced. "Not by much, is it?"

As she slid open the van door, a young man with strong arms and a husky build emerged from beneath the tent carrying a medium-sized crate. "Melanie," said Beth. "Meet Ralphie Otterbach."

Long dark bangs shadowed a pair of guileless brown eyes. There was a faint line of old acne scars along his jaw. Ralphie looked at me and nodded shyly.

"Nice to meet you," I said, then jumped as Aunt Peg pulled her station wagon in behind me and tooted the horn.

"I thought you were going to help," she complained. "All you're doing is standing around."

"I'm helping," Davey announced. He was carrying a

cardboard tray holding the doughnuts we hadn't managed to finish earlier.

"Good," said Peg. "Put those on the front seat."

Aunt Peg makes a pretty good taskmaster. It hardly took any time to load up her table, chairs, crate, tack box, and, of course, Poodle. Then again, Ralphie was no slouch either, because he and Beth finished loading her van at about the same time.

"Here, let me get that for you," I said, grasping the handle of their open van door.

"Thanks," said Beth. Ralphie was tying down a crate in back. She hopped in behind the steering wheel.

It took a bit of a tug to get the heavy door moving, but then it slid along the runners smooth as butter and latched firm. "Did that catch?" I asked innocently. "Let me try it again."

I lifted the handle, slid the door back, then forward once again.

Two tries, and it never stuck at all.

☞❧ *Seven* ❧☜

When we got home, Faith greeted us at the door with the clear belief that after a day of abandonment, we now owed her big-time. Davey and I agreed, and a game of catch in the backyard was followed by a walk in the neighborhood, then a round of dog biscuits and cookies. At last we reached the point where both dog and child were content to cuddle together on the couch and watch a Disney video.

That gave me a few minutes to go into the kitchen and call Alicia Devane. The phone rang four or five times before it was picked up, but when Alicia found out who was calling, she seemed pleased to hear from me.

"Beth told me you were at the show today," she said. "Did you find out anything?"

"A few things. Actually, I was hoping to ask you a question."

"All right."

"How come you and Barry never got married?"

For a long while there was only silence on the line. I sat and waited it out.

"What does that have to do with Barry's murder?" Alicia said finally.

"I don't know. That's why I'm asking. It seems to me that you'd invested quite a lot in your relationship with Barry. You'd left your first husband, a nice home . . ."

I was guessing about that, but considering how she felt about Barry's house, it seemed like a good bet. "Certainly your involvement had cost you a great deal more than it cost him. And now you're pregnant with his child. I was wondering—"

"If I was angry enough at Barry to want to kill him?" Alicia snapped. "That's really what you're trying to say, isn't it?"

"Well, yes."

"I answered that question yesterday."

"Answer it again."

She didn't. Instead, she hung up on me. I sat at the kitchen table for a moment and stared at the phone in my hand. It didn't ring.

I guessed this meant I didn't have to figure out who murdered Barry. I wasn't sure whether to be relieved or disappointed.

I fixed myself a glass of iced coffee and went in to join the rest of my family on the couch. Just when I was beginning to enjoy Robin Williams's manic impersonation of Aladdin's genie, the phone rang.

"I'll get it!" cried Davey. He jumped up and ran into the kitchen. Faith went along too. A step behind at the start, she beat him to the phone easily. I reached over and pushed the pause button on the VCR.

"It's for you," said Davey, sounding disappointed. Considering that he's gotten no more than half a dozen phone calls in his entire life, I don't know why he's always so surprised when it isn't for him.

"Who is it?" I asked, taking the phone.

"Some lady."

Parenthood, I've discovered, is God's way of reminding you of your inadequacies. I knew I'd taught Davey better phone manners than that; now all I had to do was figure out how to induce him to use them.

I got up and left the room before Davey could get the video's sound track booming again. Back in the kitchen, I fitted the receiver to my ear and heard Alicia's voice.

"Melanie? I'm sorry, I shouldn't have done that."

"Why did you?"

"I don't know. I'm just so tired of everyone asking questions, and treating me like I'm somehow to blame for what happened. I'm the victim here, why doesn't anybody see that?"

Alicia had played on my sympathies before and gotten what she wanted. This time I was going to hang tough.

"Why don't you tell me about your relationship with Barry?" I said.

"It was good. We were happy together."

"Even though he didn't want to marry you?"

"That wasn't an issue," Alicia said firmly. "I don't know why everyone keeps harping on that. Not every woman feels she has to be married, you know."

"You were married before."

"That was the past. Bill and I are divorced."

"So presumably you would have been free to marry Barry if he had asked."

"He didn't need to ask," said Alicia. "He knew I would have turned him down."

"That's not what I heard."

"I can't help it, it's the truth."

I wished we were speaking in person so I could have seen her expression. "What about the baby?"

"What about him?"

"Surely it would have made things less complicated if Barry were his legal father."

"Barry *would* have been his legal father. You don't have to be married for that."

True. I sat and sipped my coffee, thinking that in general nothing was any clearer to me than it had been when I'd first picked up the phone. I hate it when that happens.

"Why didn't you tell me any of this yesterday?" I asked.

"Because there was no need. It's irrelevant. Barry and I were happy together. It wasn't a perfect relationship . . ." Alicia laughed softly. "But then, what is?"

What indeed? I'd thought my own marriage was maybe not perfect, but certainly very good. And I'd continued to think that right up until the day I'd come home and discovered that my ex-husband had moved out without leaving a forwarding address.

It was hard enough keeping score when you were one of the players, much less when you were watching from the outside. I decided to accept Alicia's words at face value for the time being.

"Just one more thing. You've inherited Barry's assets, yet Beth continues to run the business. How does that work?"

"To tell the truth, we're not sure yet. As of this weekend, there are still fourteen dogs in the kennel. I'm not a handler, and I never wanted to be one. But the dogs are here, and many of them are entered over the next few weeks. Beth wanted to see if she could keep things running on her own, so I told her to go ahead."

I thought of the single point she'd won today. "It seems like a lot of work for one person."

"It is. There was plenty to do when all three of us were going to shows together. I believe Beth said her boyfriend was going today to help her out."

"Is that Ralphie?"

"Yes, do you know him?"

"We met this afternoon. Long hair? Big muscles?"

"And not a whole lot going on between his ears?" Alicia chuckled. "Yes, that's the one. During the week he works as a car mechanic, but nights and weekends he hangs around here as much as Beth will let him. They seem like a pretty unlikely couple to me, but Ralphie's devoted, I'll say that for him."

"I was thinking I might have a talk with your ex-husband," I mentioned casually. "Do you have a problem with that?"

"No, why would I?"

"No reason." If she was happy, so was I. "Is Bill a jealous man?"

She sighed softly. "Bill is a complacent man. He has his job, he has his judging, he has his field trials. That's pretty much all he wants out of life."

"And you wanted more?"

"I guess I did," Alicia agreed.

* * *

The first notice I had that Sam had arrived was when Faith ran to the front door, barking. Then I heard Davey yelling. As I was up in my bedroom putting on lipstick, I caught only sketchy details, but it sounded as though my son was trying to interest Sam in a game of catch. At the top of his lungs, naturally.

By the time I reached the hallway, the pandemonium had quieted. Of course, the house *was* empty.

I found everyone out in the backyard. Sam was tossing Davey a Frisbee and I stood on the step and admired the way his body swiveled into the throw. It took him a moment to notice me. I tried not to take it personally.

"Oh, good," Sam said. "You're up."

As I reached the bottom of the steps, Faith raced across the yard and launched herself at me exuberantly. I took that to mean that they weren't letting her join the game and ruffled my hands through her thick mane hair. "Up from where?"

"Davey said you were lying down in your bedroom. We came out here so we wouldn't disturb you."

"Davey." I slanted my son a warning look. He knew perfectly well that fibbing wasn't allowed.

"You were in your room," said my son.

"I was combing my hair and putting on lipstick."

"You might have been sick."

"And you might be looking to miss tonight's dessert."

Davey glanced at Sam, just in case there might be any support coming from that quarter.

"You heard the boss," said Sam. "That's about as far

as I'd push my luck if I were you." He turned back to me. "I'm glad you're well. Come here."

I didn't have to. As he spoke, Sam was closing the distance between us. He reached out and folded me into his arms.

"Ugh," said Davey.

"Nobody asked you to watch," Sam told him over my shoulder. "Throw Faith a ball."

Davey picked up an old tennis ball. Luckily my son doesn't have a poker face; I could read his expression perfectly. "If you hit us with that, you're really going to miss dessert."

He spun around and tossed the ball the other way. Head up, hair flying, Faith took off in pursuit. Sam and I turned to watch.

"How are your dogs?" I asked.

Sam, like Peg, breeds Standard Poodles, although his family of dogs is considerably smaller than hers. Over the winter, he'd lost Charm, his devoted friend and foundation brood bitch. She'd lived to be almost sixteen, an incredibly advanced age for a Standard Poodle, and I knew he missed her terribly.

Dogs are like children that way. No matter how many you have, you still love each one individually, and each leaves a hole in your life when they're gone. I watched Faith scoop up the tennis ball and come galloping back. With any luck, I wouldn't have to worry about that for a long time.

"Everyone's doing well," said Sam. "Callie's in coat, finally. I've never seen a bitch grow hair so slowly. I've got her entered next weekend at Trap Falls and Putnam. Want to come and give me moral support?"

"Sure." As if he needed it. Sam hadn't been in Poodles as long as Peg, but he had a good eye for a dog and an athlete's natural grace in the ring. I always enjoyed watching him show his Poodles, and I especially enjoyed it when he beat Aunt Peg.

She'd been a big fan of his since he moved to the East Coast eighteen months earlier. In fact, it was she who had originally brought us together. Actually, the truth of the matter was that she'd pushed us together repeatedly, as if we weren't adults who were capable of making up our own minds. It was nice to occasionally see her get her comeuppance.

"We're having hamburgers for dinner," Davey told Sam. "We're going to cook on the grill."

"Sounds like a great idea. Who's the chef?"

I've had Sam's cooking. He's also had mine. Believe me, there's no comparison. "You," I nominated.

"Done." Sam bowed with a flourish. "And you, young man, will you agree to serve as my assistant?"

"Done." Davey bowed as well, then turned to Faith. "And you, young dog, will you agree to serve as the assistant's dog?"

If my mother were still alive, she'd have said my son was being fresh. But I'm sorry, I found it funny. Apparently so did Faith. She cocked her head to one side and wagged her tail.

"I think that's a yes," I said.

With that many hands helping, it took twice as long as usual to get dinner on the table. Nobody cared. As we were cooking outside, the game of Frisbee continued unabated. Once the coals were hot and the burgers and corn went on the grill, whoever was closest took a turn at picking up the spatula and flipping anything that looked like it needed flipping.

With that small amount of attention being paid to the details, the meal could have been a disaster, but it turned out amazingly well. Sam had fashioned an extra little hamburger for Faith, and when it was done, I crumbled it on top of her regular food. As usual, the Poodle pushed the bowl around the floor, picking out the good parts, then begged shamelessly at the table.

Davey, who managed to stay on his best behavior for the rest of the evening, didn't have to miss dessert. All right, so I'm a pushover. So far he's turning out to be a pretty good kid, so I figure I must be doing something right.

Sam's been around so much lately that Davey and I no longer think of him as a guest. I gave him the choice afterward of cleaning up in the kitchen or helping with Davey's bath. After a bit of negotiation, the two of them trooped upstairs with Faith trailing along behind to see what kind of mischief they were going to get into.

I heard a few shrieks and plenty of splashing; and at one point Faith came skidding into the kitchen with a clutch of bubbles dangling from her tail, but I resisted the temptation to go up and see how things were progressing. Half an hour later Davey was back downstairs, clean, dry, and freshly pajamaed, with tales of how he'd soundly defeated the Spanish Armada. It was Sam whose shirt was wet clear through. It looked as though he'd fought hard and gone down with his ship.

I went up with Davey to read him a story and put him to bed—we're working our way, chapter by chapter, through *Wind in the Willows*—and snuck a peek at the bathroom on my way past. There was only one small puddle on the floor, the soap was back in its dish, and all the wet towels were hung up to dry. Another small miracle in a life that was coming to seem increasingly full of them, now that Sam was around.

I left Davey with his eyes shut, his favorite stuffed animal clutched in his arms, and Faith lying quietly at the foot of his bed. Back downstairs, I found Sam opening a bottle of Beaujolais he'd brought with him. We took the bottle and our glasses into the yard and sat outside in the warm summer night.

Sam brought me up-to-date on the highlights of the newest software package he was designing, and I told him about my visit to Barry Turk's kennel and about Alicia asking me to look into the murder.

"I never had any dealings with the man," said Sam. "But I gather he wasn't very well liked."

"Not by the other exhibitors, certainly. I've been told he was quite good at making friends with the judges. He always seemed to do enough winning."

"Although he lost Pullmans' Chow, probably the best dog he's ever had, to Crawford. Did Ron tell you why he made the switch?"

I shook my head. "No, and neither did Crawford. By the way, have you met Terry?"

"Who hasn't?" Sam chuckled. "He marched up, looked me in the eye, and said it was a crying shame that I was straight, but if I ever wanted to reconsider, I should look him up."

"Think you could give Crawford a little competition, do you?"

Sam laughed even louder. "Believe me, I'm not interested in finding out."

"I should hope not."

We sat for a few minutes and sipped our wine in silence. That's one of the things I like about Sam. I enjoy talking to him, but I also feel comfortable when we're not saying anything at all.

The moon hung low in the sky. It was nearly three-quarters full and lit my small backyard with a silvery glow. Above, the sky was dotted with stars.

"Whoever shot Turk meant business," Sam said softly. "Are you sure you want to get mixed up in something like that?"

If he'd told me not to, I'd have argued. Since he asked, I answered honestly.

"No, but I couldn't bring myself to turn Alicia down. She's alone, she's pregnant, and she didn't have anyone else to turn to. All I'm going to do is nibble around the edges of the problem a bit and see if I can make things any clearer."

"Promise me you'll be careful."

I reached over and took his hand. "I will."

Always. I'm a mother. That's what we do.

❧❀ *Eight* ❀❧

On Monday morning I dropped Davey off at camp, then drove to Patterson to meet with Bill Devane. We'd spoken on the phone the night before, and he'd told me his schedule was free. Employed as athletic director at the local high school, he had most of the summer off. He was at his leisure; I could come at mine.

I followed the same route to Patterson as I'd used to get to Poughkeepsie, but drove about half the distance. Once there, Bill's concise directions led me to a tidy, well-kept gentleman's farm on about five acres of land. The house was set well back from the road and the dirt driveway that led to it was studded with ruts. A bright yellow sign nailed to a tree proclaimed CAUTION! LABS AT PLAY! and slowed my speed still further.

The house itself was homey and cheerful-looking. Behind it was a small cranberry-red barn that probably served as a garage. There was a small amount of neatly mowed lawn, and a vegetable garden that looked as though it would be supplying half the neighborhood with tomatoes by August.

As I parked the Volvo and got out, I heard a series of low-pitched barks. A moment later, a pair of black Labrador Retrievers came tearing around the side of the barn. The larger of the two had the heft and dignity of middle age. The smaller was shiny and sleek, obviously a young adult. Though they charged in my direction with all the determination of suburban matrons at a Filene's sale, both had their tails up and wagging.

"Biff! Tucker! You two come back here!"

A small door opened in the side wall of the barn, and a solidly built man came hurrying out. Perhaps when Bill Devane was younger, the extra weight might have been muscle, but now a paunch battled with his belt for supremacy, and the roll of fat seemed to be winning. His full head of hair was cropped short and his bushy eyebrows looked as though they might have benefited from the same treatment.

"You'll be all right," Bill called, striding in my direction. "Those two look like a lot, but they're nothing but friendly. Watch they don't knock you down, though."

One Lab ran in exuberant circles. The other jumped up and tried to brace his front paws on my shoulders. From long experience with Aunt Peg's crowd of house Poodles, I sidestepped the maneuver, then reached down and patted the dog's smooth, broad head. His long tail swayed slowly back and forth and the look on his face was blissful.

Bill rubbed a hand down the side of his jeans and held it out to shake. "You must be Melanie. Alicia told me you were helping her out. I want you to know I'm grateful for that. I wish she would let me do more. Come on in the house, where we can sit down and talk."

Biff and Tucker led the way, and I fell in behind Bill. He held the screen door open until all three of us were inside, then motioned to the living room on the left. The room's decor was simple but attractive. There were braided rugs on the floor, upholstered furniture covered in a bold striped fabric, and a collection of hunting prints on the wall. As we sat down, both dogs flopped happily on the cool stones in front of the fireplace.

"First off," said Bill, leaning forward in his chair, "tell me how Alicia's doing."

"She seems well enough. Has it been a while since you've seen her?"

"Just last week. I went to Barry Turk's funeral. Couldn't care less about what happened to him, of course. I did it for her, in case she needed the support. Alicia looked awful, like she was all worn out, and I told her so too. She didn't need to be living like that, and she certainly didn't need to be cheapening herself by living with a bastard like Turk."

"You're still angry about what happened."

"Hell yes, I'm angry! And I've got reason to be. Turk was nothing, a nobody." He paused, pulling down a hard breath. "Alicia told me you showed Poodles."

"I do. I have a Standard puppy I got from my aunt. Margaret Turnbull?"

"Sure." Bill nodded. "Fine lady. If you have a Poodle, you must have known Turk."

"Not well, but I knew who he was."

"Everyone knew who he was. Turk made sure of that. That boy could kiss butt better than a redneck politician.

Don't get me wrong, I'm not saying that there wasn't some razzle-dazzle there. Just that it was all on the surface. Like some of the dogs he showed. I don't care how fancy a trim you put on a donkey, you've still got nothing but an ass underneath."

"You didn't approve of his methods, then."

"Wasn't up to me to approve or disapprove. I judge sporting dogs, Turk never came into my ring. Wouldn't have done him much good if he had, but as it happened, it never came up."

"How long did Barry and Alicia know each other?"

"You mean, when did they first meet?"

I nodded.

Bill sat back and thought for a moment. "I'm not sure I really know the answer to that. Turk's been around a good long while, you know. Alicia and I went to shows together for probably eight years. We were married for six. Living in the same neck of the woods as Turk, I guess we were bound to go to most of the same shows. To tell you the truth, I didn't pay that much attention."

There was a long pause. I wondered if we were both thinking the same thing. Maybe that had been the problem. Biff reached out with one large paw, snagged a rawhide bone, dragged it over, and began to chew.

"I'll tell you when Turk started making a play for Alicia, though, and that was last summer. He wasn't even subtle about it. Following her around at shows, bringing her little trinkets. And all of this going on right under my nose, as if he wasn't dealing with another man's wife!"

"What did you do about it?"

Bill sighed. "Looking back, I guess I could have handled things a little more forcefully. Problem was, whenever Alicia and I were at the shows, I'd be in the ring judging. We'd meet for lunch, but other than that, let's face it, she had some time on her hands.''

He was speaking more confidently now, as if this were a subject he'd devoted a lot of thought to. ''I guess my other mistake was that I didn't take Turk seriously enough. The man had the moral fiber of a snake, I figured anyone with half a brain could figure that out. And Alicia was no dummy.''

No, she wasn't. Still, she'd allowed herself to be swept away by someone who'd showered her with romance and attention. When I'd spoken to Alicia, she hadn't made it sound as though Barry's moral fiber had been a determining factor.

''So listen,'' Bill said earnestly. ''I know you've been to see her. Did she seem okay to you?''

''She was tired,'' I admitted. ''Of course, in her condition—''

''Condition?'' Bill demanded. ''What condition?''

Damn, I thought. He didn't know. And I certainly wasn't the one who ought to be breaking the news.

''What condition?'' Bill repeated. ''What's going on?''

''Alicia is pregnant,'' I said quietly.

''Pregnant?'' He slumped in his chair, his eyes large and round in his head. ''Alicia's pregnant? Are you sure?''

''Yes, she told me herself. The baby's due at the end of the year.''

''Alicia's having a baby?'' Bill shook his head, as if he hoped that would help the information sink in.

''I'm sorry. I thought you knew.''

''No, Alicia never mentioned that. I'm sure she didn't

want me to feel—" His fingers tangled into a knot in his lap. "Well, we never had any children of our own."

Abruptly, Bill stood. "I have to go see her. She said last week that she didn't want me hovering around, but this changes everything."

I stood as well. Tucker was snoring lightly on the hearth. Biff lifted his head inquiringly. "They're nice dogs," I said. "Do you hunt with them?"

Like his ex-wife, Bill Devane was no dummy. "If you're asking me if I know how to handle a gun, the answer is yes. In addition to judging at shows, I also officiate at field trials and I enjoy doing a bit of hunting myself now and then. I own a rifle and two shotguns and the police have already examined the lot. Would you like to see them?"

I shook my head. Considering how little I knew about guns of any sort, I couldn't see how looking at them would have made the slightest bit of difference.

"Just one last question. The night Barry was killed, I heard you were the first person Alicia called. Is that true?"

"Possibly." Bill shrugged. "I don't really know. She called me from the hospital. Of course, I immediately went to join her there."

"Do you know how long it was after Barry was shot that she called you?"

"I haven't any idea."

"But you were here to get the call."

"Of course I was here. How else would I have known what happened?"

Bill was talking to me but he kept glancing toward a

cellular phone that was sitting on an end table. I knew he was itching for me to leave so that he could call Alicia. The screen door had barely closed behind me before he was already hurrying back to punch out a number.

I wondered if Alicia would be glad to hear from him, or if she'd feel like wringing my neck. This changes everything, Bill had said. I wondered if he was right.

Wednesday after camp, Davey and I took Faith and went to Greenwich to see Aunt Peg. The visit was prompted by a message she'd left on my answering machine which hinted that she was feeling neglected. The fact that we'd been reduced to communicating by answering machine was telling, and it was hardly my fault. In the last few weeks, Douglas had monopolized so much of Peg's time that those of us who were merely relatives could barely get a word in.

As usual, Aunt Peg's herd of Standard Poodles was loose in the house when we arrived. They numbered half a dozen or so, all finished champions who were now retired from the show ring. Their elaborate show coats had long since been cut down to the much more manageable kennel trim, which consisted of a blanket of close-cropped hair over the entire body, with a rounded topknot on the head and a pom-pom on the tail. Aunt Peg opened the front door when we arrived and the Poodles came streaming down the steps and across the lawn to greet us.

Like the pack they were, they immediately surrounded Faith. Family member or not, she wasn't a resident, and was now considered an interloper. Peg and I both watched carefully while the Poodles milled around, sniffing noses and other assorted body parts. All were bitches, except for Beau, Peg's retired stud dog. He was king of the realm, and once he'd accepted Faith, everything was pretty much guaranteed to go smoothly.

"She looks good," said Aunt Peg, studying my Standard Poodle with a critical eye.

Compliments from Aunt Peg are as rare as perfect front assemblies, and I couldn't resist preening a bit. "I finally have her eating pretty well. I guess she's beginning to fill out."

"Of course, she needs more hair."

More hair, that was all I kept hearing. Already there were parts of Faith's mane coat that were nearly a foot long. Her topknot hung in a thick, banded ponytail down over her ear, and brushing through her took the better part of an hour because, at fourteen months, she was midway through the dreaded "coat change," in which her downy puppy coat was replaced by the thick, harsh hair of an adult.

"How much more?" Being a teacher, I like to deal in facts.

"Tons," said Peg.

"Tons." Davey giggled, holding his arms wide. "This many."

Tons, right. I looked at all the other Poodles, so neat and elegant in their kennel trims. I thought of Faith's clipper, fantasizing about running it up the length of her back and eliminating the problem once and for all.

"You promised me you'd finish that bitch," said Peg, reading my thoughts correctly.

"Are you sure?"

"Positive. I caught you at a weak moment."

Weak moment, my foot. What she'd done was introduce the puppy to Davey first and ask my permission after. By that time my son had already fallen in love and there was no way I could possibly refuse.

"Maybe I lied."

"I doubt it." Aunt Peg dismissed the possibility with great firmness.

Drat.

"Look what I can do!" Davey raced over to the thick trunk of the massive Japanese elm that stood like a statuesque sentinel in Peg's front yard.

He'd recently discovered that he was just tall enough to hoist himself up onto the lowest branch. From there, it was only a short hop to the next. Scrambling like a monkey, my son pulled himself higher than I could reach as the Poodles raced around the base of the tree and egged him on.

"Davey," I called warningly. It didn't slow his momentum a bit.

"Perhaps you'd better do something," said Peg.

This from the woman who fed my son chocolate for breakfast and let him drive her car. No doubt she was afraid he'd fall and land on one of the Poodles.

"No," I said in a loud voice. "Davey can go as high as he wants. He can stay up there all afternoon if he likes. Let's go inside and have some cookies."

We started for the house, obeying what I think of as one of the first tenets of motherhood: mayhem is fun only if there's an audience around to watch, preferably to gasp in horror. By the time we reached the front door, Davey was right behind us.

"What kind of cookies?" he asked.

"Mallomars," Peg told him. "How was camp?"

Davey's recitation of the highlights of his day took us through the pouring of milk for him, and the brewing of tea and coffee for Peg and me. By that time, I think both adults involved knew more about the workings of Camp Graceland than either of us had a desire to. Fortunately once Davey got a fistful of Mallomars, he was content to go off and do some exploring in Peg's big, old-fashioned house. To no one's surprise, the Poodles trailed hopefully in his wake.

"So," said Peg when we were alone. "Have you figured this thing out yet?"

A mouth filled with cookie prevented me from answering, but it didn't really make much difference. It wasn't as though I had any brilliant deductions to impart.

"Dog show scuttlebutt has it the police aren't the only ones who think Alicia did it."

I swallowed hastily. "Why?"

"Half her detractors seem to think she was angry that Barry got her pregnant and still wouldn't marry her. The other half think she was interested in his money."

"According to Alicia, Barry Turk didn't have any money, and it certainly doesn't look as though she stands to inherit much. Not only that, but Alicia claims that she was the one who didn't want to get married."

"She lived with Barry for nearly a year!"

"She says she was happy the way things were."

"Of course she'd say that," Aunt Peg huffed. "What choice did she have?"

"She had the choice of leaving," I pointed out.

"With a baby?"

"All right, that would have made things tougher. But how about before she got pregnant? She could have left at any time."

Aunt Peg picked up a Mallomar—her fourth, I might point out—and dipped in it experimentally in her coffee. "Say Alicia did want to leave Barry. Where could she have gone?"

"Back to her ex-husband, for one thing. From what I saw on Monday, I'd say that door is still very much open."

Beau, who'd remained behind when the other Poodles left, laid his head on Aunt Peg's lap and gazed upward with imploring eyes. "It's chocolate," she told him sternly. "You can't have any." Then she relented, scooped out a bit of marshmallow, and fed it to him from her fingertips. "So it *is* true that Bill wants her back."

"He couldn't wait to call her yesterday after I told him she was pregnant."

"You told Bill Alicia was pregnant? Are you sure you should have done that?"

"Actually, I imagine I probably shouldn't have. It just sort of slipped out. But even before he knew, Bill was asking me all sorts of questions about her. Alicia might profit from Barry's death in a small way, but if getting Turk out of the way is the impetus that drives her back to Bill, then I'd say he's the one who ended up getting exactly what he wanted."

Aunt Peg thought about that for a moment. The silence called for another Mallomar. No doubt she hoped the sugar rush would go straight to her brain and help her sort things out.

"Bill's never struck me as a violent man," she said finally.

"Maybe not, but he definitely struck me as an angry man. Think about it. Barry was shot in the back, in the dark, by someone who seems to have been a fair distance away. If I wasn't a violent person but I wanted to eliminate someone, that might be the way I'd choose to do it. Especially if I was experienced in handling guns."

"What about Beth?" asked Peg, changing the subject. She tends to do that whenever I say something she'd rather not hear.

"What about her?"

"She was showing Barry's string at the show last weekend. If she's able to make that work, I'd say she profited from his death too."

"She had part of his string. Some of the dogs have already gone home. And she managed to pick up only one point all day. I'd hardly say that's making things work. But here's something else that's interesting. I ran into Bertie at the show, and she told me that Barry Turk was notorious for harassing women handlers in the ring."

That made Aunt Peg sit up. Her hand, holding a Mallomar, paused on the way to her mouth. "Harassing how?"

"She said he was apt to rub up against them or make some sort of sexually suggestive remark. According to Bertie, it's been going on for years."

"And nobody ever reported him for it?"

"Apparently not. The women involved all seemed to think that Barry had enough friends in high places who'd protect him."

"He was pretty chummy with the people who counted," Aunt Peg snorted. "But that doesn't matter, it's still outrageous!"

She was so busy being indignant, I was able to use the opportunity to snag the last Mallomar. A full box to start with, three people eating. Doing the math would have only depressed me.

"And don't forget about Ron Pullman," I said as I chewed.

"Ron? What's he got to do with any of this?"

"Possibly nothing. But he did yank Leo out of Barry's kennel not too long ago, and nobody seems to want to discuss why. You don't have to be psychic to figure out that they had some sort of a problem with each other."

"A psychic," Aunt Peg mused. "Maybe that's what we need to figure all this out."

"Maybe the police are doing better than we are," I mentioned hopefully.

"Have you spoken with them?"

"No, I was thinking that could be your job."

"My job?" She looked affronted. "I have plenty of better things to do than travel to Poughkeepsie to talk to authorities who probably won't tell me a thing. Besides, you were the one who told Alicia you'd help."

"Right," I said, standing firm. "And you were the one who sent me to Alicia in the first place. It's time to put some effort where your mouth is."

"I believe that's supposed to be money."

"Try bribing them if you like, but I doubt if it will help."

She seemed too surprised by my show of strength to

argue any further, so I took that to mean that the matter was settled. It felt good to be giving the orders for a change. It didn't necessarily mean that she'd follow them, but at least it was a start.

ᥱ✻ *Nine* ✻ᥱ

My younger brother, Frank, lives in Cos Cob, a small town on the Connecticut coast between Stamford and Greenwich. In other words, he's right around the corner. In our case, however, mere convenience isn't enough to compel us to spend much time with each other.

Some siblings hate each other as children but become friends when they reach adulthood. Frank and I haven't achieved that state of equanimity yet, though we do finally seem to be working our way in that direction. My brother scoffs at my tendency to work too hard, and I can't understand his to continually slack off. Luckily, there is one thing we've always agreed upon: that Davey is entitled to the best upbringing we can figure out how to provide.

With this in mind, Frank has spent the last five years acting as the one constant male influence in my son's life. At least once a month, the two of them get together on a Saturday and spend the entire day doing something they both enjoy. Their **excursions** have included everything from soccer matches to the local Scottish games. They have not, so far as I can tell, been to any museums.

When Frank arrived early Saturday morning, however, I was in for a surprise. He had spoken to Davey on the phone the night before—my son pushing me out of my own bedroom and closing the door for privacy while they spoke. Davey likes to keep their plans a secret, so I hadn't pressed for details, even though he'd seemed suspiciously smug.

We were in the front yard when Frank got there. It was just past eight on a beautiful summer morning. Heat had been promised for later on, but for now the temperature hovered in the low seventies and the sun felt like a warm caress.

Davey, whose shorts and T-shirt had been clean only half an hour earlier, was playing tag with Faith. The game seemed to involve quick sprints, hairpin turns, and a great deal of rolling in the grass, which accounted for most of the stains now decorating my son's clothing. As I was leaving for the Putnam dog show as soon as Frank picked up Davey, this was Faith's last chance for exercise and she was making the most of the opportunity.

"He's here!" cried Davey.

He grabbed Faith and held her while Frank pulled his shiny black Eclipse into the driveway. Considering my brother's spotty employment record, I figured he must have bought the sports car on a twelve-year plan, and was hoping it would last that long.

"Guess where we're going?" Davey said. That smug look was back, leading me to believe there was every possibility that the two of them were up to no good.

"Where?"

"Guess," Davey demanded.

"Hi, guys." Frank sketched a wave as he unfolded his long frame out of the low-slung car. His hair is brown and straight like mine, but cut considerably shorter. We also share the same hazel eyes and strong bone structure. Unfortunately, I think the effect works better on a man.

Frank opened his arms and Davey ran into them for a hug. Faith, who is almost always hard on his heels, followed suit. Only a rather nifty balancing act on Frank's part kept all three of them from going down in a heap. Considering how many times Faith had come out on top in their previous encounters, I was glad to see that my brother was finally working his way up the learning curve.

"Did Davey tell you where we're going?" asked Frank.

"He's trying to make me guess." I regarded the two of them thoughtfully. "Bungee-jumping? Parasailing?"

"No!" Davey crowed.

"You have an appointment to get matching tattoos?"

"Not even close."

"I think we'd better tell her," said Frank.

"You're right, you'd better tell me. I have a dog show to go to."

Davey began to giggle, then quickly clapped a hand over his mouth.

"As it happens," said Frank. "So do we."

"So do you what?"

"Have a dog show to go to. That's where we're going today. With you."

"You're not," I said quickly. Nobody jumped in to agree with me.

"It was Davey's idea," said Frank. "You've been spending so much time at these dog shows lately, I figured I might as well try one out and see what they're like."

"You told me you thought they were stupid," I pointed out.

"I'm ready to be proved wrong."

"I thought this was supposed to be Davey's chance to get away from me for a change."

"He will be away from you," said Frank. "He'll be with me. You won't even see us all day."

Which didn't necessarily mean I wouldn't hear about their exploits from other exhibitors.

"You're sure that's what you want to do?" I asked weakly.

"Positive," said Frank. "It'll be great. You can pretend you don't even know us. We'll even take our own car."

Davey was already racing toward the black Eclipse. When it comes to hot wheels, nobody has to twist his arm.

I lifted a brow. "Do you know how to get to the dog show?"

"No," Frank admitted. "I was thinking we'd follow you."

Right.

I took Faith inside and got her settled while doing a great job of ignoring the imploring looks she cast my way. Trust me, when it comes to inducing guilt, kids have nothing on Poodles. "Next time," I said finally. "Okay?"

When I got back outside, I saw that Frank and Davey had put down the convertible top on the Eclipse. I stood in the driveway and looked from the shiny little sports car to my nice, solid Volvo station wagon.

There was a small area behind the bucket seats in the Eclipse that only an optimist would have called a seat, but I noted that it did have seat belts. What the hell, I thought. Why should they have all the fun?

"Climb in back," I said to Davey. "I'm coming with you."

The Putnam dog show is held in Pound Ridge, an easy twenty-minute drive from Stamford over back-country roads lined with the sumptuous estates of the very rich. Skimming along in a low-slung convertible, the sun in our faces, the wind in our hair, it was hard to see how the trip could have been improved upon. Bearing in mind that I'd invited myself along, I didn't even say a word about my brother's flagrant disregard for the posted speed limits.

Frank did blanch slightly when we arrived at the show ground and he saw that the parking area consisted of a badly mowed and rather steeply inclined meadow. He got out, surveyed the situation, and came to a decision. We parked at the top on the road and hiked down. Then, true to his word, my brother took Davey's hand and they set off to find their own adventure.

Alone at last, but not for long. The handlers' tent was just at the edge of the parking area, and the first person I saw was Ralphie Otterbach, Beth's boyfriend. He was unloading the maroon van and wearing a ferocious scowl.

"Need some help?" I asked, pretty sure that he did. It was almost nine o'clock, which meant that the judging had already started. The rest of the professional handlers would have had their vans unloaded and their setups in place hours before.

"Screw this," said Ralphie. The scowl turned in my direction. "Who are you?"

"Melanie Travis." I tried out a sunny smile, which had not the slightest effect on his expression. "We met last week."

"You dog people are crazy, you know that?"

"It's been said before," I agreed. "Is Beth under the tent?"

He waved vaguely to the right. I picked up a box of supplies that was sitting on the ground and set off to see for myself. As Standard Poodles weren't scheduled to be judged until afternoon, most of the owner-exhibitors like Sam and Aunt Peg had yet to arrive. All the pros, however, were already hard at work. I passed Crawford's setup, where Terry was blowing dry the legs on a Tibetan Terrier.

His memory was obviously a good bit better than Ralphie's, because when he saw me, he leaned out into the aisle and gave my cheek a loud smooch. "Are we having fun?" he asked.

"I don't know yet," I said, smiling. "I just got here. Is Beth Wycowski over here?"

"Barry's Beth?"

I nodded.

"Keep walking."

I found her a moment later. She looked frazzled and her small setup was a mess. Crates were stacked haphazardly; there were two Miniature Poodles out on grooming tables, and Beth was standing between them, holding a brush in each hand. I set the box of supplies down and pushed it out of the way under a table.

"Did you see Ralphie?" she asked.

"Yes. He's not happy."

"He's not a morning person." Beth shrugged, as if she had more important things to worry about. And as it turned out, she did. "I know you show a Standard. How are you with Minis?"

"Doing what?"

"Brushing, topknot, spray."

I looked at the two medium-size Poodles. Both were clean and clipped, but they were a long way from being ready to go in the ring. "When do they show?"

"Half an hour."

The chances of my being able to get a Poodle ready to be shown in that amount of time were right up there with the possibility that I might scale Mt. Everest. Actually they were worse, because I happen to like heights.

My answer must have shown on my face, because Beth shoved a brush in my hand and said, "Don't make me beg, I don't have time. Whatever you get done is better than nothing."

With confidence like that, how could I help but be inspired?

I had the Mini lying on her side and was brushing quickly through her coat, when Ralphie came puffing up the aisle, carrying a large crate in his hands. He maneuvered the crate in next to the tack box, then stacked two smaller ones on top.

"That's the last of it," he said to Beth. "I'm outta here."

"You'll be back around four?"

"Yeah, sure." He lifted a big, meaty hand and brushed his bangs up off his forehead. Almost immediately, they fell back down. "Unless something comes up."

If Ralphie had been my boyfriend, I would have protested an arrangement like that. Actually, if Ralphie had been my boyfriend, I'd have been thinking of slitting my wrists. Beth, however, didn't seem to mind. She just kept right on brushing as Ralphie lumbered away in the direction of the van.

I picked up my little black bitch and turned her over so I could do the other side. It wasn't up to me to make disparaging comments. Of course, that's never stopped me before.

"Ralphie seems like an interesting guy," I tried, aiming for a diplomatic approach.

"Yeah, sometimes," said Beth. "When he isn't acting like an ass."

So much for diplomacy.

"Have you known him long?"

"About a year. The van broke down last summer and Barry took it in for servicing. I went with him to pick it up. Ralphie was the guy who fixed it."

I thought of my old Volvo that had been traded in that spring. With more than two hundred thousand miles on the odometer, I knew plenty about all the things that could go wrong with cars. "Must be kind of handy having your own mechanic around all the time."

"Oh, he's handy all right."

The tone of her voice made me look up, and I saw that Beth was smiling. "That good, huh?"

"You wouldn't think it to look at him, would you?"

"Well, no."

"Catch Ralphie in just the right mood," Beth confided. "And he can be positively inspired."

At least that cleared up one mystery. Now I knew what she saw in him. I raked a slicker through the bracelets on the bitch's legs, then rolled her upright so she was lying straight. Luckily, she'd been shown before and knew the routine.

Some Poodle people wrap ear hair and band topknots. Some wrap the hair on both. Beth was of the latter school. Using the last tooth in my comb, I snagged the rubber band holding the first wrapper in her topknot and yanked it hard enough to pop.

As I moved on to the next wrap, I said, "Mind if I ask you a few questions?"

"About Barry?" Beside me, Beth was moving faster than I was. She already had her Mini's topknot undone and was brushing through it to straighten and untangle the long strands. "Sure, go ahead." She glanced down at her watch. "Just as long as you can brush and talk at the same time. That doesn't have to be perfect, you know."

I popped the last rubber band and quickly unrolled the wrappers. The hair was curly from being folded. I spritzed it with water and began to brush. Beth was already fishing around in the tack box for the knitting needle she'd use to make parts for the new, tighter topknot that the bitch would wear in the ring.

"Do you know Alberta Kennedy?" I asked.

"Bertie? Sure. I see her around all the time."

"She told me she'd had some trouble with Barry."

Beth's brow furrowed. "What kind of trouble?"

"She called it sexual harassment."

"Barry?" She sounded as though she were aiming for outrage, but the act wasn't very convincing.

"According to Bertie, she's not the only one who had a problem."

Beth was holding some rubber bands between her lips

while her fingers were busy with the hair. Handlers did it all the time, but now she used the fact that her mouth was full as an excuse not to answer.

"Well?" I said finally.

"You know Barry," Beth mumbled.

"Actually, I didn't know him. At least, not very well. Why don't you tell me about him?"

"He was a pretty simple guy. He figured he worked hard, so he was entitled to play just as hard. To him, sex was playing."

"I doubt that any of the women he rubbed himself up against in the ring were amused," I said dryly.

"He was just trying to have a little fun."

I wondered how much Alicia had known about Barry's propensity for having fun.

"Why are you defending him?" I asked.

"Because it wasn't any big deal," Beth insisted. "Now that he's not here to defend himself, people can say all sorts of things. There's no reason to let it all get blown out of proportion."

"Did he ever try anything with you?"

Beth shrugged. "How's that bitch coming?"

"Topknot's in."

Luckily she didn't bother to look. The bubble over the Mini's eyes had turned out flat and the whole thing had a serious list to one side. If there'd been time, I'd have redone it. There wasn't, so I took the can of hair spray Beth held out to me and went on.

"I'll tell you something," she said as we sprayed. "But it's just between you and me. I don't want you spreading it around, okay?"

"Okay."

"Barry and I . . . we kind of had a fling."

Why wasn't I surprised? "When?"

"Last winter."

"After Alicia had moved in."

"Yeah," Beth admitted. "I guess."

I wondered if Beth realized her involvement could be construed as a possible motive for murder. "Didn't it bother you that Alicia was living with him?"

"I figured if it didn't bother him, why should it bother me?"

"Did he tell you he was going to leave her?"

"Why would he have done that?"

This was like walking through deep mud with suction cups on my feet. "Well, since the two of you were having an affair . . ."

"You thought I might be looking for something more permanent with Barry?" Beth shook her head emphatically. "Believe me, that wasn't what I was after. Barry wasn't that big a prize."

"Then why were you sleeping with him?"

"It just kind of happened. You know."

No I didn't, thank goodness. I waited a little, keeping busy with my hair spray. When her Mini was finally looking like it was almost ready, she elaborated.

"We went away with the dogs on a long circuit," said Beth. "And let me tell you, there just isn't that much else to do in the winter in upstate New York."

Well, that explained everything, didn't it?

"Did Alicia know?" I asked.

"No. Do you think we're crazy? And you're not going to tell her either."

"You're right, I won't. What about Ralphie?"

"He didn't know either, which is a damn good thing. You might not be able to tell by looking at him, but Ralphie has a real hot temper."

Big muscles, little brain, hot temper. That sounded like a winning combination. Good thing Ralphie was good in bed, otherwise he might have had a hell of a time getting dates.

Beth looked at her watch again. "It's time to go up to the ring. Can you bring her for me?"

I nodded.

As Beth pulled off her apron and ran one of the dog combs through her hair, she appraised my work with a critical eye. "She'll do. You did a pretty good job."

"Thanks." I picked up my Mini, waited until she'd picked up hers, then said casually, "Now that Barry's out of the way, do you think you'll be able to make a go of it with his clients?"

Beth smirked. "You mean, now that you know he and I were more than just coworkers, did I blow him away over some imagined slight so that I could let my ambitions run wild while taking over his business?"

Like I said before about Beth, no bullshit.

"Yeah," I said, grinning back at her. "Something like that."

"Barry was my meal ticket. Trust me, there's no way I would have messed that up."

We got both Minis up to the ring in time for judging, but as things turned out, it didn't make much difference. In a small entry, the male managed to go Reserve. The bitch was unplaced in a big Open class. After all the work she'd put in, Beth had to have been disappointed.

"All right, the bitch maybe," she said as we strolled back to the setup. "But the dog should have won in a walk. Jeez, if I'd have wanted to murder someone, it wouldn't have been Barry. I'd have sicked Ralphie on the judges."

❦❖ *Ten* ❖❦

I delivered the Miniature Poodle back to Beth's setup, then headed over to the concessions to get myself a cup of coffee. It felt strange to be at a dog show without Davey, and stranger still to know that he was somewhere on the grounds without me.

I wondered if he and Frank were enjoying themselves. Since my brother's main interests in life are women, team sports, and beer, it didn't seem likely. If Frank was grinding his teeth in boredom, however, at least I didn't have to witness it. That in itself made for a pleasant change.

Since it was mid-morning, the line at the food concession had dwindled to a mere five-minute wait. The breakfast rush was over, lunch had yet to begin. I did notice, however, that they were already cooking hamburgers on the grill—heating them through, then stacking them on one side to be sold later. No wonder the food at dog shows tastes so bad.

I'd just paid for my coffee, when Douglas Brannigan came strolling up behind me. "Good morning," he said. "Isn't this a lovely park?"

"Lovely," I agreed, rolling the word off my tongue. It isn't one I get to use in conversation often, but something about Douglas's dignified demeanor made it seem entirely appropriate. "Did you come with Peg?"

"Yes. She's gone to park the car, and I've been sent to find tea." He grimaced slightly as the aroma of over-cooked meat wafted toward us from the grill. "I assume this would be the place?"

"The only food concession on the grounds. Buy at your own risk."

"Yes, well." Douglas eyed the growing stack of mud-brown hamburgers with about as much enthusiasm as I had. "As long as the water's hot and the tea's in a bag, I imagine it's hard to go wrong."

He placed his order and I waited with him while it was filled. Lemon seemed to be out of the question. Douglas picked up several extra packets of sugar instead. I had to smile at that. Buying for Aunt Peg, it was exactly what I would have done.

"I'm very new to all this," he said as we headed across the lot toward the grooming tent. "Two months ago, the only dog show I'd ever heard of was Westminster. If somebody had asked me how many shows there were in a year, I'd have said one. So obviously I'm under-informed. Would you mind if I ask you a question?"

"Not at all," I said, taking a cautious sip of coffee. It was hot and dark, which was about the best that could be said for it.

"Peg seems very involved in showing her Poodles. Sometimes, perhaps, to the exclusion of other things in life. So I was wondering whether this sport has a season, like so many others do. Might it be something one does all summer, and then the activity would taper off in the fall?"

He sounded so hopeful, this nice man carrying my aunt's tea and her extra packets of sugar, that I was almost tempted to lie. But that would have only postponed the bad news.

"I'm afraid not. People show dogs all year round. In the Northeast, there are shows every week of the year except Christmas."

"Every week?" he mumbled. "You don't say."

"Of course Peg doesn't go every single week. Nobody does, except the professional handlers, or the exhibitors whose dogs are trying for year-end awards. Peg enters a show only when the Poodle judge is someone whose opinion she respects."

"You mean, one she thinks she can win under," said Douglas, who obviously wasn't as much of a novice as he thought.

"Exactly. And then of course there are times when Aunt Peg doesn't have a Poodle in hair that she wants to show. Like me, right now. My Standard, Faith, is fourteen months old. She's sitting at home, waiting to grow up."

"That would be Hope's sister."

He was right again, which meant that he must have been doing a good job of paying attention. Even I sometimes still have difficulty telling all of Aunt Peg's Poodles apart, much less figuring out who's related to whom, and how.

"And when will Faith be ready?" asked Douglas.

"Probably three or four months."

He thought for a moment. "In the meantime, Peg has Tory in the ring. And when Tory has finished her championship . . ."

I saw where he was heading with that idea and finished for him. "Hope will be ready to start showing again."

Poor Douglas looked morose. "Not to give you the wrong impression," he said quickly. "I'm enjoying the dog shows, really I am. It's just that I wish Peg and I could do other things together as well.

"For example, last night I had tickets for Shakespeare in Central Park. I thought we could go into New York early and enjoy dinner beforehand, maybe have drinks at the Palm Court afterward. Instead, it turns out that she's made plans to show both days this weekend, and feels that trying to sandwich a trip into the city in the middle of all that would be too much."

He didn't sound angry, just disappointed, which made me all the more determined to try to explain how committed Aunt Peg was to her Standard Poodles. First, however, I needed to fill in some background.

"Does Peg ever talk to you about her husband?" I asked.

"Max? She's mentioned him. I know they were married for many years, and I gather they had a very good relationship."

Surprisingly, he probably knew almost as much about

their lives together as I did. Max had been my uncle, my father's brother. A third sibling, Rose, had joined a Catholic convent at an early age and remained there for thirty years, before choosing to resume a secular life the summer before.

An old argument over money had driven the three of them apart, and for much of my life the family had been estranged. My parents had been killed in a car accident when I was pregnant with Davey, and it wasn't until a year ago that I'd discovered the reason for the rift. By then Max was gone, and much of what I knew about him, I, too, had learned from Aunt Peg.

"Max was very much involved in breeding and showing the Poodles," I told Douglas. "It was something that he and Peg did together. Now people think of the Cedar Crest line as being Aunt Peg, but it wasn't always that way."

We were nearing the grooming tent, which was, as always, a hub of activity. Douglas paused outside the row of exercise pens that marked the boundary of the handlers' area so that we could finish our conversation. "So perhaps this is her way of keeping his memory alive?"

"At least in part, yes. Maintaining the quality of the Cedar Crest Standard Poodles is something that was important to both of them. In a sense, I'm sure Peg feels that she's carrying on Max's work. But there's something else.

"After Max died, Peg was very lonely. She threw herself into the breeding and showing as a way to take her mind off what had happened. Going to dog shows kept her busy at a time when there were other gaps in her life that she didn't want to think about."

Douglas smiled. "You mean gaps like the one I'm currently filling?"

"Well . . . yes. After Max died, Peg needed to fill her life with other things, and she did. Maybe now she needs to create some openings. She just hasn't figured out how to do that yet."

"You're telling me to be patient," said Douglas.

"Oh no, I'm not." I held up a hand. "I would never presume to give advice—"

"Yes, you would." His smile widened. "You're not Peg's niece for nothing. I thank you for our chat. It gives me much to think about, and it's been most enlightening."

I followed him under the tent, and we cut across to the other side, where Peg had set up her table and crate. When we got there, Sam was just unloading his things into the space she'd saved for him. He looked all around me, then shook his head. "It's the strangest thing. I could have sworn I just saw Davey over by the rings."

"You probably did," I said.

Aunt Peg looked horrified. "Melanie, that child's five years old. Don't tell me you're letting him run around the dog show all by himself."

"Not at all. He's with Frank."

"My nephew Frank?" Peg looked no happier than she had a moment before. "What is *he* doing here?"

"Taking good care of my son, I hope. Today was their day to do something together. According to Frank, Davey wanted to come to the show."

"And Frank agreed?" Sam laughed.

"What's the matter with that?" asked Douglas.

"Frank doesn't like dogs!" Peg snorted. "That's what's the matter with that. I'll have you know that boy once sat me down for a heart-to-heart talk in which he recommended that I get rid of every single one of mine."

"He was trying to help," I pointed out. "It was right after Max died, and Frank seemed to think that you would want to simplify your life."

"The only thing that needed eliminating from my life at that point was Frank."

"He meant well. And he's getting better. He's even starting to like Faith."

"Says you." Sam was still laughing. "He calls her 'that bear' behind your back."

"He does?"

"You see?" cried Peg. "That boy is impossible!"

"He's not a boy, Aunt Peg. Frank is twenty-seven."

"Physically, perhaps. Not mentally. Just to be on the safe side, I think you'd better hunt them down and make sure Davey is being well taken care of."

"You don't understand," I protested. "This is my day off."

"I don't care. You've entrusted my grandnephew's well-being to someone who'd probably benefit from having a keeper himself."

"Frank's not *that* bad. . . ." My voice trailed off, probably due to lack of conviction. I'd spent a lifetime alternately defending my brother or cleaning up after him. Besides, Peg wasn't the only one who'd suspected that a dog show might not be the best idea.

Peg's glare never even wavered.

"All right," I said, sounding every bit as grumpy as I felt. "I'm going."

I started my search at the section of the show grounds devoted to the obedience competition. Dogs who show in obedience have been trained to follow a variety of commands. Rather than simply remaining at their owner's side as the breed dogs do, these competitors jump, retrieve, and stay on command. Because the routines are entertaining and easy to follow, novice spectators are often drawn there first. The ringside was crowded, and there were several family groups in evidence, but no sign of Davey and Frank.

After watching a Sheltie turn in a near-flawless performance, I headed back the other way. As at most dog shows, the breed rings had been set up in two parallel rows with a tent running down the middle between them. At the near end were the big rings, where the large breeds from the Sporting, Working, and Hound groups were judged. The first one I came to was filled with Irish Setters.

Six of the beautiful red dogs were gaiting around the perimeter of the ring, seeming to move almost in unison. With their heads up and tails out, they were the picture of canine good health and exuberance. Dogs are judged at a trot because it's a functional gait for assessing soundness, but watching these Irish Setters move was like reading poetry. There was elegance, there was simplicity, and a perfect blending together of parts into a harmonious whole.

The line finished its circuit, then came to a stop in the portion of the ring that was shaded by the tent. Handlers toward the back of the line began to chat and run combs through their dogs' windblown coats. The first Irish Setter was walked out into the sunlight and stacked for his individual examination. I'd been so busy watching the dogs that it wasn't until the judge approached the Setter that I realized it was Bill Devane.

At home Bill had struck me as easygoing, but inside his ring he was all business. He'd donned a jacket and tie for the occasion, though he didn't look particularly comfortable in either. The jacket was rumpled and his cuffs were slightly frayed, but Bill assessed the Irish Setter entry with an air of authority that left little doubt, at least in my mind, that he knew just what he was looking for.

As he moved the first dog, I glanced around the ringside. No sign of Frank or Davey, but I did find one familiar face I hadn't expected to see. Alicia Devane was sitting just outside the tent on one side of the ring, watching her ex-husband work.

Hair freshly washed, makeup neatly applied, she looked markedly more composed than she had the last time I'd seen her. In keeping with the warm weather, she was wearing a sleeveless cotton shift that was loose enough to hide any changes in her figure. On her face was the rapt expression of a groupie at a rock concert. I pulled a chair over beside her and sat down.

Alicia glanced in my direction, smiled briefly, then turned her eyes back to the ring. "I've gotten some calls. I hear you've been talking to people."

"That's what you wanted me to do, isn't it?"

In the ring, Bill awarded the Open Dog the purple ribbon for Winners. His judging was careful and precise, but he took time out every few minutes to glance over to where Alicia was sitting. When he caught her eye, they both smiled.

"I thought so. Now I'm not so sure."

"Have the police turned up anything?"

"If they have, they aren't sharing it with me." Alicia sighed softly. "I do want to know what happened to Barry. It's just that for the baby's sake, I wish I could simply put all this behind me. Bill called me after you spoke with him."

"I figured he would. Were you angry?"

"That you told him about the baby?" She shook her head. "I should have told him myself. This forced the issue, that's all."

"He seemed very concerned."

"He would. Bill doesn't take responsibility lightly."

This time, we both looked into the ring. Bill nodded slightly in our direction. It was clear he was keeping tabs on his ex-wife.

"Surely he no longer feels responsible for you?"

"You wouldn't think so, would you?"

Alicia hadn't answered my question, and we both knew it. Instead, she changed the subject. "Tell me what you've found out."

"Not very much, I'm afraid." And the things I did know were not necessarily the sort I wanted to tell her. "Barry did seem to have the unfortunate capacity to rub people the wrong way."

I blanched, realizing what I'd said, but Alicia didn't seem to notice. Quickly, I pressed on. "I know he lost the Pullmans' Chow in the spring. Have there been other clients who left him recently?"

She thought for a moment. "None worth mentioning. You know how it is, people are always moving their dogs around. No matter how much you're doing for them, they always think they can get a better deal somewhere else. We'd lost a few dogs in the last couple of months, but we'd gained some too. Actually, overall our numbers were up."

"So what happened with Leo?"

Her eyes darted my way, then back. "What do you mean?"

"When a specials dog changes handlers like that, it's news. Something must have gone wrong. What was it?"

"What makes you think I'd know the answer to that?" Alicia's tone was brisk and, I thought, somewhat defensive.

"You and Barry were living together. Not only that, but you came to all the shows with him. You must have known what was going on."

"About some things, yes. But not everything. Barry and I weren't business partners, we were in love. Believe it or not, we didn't discuss work all that much."

I picked at a splinter on my chair and said casually, "So I guess you wouldn't know whether or not Ron Pullman left an unpaid bill behind when he moved Leo to Crawford's."

"Everybody knew about that," said Alicia. "Barry complained about it often enough."

Before I could ask another question, a shadow fell across our faces. I looked up and saw Austin Beamish standing over us. An experienced show-goer, he had a canvas folding chair under his arm, which he opened out and placed beside Alicia's seat.

"What a pleasure it is to see you, my dear," he said, taking both of her hands in his. "I'm so glad you've found your way back to the shows."

"It's nice to be here." Alicia smiled. "I've missed seeing all my friends."

"If there's anything I can do, anything at all, you must call me. I'd be happy to help."

"Thank you. I'm doing fine, but I appreciate the offer."

"Hello, Melanie," Austin leaned forward and gave a small wave. "I didn't know you had an interest in Golden Retrievers."

I looked into the ring. While Alicia and I had been talking, the Irish Setters had finished being judged and Golden Retrievers had taken their place.

"I enjoy watching all the breeds. Is Midas entered today?"

"Today and every day," Austin said lightly, a clear indication of the size of his wallet. "He won Best in Show yesterday. I've got my fingers crossed for a repeat performance this afternoon."

"Congratulations," I told him. "And good luck."

I was sincere in my good wishes, but Midas certainly didn't need them. In a ring filled with pretty Golden Retrievers, he was once again a standout. Bill wasted no time in awarding him Best of Breed.

"That's the first step," said Austin, standing up and folding his chair. "The Sporting group's at three. Stop by the ring and cheer us on, if you can."

Call me a cynic, I thought as he walked away. But I doubted I was the only one who'd noticed that Bill was keeping an eye on his ex-wife from inside his ring. Was it mere chance that had Austin sitting by Alicia's side, offering condolences while his dog was being judged, or an opportunity seen and taken?

I watched Austin pause by the gate to have a word with Tom Rossi as the handler exited the ring. Midas stopped at the end of his lead and stood quietly. If I'd let someone else show Faith, she would have turned handsprings with joy when I reappeared. The Golden Retriever, however, barely spared Austin a glance. He might be the dog's owner, but it was clear they'd never spent any time together.

Beside me, Alicia was gathering up her things. The morning's judging was over, and once Bill had finished having his picture taken with the dogs he'd put up, he'd be free to go to lunch.

"Did Barry ever show any of Austin's dogs?" I asked.

"Not that I know of," Alicia said, standing. "If he did, it was before my time. I don't think Austin and Barry liked each other very much."

"Barry told you that?"

"Actually, it was Austin. Ron Pullman introduced us and Austin made some sort of tacky comment about how I needed to improve my taste in men. At the time, he seemed to find it amusing." She frowned distastefully. "I certainly didn't."

"Funny, I just met Austin a few weeks ago, but he's always been rather charming to me."

"You must be every bit as young as you look," said Alicia. "Trust me, all men are charming until they get what they want. After that you're on your own."

When Bill was finished with his photos, he and Alicia

left the ringside together. A casual observer would have taken them for a happy couple.

As I watched them leave, I thought about what Alicia had said. She seemed to know a lot of men who were used to getting what they wanted. What about Bill Devane? I wondered. Did he fit the mold as well?

❧✿ *Eleven* ✿❧

Ten minutes later, I found Frank and Davey standing in line at the Good Humor truck. Lunchtime? No mother around? In their minds, I guess that called for ice cream.

Davey waved when he saw me. "We saw a motor home get stuck in a ditch," he cried. "It was awesome!"

And to think I'd been worried that they might not find the dog show entertaining enough.

"Want something?" asked Frank. He'd worked his way to the front of the line and had his wallet out. That was a rare sight. Besides, I'd already seen what the food concession had to offer.

I got a toasted almond bar and three napkins, one for each of us since nobody else seemed to be thinking about things like that. Davey went for a chocolate eclair, while Frank opted for something covered in coconut.

"Listen," he said as we moved off to one side. "There's someone I want to meet. I figured you could introduce me."

"Really?" I asked curiously. "Who?"

"A woman, a redhead. She handles other people's dogs. Davey told me you knew her."

Bertie, it had to be.

Of course, we wouldn't have been brother and sister if I hadn't still harbored the childish urge to make him squirm. "Any particular reason why you'd like to meet her?"

"She looks like a nice person."

"You could tell that from watching her show dogs?"

"Maybe not." Frank grinned. "But I could sure as hell tell I wanted her phone number."

"You sure as hell could," Davey echoed. He's just beginning to figure out that swear words have a fair amount of shock value when spoken by a five-year-old. Accordingly, he throws them into the conversation as often as he thinks he can get away with it.

I glared in his direction, but my son didn't notice. He was too busy trying to lick the ice cream off his stick before the rest of it could dribble down onto his hands. Good thing I'd picked up those extra napkins.

"About this handler . . . ?"

"Bertie," I supplied.

"Bertie. Is she seeing anyone?"

"Not that I know of, but she and I aren't exactly confidantes. You'll have to ask her that yourself."

"Great," Frank said enthusiastically. He's never been low on self-confidence. "Let's go."

We found Bertie under the grooming tent. She was munching on a handful of carrot sticks and running a damp towel over the back of a Basset Hound. Looking at her, I was reminded of the Irish Setters I'd admired earlier. She was sleek, elegant, and definitely eye-catching.

"You again," she said, but a smile softened her words. "More questions, right?"

"Maybe a couple. But first I want you to meet my brother." I performed the introductions. "This is Frank's first dog show."

"This is fascinating," he gushed. I wondered if it was as obvious to her as it was to me that he was lying through his teeth. "I'm really enjoying the whole scene."

"Glad to hear that," Bertie was noncommittal as she went back to work. For her, being approached by enthusiastic males was probably nothing new. "What breed do you have?"

"I don't actually have a dog of my own at the moment . . ." Frank faltered, but then quickly recovered. "But of course, Melanie and my aunt have Standard Poodles. They're magnificent animals."

Magnificent animals, my foot. "He calls them bears," I mentioned.

"Only when I'm kidding around," Frank said. "Listen, I was wondering—"

"I'm bored," Davey announced. "Come on, Uncle Frank. I want to go watch the dogs in the ring."

"Just a minute, Davey."

"No, now!"

When my son gets in that mood, he can try the patience of a saint; and if there was one thing my brother wasn't in line for, it was sainthood.

Davey grabbed Frank's hand and began to pull. Considering his size, he's pretty strong. Frank had a pained expression on his face.

"Maybe your mother would like to take you over to the rings," he said somewhat desperately.

"Then again, maybe she wouldn't." I smiled sweetly.

Out of the corner of her eye, Bertie watched the family interplay with interest. Quickly Frank reevaluated his options. I knew what he was thinking. Would he score more points by staying and talking, or by playing the role of the doting uncle? When Davey's next, outraged shriek caused Bertie's dog to jump up in a startled reaction, my brother saw the wisdom in moving on.

"I guess we're going." Frank turned a hundred-watt smile in Bertie's direction. "Will you be around later?"

"All day," she told him.

Together, we watched them walk away.

"He seems like a nice guy," said Bertie.

"I'm sure he was hoping you'd think so." There was an unoccupied grooming table behind me. I curled my fingers around the rubberized edge and hopped up to have a seat. "Don't get me wrong. Frank *is* a nice guy. I guess it's just hard for a sister to be too complimentary."

Bertie picked up a pair of carrot sticks from the top of her grooming box and offered me one. "What does he do?"

"At the moment, he's tending bar in Greenwich. Frank has what you might call a diversified career history."

"Nothing wrong with that," said Bertie. "So was he interested, or what?"

"Frank asked for the introduction. I'm sure he hoped to get your phone number."

"That's easy enough." Bertie reached around, fished around the top tray of her tack box, and came up with a business card, which she handed over.

"I should tell you, he doesn't really like dogs."

"That's okay. Sometimes I'm not so sure I do either." She caught my look and smiled. "After a while, enough is enough, you know? Besides, it's not like it's easy to meet guys. Around here, all the interesting men are either married or gay. I'm not saying I want to spend the rest of my life with your brother, but I'll meet him for a drink. It might be fun, and it would certainly be a relief not to spend the whole night talking about dog shows."

I pocketed the business card. I figured Frank now owed me one. It wasn't the worst position to be in.

"So what else?" asked Bertie. "It seems like you never show up unless you want to know something. What is it this time?"

Was I really that much of a pest? I hoped not. But she was right, I did have questions.

"Would you be willing to give me the names of the women who were going to report Barry Turk for harassment?"

"I might." Bertie thought for a moment. "Although I doubt they had anything to do with his murder."

"Maybe, maybe not. It must be awfully frustrating to have something like that happen and then find out you have no recourse through official channels. Could be they decided to take matters into their own hands."

"Let me check with them," said Bertie. "One's a new client of mine, and I don't want to ruffle any feathers. If they say they wouldn't mind talking to you, I'll give you a call."

"Great." I scooted forward and slid down off the table-top. "Speaking of clients, it looks like business is going pretty well for you."

"So far, so good. I wouldn't mind having a group dog or two to round things out."

Like every other pro, Bertie was constantly searching for the big dog and big client that could make a handler's career.

"I just saw Austin Beamish over at the Golden ring. Have you ever thought about going after his dogs?"

"Briefly." Bertie smiled. "Very briefly. That man's too tough for me. He wants what he wants and nobody better get in his way. Besides," she said ruefully, "Austin hires only the best. I'm much too small-time for him."

"Now maybe. Not forever."

"Hold that thought," said Bertie. "I sure am."

I strolled back over to Aunt Peg's setup, where I delivered the news that Frank and Davey were fine, and found myself pressed into service holding Poodle noses while Tory and Callie stood on their tables to be scissored. Standard Poodles are tall. By the time Sam and Peg were finished, I had a cramp in my arm and a crick in my neck.

"Do you want me to check the ring?" I asked, angling for easier duty.

"It's not necessary," said Peg. "Crawford will be back with Leo any minute. He'll let us know what's going on."

Most judges are licensed for a variety of breeds, but in general they tend to branch out within the same group. Practically speaking, this often means that at a single show an entire group might be judged by the same person. Chows, also in Non-Sporting, were scheduled two breeds ahead of Standard Poodles.

As Peg and Sam began to spray up, Crawford came

back to the tent clutching the purple and gold Best of Breed rosette in his hands. Terry, the assistant, was leading Leo. Ron and Viv, the proud parents, followed along behind.

"We won!" Terry crowed, just in case there had been any doubt.

"Big deal," I teased him. "You always win."

"That's because Leo's the best." He lowered his face and nuzzled the Chow's nose with his own. "Aren't you, little boy?"

Leo wagged his tail, and the back end of his stocky body wriggled back and forth at the same time. Maybe he was agreeing. Or maybe it was the piece of dried liver Terry slipped him from his pocket that got him so excited.

"Not now," Crawford said sternly. He had two Standard Poodles lying on their grooming tables, awaiting the finishing touches.

"Need help?" I asked.

"We should be okay. Terry's a wiz with hair." Crawford cast a meaningful glance at his assistant. "When I can get him moving."

"I'm moving, I'm moving. See?" Terry wiggled his butt back and forth a few times, much like Leo had just done.

Viv and I laughed. Crawford sighed loudly, but he didn't look too upset. Everyone went to work, and ten minutes later we all trooped up to ringside. Sam and Aunt Peg were both entered in the Open bitch class. Crawford had an Open dog and a Puppy bitch. Ron stayed back at the setup, but Viv came with me to watch.

While Crawford showed the Open dog, Terry held the puppy near the gate. He took a comb out of his pocket and ran it through the pom-pom on her tail.

"You *are* a wiz with hair," I told him with no small amount of envy. "Aunt Peg's been working on me for a year now, and I still can't get the scissoring just right. How did you ever pick it up so quickly?"

"Talent like this is in the genes."

I gave him the look the comment deserved.

"Don't tell me you want the truth!" Terry said. "How dull. Hon, I've been doing hair for years. Before I met Crawford I was a hairdresser. You know, saving up to buy my own shop and never quite getting there? Being forced to work for Medusa to earn my daily bread? Then poof! True love hit me right between the eyes, and next thing I knew Crawford had taken me away from all that."

"How nice for you."

"Nice for Crawford too. Honey, I'm good."

He reached up and ran the tips of his fingers through my hair. It fell, thick and straight, to my shoulders, the same as it had since I was a teenager. Since nothing I did to it seemed to make much difference, I'd pretty much given up trying.

"I'll do you sometime if you like," Terry offered. "Maybe a few layers in the front to frame your face?"

"You should take him up on it," said Viv. "He *is* good. You know how things slow down late in the day, when everyone's just sitting around waiting for Best in Show? I've seen Terry pull out a pair of scissors and go to work. He did Tom Rossi's assistant at Greenwich, and next thing you know, a line had formed."

"Only two people," Terry said modestly, then ruined the effect by adding, "Of course, they were two very satisfied people by the time I got done with them."

In the ring, Crawford won the Open class and then

took the points. Terry unrolled the puppy's leash, had a last critical look, then switched Poodles with Crawford, who went back in the ring. I ambled down the sideline to where Peg and Sam were waiting.

"That will help," said Peg. "I always feel better when Crawford wins right before I have to show against him. With any luck, Winners Dog will be his piece for the day."

Judges are only human. They like to make as many people happy as possible, especially since satisfied exhibitors tend to come back and enter under them again, and most shows try to hire judges that they know will draw the largest number of entries. In theory, Crawford had now had his win in Poodles for the day, which meant that he would be less likely to beat the winner of the Open Bitch class with his puppy.

Sam smoothed down Callie's ears with a damp comb. "I don't know why you're worried about Crawford. I'm the one you're going to have to beat."

"Says you." Peg harrumphed.

"Good luck to both of you," I said diplomatically when the Open class was called. As they entered the ring, I went back to watch the proceedings with Viv.

"I swear, I don't know how you Poodle people stand that trim," she said. "You must be brushing and clipping day and night."

"Sometimes it feels that way," I agreed. "Believe it or not, the continental is a direct descendant of a traditional German hunting clip."

"You're pulling my leg." Viv was obviously amused. "I used to go hunting with my daddy and brothers when

I was little, and none of our hunting dogs looked like that."

"It's true," I said.

In the ring, Tory had reached the head of the line and was being examined by the judges. I smiled to myself as Aunt Peg placed her hand around Tory's muzzle and foreface. To the uninitiated, it might have looked as though she needed that grip to hold the bitch still. I knew better, however. Tory was very well trained; she wouldn't have dreamt of moving while the judge's hands were on her.

The problem was that for a Poodle, Tory didn't have a very pretty head. Aunt Peg wasn't actually obstructing the judge, she was just restricting his view. By the same token, when the man put his hands on Tory's very correct shoulder assembly, Peg stepped back out of the way and let him have all the time he wanted.

"There's a rumor that's been floating around," Viv confided in a low tone. "I heard the police are going to arrest Alicia for Barry's murder."

"Really? Who told you that?"

Viv shrugged. "You know how people talk."

"Well, today they can talk directly to the source. Alicia's here."

"She is?"

I nodded. "She was watching Bill judge. Last time I saw them, they were on their way to the judges' tent to get some lunch."

"It hardly sounds like she's running from the law, does it?"

I glanced over at Viv, who kept her eyes firmly trained on the ring. "You sound disappointed."

"Do I? I didn't mean to. I don't know Alicia well, but I'd be surprised to find out that she was behind Barry's murder. She strikes me as the type of woman who needs someone to take care of her. Barry wasn't much, but he was probably better than nothing."

"Apparently he was good enough to leave Bill for," I pointed out.

"I doubt there are many women who would agree." Viv shook her head. "Talk about adding insult to injury. Now, if someone were to tell me that Bill was the one who shot Barry in the back, that wouldn't surprise me one bit."

Peg finished gaiting Tory and took her to the end of the line. Sam was next, and I watched as he presented Callie to the judge. Aunt Peg has shown dogs for years and she's very good at it. Sam, however, was all fluid motion and deft grace. It was a joy just watching him move.

"I take it that one's yours," said Viv.

"The bitch? No, she belongs to—"

"Not the bitch." Viv laughed. "The man. You're all but drooling."

"I am not." All right, so maybe I had to snap my mouth shut.

"That's okay. I guess I might be too if he were mine. What's his name?"

"Sam Driver."

"Driver," she purred, drawing the word out. "I like that."

"Naughty, naughty," said Terry, coming up behind us. "I heard that."

"You're just jealous," I told him.

"Not me. I'm spoken for."

In the ring, the judge put Callie at the head of the line, followed by Aunt Peg's Tory. He had one last look, reaching out to cup each of the Poodles' heads briefly in his hands before sending the line around the ring and pointing to them the way they were. Sam was awarded the blue ribbon and Peg had to be content with the red.

Callie beat Crawford's puppy for the points, and Tory went Reserve. "Serves you right," I said to Peg when she emerged from the ring. "What were you thinking, bringing that bitch to a headhunter?"

"He gave Tory's mother points."

"Did Tory's mother have this head?"

"Go ahead," said Peg. "Kick me while I'm down."

Peg and I waited while Sam had his picture taken, then trooped back to the handlers' tent. Terry, Crawford, and Viv had gone on ahead. Ron was just where we'd left him, thumbing through a new issue of *Dog Scene* magazine. Austin and Douglas arrived a moment later.

Peg hopped Tory back up on her table and started taking her apart. Douglas took my arm and pulled me aside. "Don't tell me I missed it," he said in a horrified whisper.

"Standard Poodles just finished."

"Oh, Lord. Did Peg win?"

"Reserve."

Aunt Peg looked pointedly in our direction. I felt like a second-grader who'd been caught passing notes in study hall.

"Maybe you could tell her you were watching from the other side of the ring."

"You mean lie?" Douglas shook his head. "That

wouldn't be right. No, I think an abject apology will do better."

Before he could make the gesture, however, the sound of raised voices coming from Crawford's setup drew everyone's attention.

"You've got a lot of nerve!" Ron Pullman snapped.

"Let's let the judge determine that, shall we?" Austin fired back.

"Excuse me." Viv stepped between the two men. "Maybe I've misunderstood. Has either one of you won your groups yet?"

There was a moment of silence. Since we all knew the group judging had yet to start, the question was purely rhetorical.

"That's what I thought," said Viv. "So this discussion is a little premature, don't you think?"

"All right, everybody." Terry clapped his hands. "Kiss and make up."

Viv looked at Ron. Austin looked at Viv. Terry made cow eyes at Crawford. Douglas slipped an arm around Peg's shoulders, and Sam just keep brushing his dog.

It was just like elementary school, only with grownups. There are days, even in summer, when you just can't leave the office behind.

∽❋ *Twelve* ❋∽

Ron's Chow and Austin's Golden Retriever probably went on to win their respective groups and duke it out in the Best in Show ring, but we didn't stay around to watch.

By the time Sam and Peg had their Poodles brushed out and their supplies packed up, it was mid-afternoon and I was itching to get home to Faith. Davey's nose was sunburned and he was complaining of a stomachache. Frank's nose was similarly sunburned, and now that he had Bertie's business card tucked away in his pocket, he seemed to think that the show had little else to offer. It was time to call it a day.

By common consensus, we all went back to my house. Douglas had an appointment and dropped Peg off, after securing a promise from me that I would drive her home later. After he left, we put Faith, Callie, and Tory outside together in the fenced backyard. The three black Poodles raced around the small area, bouncing from steps to swing set to fence like a pinball game gone amok. Davey added to the excitement by acting as referee.

Frank stayed for a beer but left soon after. It was just as well. Having him and Sam around together can be wearing. It's not that they don't like each other, just that each feels protective of me in his own way, and isn't necessarily sure that the other has my best interests at heart. That left Peg and Sam and me, sitting around the kitchen table, sharing chips and salsa and discussing the day's events. I started by bringing them all up to speed on what Beth had said.

"Goodness!" said Aunt Peg. "For an obnoxious man, he certainly was successful when it came to making romantic conquests."

"Maybe he had hidden talents," said Sam.

I scooped salsa onto a chip and aimed it for my mouth. "Speaking of which, have either of you met Beth's boyfriend, Ralphie?"

Both heads shook back and forth.

"Does he have hidden talents too?" asked Peg.

"Apparently so. At any rate, Beth thinks so. And in his case, they'd have to be hidden, because they're certainly not visible to the naked eye. According to her, he also has a ferocious temper."

"A ferocious temper and a girlfriend who's just had an affair with her boss. That sounds like a recipe for murder to me," said Sam.

"To me too," I agreed. "But Beth claims that Ralphie doesn't know what went on. She says no one does."

Aunt Peg glanced out the back door, checking for potential mayhem, then turned back to the conversation. "Do you think she's telling you the truth?"

"I certainly think she had no reason to tell him. Any more than Barry would have wanted Alicia to know."

"It doesn't mean Alicia didn't, though," said Sam. "You know how people gossip at shows. Ralphie isn't part of the dog scene. He might well have been kept in the dark. But Alicia went to nearly every show with Barry and Beth. What are the chances that she didn't find out?"

"If she did, she didn't mention it to me," I said.

"Of course she didn't mention it to you," said Peg. "She wants you to believe in her innocence. But think about this. Alicia's been living with Barry for a year. Now she's pregnant with his child. If she'd just found out about his affair with an assistant, I can see how that might be a dandy motive for murder."

"Didn't you tell me that the police already suspect her?" Sam asked. "I wonder if they know about this."

I got up, went to the refrigerator, and got out three more beers. In the yard, Davey and the three Standard Poodles seemed to be playing monkey-in-the-middle. My son was the monkey; not surprisingly, he was getting creamed.

"That was supposed to be your department," I said to Peg. "Did you have a chance to talk to them?"

"Have a chance? I made the chance. I got in my car and drove all the way up there, and for what? I didn't learn a blessed thing. The detective in charge of the investigation asked me whether I was related to any of the pertinent parties, and if not, what my interest was in the case. I'm afraid he didn't find my answer a compelling enough reason to continue the conversation."

"I can't understand it. You always seem to find a way to make me do things I don't want to do. I thought you'd be the perfect person to ferret information out of the police."

"Apparently not," said Aunt Peg, reduced to smothering her disappointment in salsa.

"Think about this for a minute," said Sam. "First there's Beth. She's been working for Barry for several years, making some money, learning the trade, probably reasonably happy with things the way they are."

"And then Alicia shows up," I said, seeing where he was going. "Suddenly Beth's no longer second in command, but somewhere lower down the ladder. She told me she didn't mind, that she and Alicia got along fine, but still . . ."

"The timing of her affair with Barry is very interesting," Peg mused aloud. "If they'd felt the urge, presumably they could have done something about it years ago. But they didn't. Not until Alicia came on the scene."

"Did Beth resent the change in her situation?" I wondered. "Did she think that maybe if she slept with Barry she could use that as a wedge to drive Alicia away?"

"Except that Alicia didn't leave," Sam pointed out. "Because Beth didn't tell her."

"Maybe she threatened to," Peg said.

"And maybe Barry threatened to fire her if she did."

"So she decided to shoot him?" Sam sounded skeptical. "That seems pretty drastic. It also assumes that she planted a gun in the van that morning before they left for the show."

"She could have done it," said Peg. "Maybe Ralphie helped her."

Even I frowned at that. "Ralphie doesn't seem very

bright, but only a real moron would kill his girlfriend's boss because she was jealous that he had a live-in lover."

"I see what you mean." Peg frowned too. She rifled through the chips in the basket, taking her time selecting the largest one. "Clearly we need more information. The Elm City show's next week." She looked at Sam. "Is Callie entered?"

"No, I have to be in California during the week. I figured I'd tack on a few extra days and stop off and see my brother and his family."

"Too bad," said Aunt Peg, not looking disappointed in the least. She was probably already counting her points.

"So who do you suppose won the show today?" I asked.

"Fifteen hundred dogs were entered," Aunt Peg said primly. "It could have been any one of them."

She likes to remind me that although the top winning dogs sometimes seem like sure things, judging is a complex equation. It takes into account not only a dog's good points and faults, but also its performance on the day. Not only that, but it's subjective as well, with each person free to interpret the breed standard in his or her own fashion.

While nearly all judges would agree if asked to choose between a good dog and a bad one, once the competition gets as far as the group ring, the choices are never that simple. Instead, a judge is often required to sort out the minute differences in a collection of very good dogs. Based on the winning they'd done lately, Leo and Midas might look as though they each had a lock on their respective groups, but in truth, anything could happen.

"What were Ron and Austin arguing about?" I asked curiously. "Did either of you hear?"

"Not the beginning," said Sam. "Only the final outburst."

"It's funny," Peg mused. "For two men who don't seem to like each other very much, they certainly end up spending a lot of time together."

I bypassed the bowl of chips, knowing full well that was where the calories lay, and dipped my finger in the salsa. "That's because their dogs are going head-to-head at the moment. Both of them strike me as very competitive men. In other circumstances, I could see how they might be friends. One thing's for sure, neither one of them likes to lose."

"That's true of all of us, isn't it?" Peg asked. "I'm just glad it's Viv who has to keep them apart, and not me."

She stood up and pushed back her chair. "I've got a bitch with hair spray in her coat that needs a bath this afternoon. Who's going to drive me home?"

Sam and I both volunteered, and in the end we all went. My new Volvo station wagon had room for four people and a Standard Poodle if you didn't mind sitting close, which nobody did. At Peg's house, Sam was invited in to take a look at her new litter of puppies. Davey and I got to go along too. The difference was that Sam, as a fellow breeder, had a valuable opinion. Nobody was going to pay any attention to ours.

The puppies were seven weeks old and Aunt Peg had moved them into her kitchen a few days earlier. Very young puppies require warmth, and privacy, and lots of maternal care. Older puppies need socialization, and all six of these were obviously off to a good start, because they rushed to the baby gate that blocked the doorway, tails wagging joyously, when they saw us coming.

Since we'd all been at a dog show earlier, Aunt Peg made us remove our shoes before entering the house and wash our hands with a solution containing bleach. At their age, the puppies' immunity to disease was uncertain as the antibodies they had received from their dam's milk were wearing off, but they had yet to have their first shots. Considering the number of dogs we'd just been exposed to at the show, Aunt Peg wasn't taking any chances.

One by one, we climbed over the gate and sat down on the kitchen floor. Davey went first. To his delight, he was immediately set upon by all six puppies. There were four girls in the litter and two boys, all black, the only color Aunt Peg breeds. In order to be able to tell them apart easily, she had tied different color shoelaces around their necks like little collars.

Aunt Peg gave Sam a few minutes to form an initial impression of her litter. She tried to contain her curiosity, but I knew she was watching him closely. "So," she said finally. "What do you think?"

"The red boy's a standout." By that he meant the black boy who was wearing the red collar.

"I don't need another boy. Find me a girl you like."

"Yellow is pretty," Sam said. "I like her carriage, but she doesn't seem to do much with her front, does she?"

"She's seven weeks old!" Aunt Peg cried. "Give her time."

Davey giggled. I looked over at him and shrugged. As far as we could tell, the puppies all looked alike, cute and floppy, with endearing little faces, dark eyes, and long pink tongues. My son wasn't wearing any socks. Since he'd taken off his shoes, he now had a puppy licking his bare toes.

"Green has the prettiest head," said Sam. "And they all have nice feet. Pink's a little long for me."

"She's too long for me too," Peg agreed. "But she has a lovely temperament and I have a wonderful pet home waiting."

Sam rolled a ball across the floor and watched as the puppies scrambled after it. If Aunt Peg had wanted an in-depth evaluation, they'd have taken each puppy and set it up individually on a grooming table. Even without that, however, much could be told just by observing them as they played.

"Red," Sam said again. "That's the one."

He patted the floor in front of him and the puppy wearing the red collar trotted over to see what was going on. Even I could appreciate the boy's ground-covering movement and elegant carriage.

"Too bad I don't have room for another boy," said Peg, staring up at the ceiling. "Especially one as pretty as that."

"Make room," said Sam. "You'd be crazy to let him go." He waggled his fingers and the puppy climbed up into his lap. Sam lifted the Poodle's lips and peered briefly into his mouth, checking the teeth and bite.

"Well, you know I have Beau, of course."

Beau had been Peg's top-producing stud dog before his theft the previous summer. He'd been missing for three months, and at the time I'd suspected that Sam, whom I'd just met, might have had something to do with the disappearance, since he'd offered Peg a blank check for the dog shortly before he was stolen.

"And now I have Joker too," said Peg, referring to her new, young stud dog. "I have a dog in the house and a dog in the kennel, that's plenty. That boy needs to go to a home where there are only bitches, where he can be top dog right from the start."

Something flickered briefly in Sam's expression. Surprise, or maybe realization. Then suddenly I, too, realized what Aunt Peg was up to and cracked a grin.

"His parents have had all their genetic testing done," said Peg. She'd stopped staring at the ceiling. Now she was looking innocently out the window. "He doesn't come down in a direct line from Beau, and yet I can see a number of traits they have in common."

Sam glanced downward. The puppy had wiggled himself into a comfortable position and gone to sleep, his long muzzle resting between his front paws on Sam's knee. "When do you want me to pick him up?" he asked.

"After you come back from California?"

"Done."

We left Aunt Peg to her puppies and her Poodle bath and took ourselves back home. Of course, Callie had also been shown and needed a bath too. But Sam didn't look too perturbed about the fact that hair spray was still sitting in her coat, and I certainly wasn't about to bring it up. Instead, we ordered takeout pizza and Greek salads and had a picnic in the backyard.

"Is he really going to be your new puppy?" Davey asked Sam for what seemed like the hundredth time.

"It looks that way." Sam speared an olive with his fork and popped it into his mouth.

"What are you going to name him?"

"I don't know yet. Maybe you'd like to help me think of something."

"Cool!" cried Davey. "How about Zoomer?"

"Zoomer," Sam tried the name out. "It has possibilities."

"Or Bob."

"Bob?" I asked.

"After Daddy."

Oh. After a four-year gap in their relationship, Davey's father had recently come back into his life, if mostly from a distance. They exchanged cards and letters now, and as long as Bob behaved himself, I was more than willing to keep the lines of communication open. But this was a little much.

"I don't think your daddy would like having a Poodle named after him," I mentioned.

"Cedar Crest Bob," said Sam, adding Peg's kennel name as a prefix. "I think maybe we can do better than that."

"Cedar Crest Scimitar," I suggested. "That's a kind of sword," I added for Davey's benefit.

"Scimitar!" Davey slashed his arm through the air. "You could call him Tar."

"That's not bad." Sam helped himself to another slice of pizza. "Tar it is, then."

Faith and Callie came over to see what we were so excited about and each got a piece of pepperoni for her trouble. Thus bribed, neither offered any disagreement with our choice, and so the puppy was named.

* * *

Tuesday morning the telephone rang early. I'd just wandered downstairs in my pajamas to get the coffee started. Faith was taking a stroll around the backyard, and Davey, who was due at camp in forty minutes, was sitting in front of the television with a bowl of Cheerios. Bert and Ernie were singing the alphabet, which qualified the experience as educational, not just mind-numbing.

"Oh, good," said Alicia. "I was afraid I wouldn't catch you."

At seven forty-five?

"I was hoping we could talk. Maybe you could give me directions and I'll stop by later this morning?"

"Sure," I said. "Is there anything in particular you want to discuss?"

"Beth and I had a long talk last night," said Alicia. "There are some things I think you need to know."

∽❀ *Thirteen* ❀∽

After she'd left me dangling like that, I couldn't wait for
Alicia to arrive. In the meantime, I got Davey dressed
and drove him to camp. When I got home, Faith was
waiting for me with a mischievous gleam in her eye and
a tennis ball in her mouth. It's bad enough when your
child can manipulate you, but when the dog starts, you
know you're in trouble.

It was too hot to play catch for long. After half a dozen
tosses, I brought Faith inside and brushed through her
coat and topknot, then put everything back together. I
checked the clock eight or nine times, paid some bills,
balanced my checkbook, and seriously considered washing the kitchen floor. By that time it was nearly eleven.
Alicia had sounded eager to speak to me; I wondered
what was keeping her.

"Car trouble," she said when she arrived. "I was driving along fine, and next thing I knew, there was steam
pouring out of the engine. I had to get out and walk.
Luckily I was only about a mile from a service station."

"What was the matter?"

"Broken hose. Once they'd towed the car in, it was pretty easy to fix."

I nodded, sensing there was more she wanted to say. Instead of continuing, however, Alicia glanced around. We were standing in the front hall, and she could see most of the first floor of my small house. "Cute place."

"Thanks." No point in pushing. I didn't have to pick Davey up for another two hours. "I thought we might sit out back. Most of the yard is shaded and it stays pretty cool."

When we reached the kitchen, Faith, who'd been in the yard when the doorbell rang, was throwing herself against the back door. Like my son, she hates to be left out of anything.

"That's Faith," I said. "Appearances notwithstanding, she's very friendly. How about something to drink? Iced tea or coffee? Juice? Water?"

"Don't worry, I love Standard Poodles. Can she come in?" Alicia walked to the door. I nodded on my way to the refrigerator, and she let the bouncing dog into the room. "Iced tea would be great, but caffeine's off limits. How about a glass of water?"

I poured our drinks and we carried them outside. Faith bounded through the door behind us.

Over near the grill, two wrought iron chairs flanked a small table. A chaise longue sat in the shade. Davey's swing set was on the other side of the yard with a small round wading pool beside it. Alicia walked straight there.

"Do you mind?" She slipped her feet out of their sandals. "Being pregnant seems to have raised my temperature by about ten degrees. I'm always hot these days. And on top of that, my feet are killing me. I hadn't planned on taking a hike this morning. Otherwise, I'd have worn different shoes."

"Go right ahead. In fact, I'll join you."

I put down my drink and dragged the two chairs over beside the small pool. Now we could sit and dangle our feet at the same time. I kicked off my shoes, then picked up a rope chew toy and tossed it to Faith, who caught it on the fly. She carried it into the shade and lay down.

I waited until Alicia looked comfortable, then said, "So, what do you suppose happened to your car?"

"It's no big deal." Alicia shrugged. "A broken hose can happen to anyone."

"Sure," I said agreeably. Judging by her tone of voice, there was more to come.

"It's just that . . . it's not the first thing."

"What do you mean?"

"I don't know. Maybe I'm imagining things. I've heard that pregnant women can be fanciful. Or maybe I'm just having a run of bad luck."

I set my drink down in the grass. "Why don't you tell me what's going on?"

"You don't have to make it sound so ominous. Nothing's exactly *going on.* I've just had a couple of accidents around the house. Small things. The kind that could happen to anyone."

That was the second time she'd said that. I wondered how often she'd been repeating it to herself. "Like what?"

"There was a broken step outside in the back. I guess maybe it was loose and I just never noticed. Anyway, the tread broke and I fell down."

"Were you hurt?"

"I wrenched my ankle. Other than that, I was just bruised a bit. There are only a couple of steps."

I thought of the way Barry Turk's house had looked when I'd seen it a year ago. Then it had been pretty rundown. Last time I was there, it had looked considerably better, but it wouldn't have surprised me to hear that there were pieces still in need of repair.

"What else?"

Alicia helped herself to a sip of water. "I guess I had a little fire."

"You *guess* you did?"

"Well, I'm sure I did. I just don't want to make it sound like more than it was. It started when I was asleep. Somehow the toaster oven got left on and it overheated. When I moved in, I made Barry install smoke alarms, thank God. The noise woke me right up. I ran downstairs and put the fire out with water from the sink." She leaned back in her chair and wiggled her bare toes in the cool water. "I'm not exactly helpless, you know."

"Good thing," I muttered. "Was anyone else in the house at the time?"

"No. Beth has a room and bath off the kennel. She uses my kitchen, but she sleeps in the other building."

"Could she have left the toaster oven turned on?"

"I asked her about it," said Alicia. "She said she hadn't."

"And you don't remember doing it either?"

"No, that's what's so odd. That and the fact that there was a stack of paper napkins sitting on top of it. That's what caught on fire. Why would I have left napkins there? Luckily they made a lot of smoke and set off the alarm."

"Luckily," I repeated. "Just like it was lucky you were

near a gas station today when your car broke down. What if your curtains had caught fire? What if you'd broken down at night on a deserted road?"

"I know." Alicia sighed. "I've thought about that. It wouldn't be so bad if I had only myself to worry about, but I don't."

"Maybe you should have someone move in with you," I suggested. "Do you have any family around here, anyone that you're close to?"

"No one whose lives I could disrupt that way."

"Maybe Beth could move into the house with you."

"I can't see how that would help," Alicia said flatly. "Actually, she's the reason I came to talk to you today."

"You mentioned that on the phone. You said that you and she had had a talk." I kept my voice carefully neutral, which was hard when I considered all the things these two women might have had to say to each other.

"What we had was more like a soul-baring." Alicia didn't sound pleased. "I gather you two spent some time together at the show on Saturday."

"Beth got off to a late start and fell a little behind. I helped her get a Mini bitch ready for the ring."

"I guess you also got her to talk too, because apparently she decided after the fact that she'd said entirely too much. Last night she showed up in my living room with half a bottle of cheap wine. She'd already drunk the other half, and was ready to spill her guts."

"That must have been interesting."

"The most interesting thing about it was that it happened at all. Beth and I have been living on the same grounds for nearly a year. We get along okay but we're not exactly friends. This was what you might call our first heart-to-heart chat." Alicia frowned. "I'm hoping it will be the last."

"What did you two talk about?"

"I imagine you already know the answer to that. Barry, of course. Specifically the fling he and Beth seemed to have had last winter."

I searched her expression for signs of distress and was surprised not to see any. "She told you because she was afraid I might?"

Alicia nodded. "That, and because she was drunk. Beth isn't a drinker. On one glass of wine, she was probably high as a kite. After two, it was true-confessions time."

"You don't sound too upset."

"Don't I? Maybe it's because I've had a night to get used to the idea."

"Maybe it's because you already knew," I guessed.

Alicia sipped at her water, then set her glass aside. "I wouldn't say I knew, exactly. I did have my suspicions."

"And it didn't make you angry?"

"Of course it made me angry. But it didn't surprise me. If you'd known Barry, you'd know what I mean."

The more I learned about Barry Turk, the more it seemed to be just as well that I hadn't known him any better when he was alive.

"You're carrying his baby," I said. "You must realize there are people who would see this as a motive for murder."

"Not exactly." Alicia's lips curled upward in a small smile. She looked like a cat contemplating a bowl of cream. "You see, Barry isn't the father of my baby."

It's a good thing I was sitting down. As it was, I nearly fell off my chair.

"Yes, he is," I said stupidly. As if I would know.

"No," Alicia repeated. "He's not."

I contemplated that information for a moment. It seemed to put a slightly different spin on everything.

"I guess Beth isn't the only one who had a confession to make."

"Oh, don't go getting all melodramatic," snapped Alicia. "I'm certainly not the first woman to be living with one man and pregnant by another."

"Did Barry know?"

"Of course not, and he never would have either. I'd have made damn sure of that."

"What about the baby's father? Does he know?"

"He does now. I guess maybe he suspected before but he never said anything. With Barry gone, there didn't seem to be any reason to keep it from him."

I reached for my glass and took a long, cold swallow. "Are you going to tell me who he is?"

"No."

"You asked me to figure out who shot Barry. Now I find out you've given me only part of the story."

"I answered your questions. I told you everything that was important. So I had an affair. So what? It happens. And it had nothing to do with Barry's murder."

"How can you be so sure?"

"Because I know this man, and I know he wouldn't have done anything to hurt Barry. He wouldn't have had any reason to."

Everything about Alicia—her demeanor, her tone of voice—implied that she thought what she was telling me made perfect sense. Was I the only one who was floundering here?

"If Barry wasn't the father of your baby," I asked, "why were you still with him?"

Alicia looked down into her lap. Although the temperature hovered in the mid-eighties, she rubbed her arms as if she were cold. "It's just the way things worked out. The other man is a good man, a decent man, but . . ."

Not decent enough to stand by her when she was carrying his child apparently. I went for the obvious reason. "Is he married?"

She let the question dangle so long that I thought she wasn't going to answer. Finally, she did. "As it happens, he is. And he has no intention of getting a divorce. I knew that going in. We both did. We were two consenting adults doing something we wanted to do."

"How did a baby figure into that?"

"The baby was an accident," Alicia said with a small smile. "An unexpected bonus. Bill and I wanted children for years, but it never happened. Barry didn't want kids, so we were using birth control. But no system's perfect. You know how it is."

She looked at me, woman to woman, and I nodded.

"Besides, a stolen moment of pleasure is no time to be worrying about whether or not your diaphragm's in place."

Actually I'd have thought that was exactly the time, but I kept that thought to myself.

"Who is he, Alicia?"

"No." She shook her head emphatically. "It's none of your business, and I'm not going to violate his privacy by discussing it with you."

"You're awfully concerned about protecting him. It's a shame he isn't as concerned about you."

"Nice try." Alicia gave me an assessing look. "But it won't work."

Too bad.

"How much of this have you told the police?"

"None of it," she said. "They're doing enough poking around in my life as it is."

Behind us, Faith tired of merely chewing her toy and tossed it up in the air. The thick rope knot flew in a high, soaring arc over our heads and landed with a splash in the pool. That wouldn't have been a problem if Faith hadn't gone in after it.

"Oh!" shrieked Alicia, jumping up. Her legs and the front of her sundress were soaked.

I was wet, too, but that was the least of my concerns. Faith followed her initial leap into the pool with a dive underwater to retrieve her toy. The water was less than a foot deep, but it was enough to soak her face, topknot, and ears thoroughly.

I scrambled up and jumped in after her. The plastic floor of the pool was slick and slippery. When my feet shot out from under me, it was reflex to try to save myself by reaching for Faith. Great idea, right? When we both went down in the water together, I had only myself to blame.

Faith's ancestors were water dogs. The dunking didn't bother her a bit. True to her roots, she hung on to her toy and quickly found her feet. Sitting in the waist-deep water, it took me longer to regroup. Which is why the mighty shake she gave hit me full in the face.

I reached over and gave the Poodle's hindquarter a strong shove. "Get out of here, you big bear!"

Alicia was standing beside the pool, trying hard not

to laugh. She reached down and offered me a hand. I took it and hauled myself out.

Faith stood by the pool, waiting to see what new form of excitement we would come up with next. Her long, luxurious mane coat hung in streaming clumps.

Alicia looked at her and grinned. "I guess I know how you'll be spending the rest of the day."

"Maybe I could towel her dry," I said hopefully.

"Don't count on it. I'm no Poodle expert, but even I can see that if you don't want that coat to mat, it's going to need to be bathed and blown dry. I'll get out of your way and let you get started."

Accompanied by Faith, we walked around the front of the house to her car. "You be careful," I said. "Okay?"

"I will."

"If you need help, call me. I'll come."

"Thanks for the offer, but I'm sure I'll be okay. Now that we've talked things out, I feel much better."

I stood in the driveway, my hand resting on Faith's back, and watched Alicia drive away. I was glad that she felt better, but unfortunately, that made one of us.

When Faith and I went inside, the phone was ringing. I wasn't surprised. Aunt Peg seems to have a sixth sense where Faith's coat is concerned. Whenever I've really screwed up and I'm tempted just to let the coat go, there she is.

"I have an idea," she said.

"I have all sorts of ideas," I told her. I was hoping that might slow her down, but it didn't.

"Why don't you take that new Volvo of yours in for servicing?"

Of all the things she might have said, I wasn't expecting that. "Why?"

"Maybe Ralphie Otterbach could look at it for you. I've done a little checking around. Did you know he's a car mechanic?"

"Yes, but—"

"So I was thinking that even a new car must have something it could have done. Something innocuous. How about an oil change?"

"I take it you think I ought to talk to Ralphie."

"Melanie dear, catch *up*. Of course I think you ought to talk to Ralphie. It occurred to me that he's been an objective observer of much of what's gone on at Barry's kennel recently. Maybe he has something interesting to say."

Knowing Ralphie slightly better than Peg did, I sincerely doubted it. Still, it couldn't hurt. Besides, in a pinch, I could manage an oil change myself, so the job shouldn't be beyond Ralphie's capabilities.

"I'll have to track him down," I said.

"Already done. He works at Premier Motors in Brewster."

Brewster? "Nobody drives an hour to get their oil changed."

"So don't tell him how far you've come." Another objection disposed of in Aunt Peg's usual high-handed fashion. "Here's the phone number."

"You mean you haven't already made the appointment?"

"I may be pushy, but I'm not totally manipulative."

That, I thought, was open to debate, but when she

rattled off a phone number, I dutifully copied it down. Then I told her about the visit I'd just had with Alicia.

"What do you mean, Barry isn't the baby's father?" she cried. "Then who is?"

"She wouldn't tell me. Apparently he's married, and his wife doesn't know a thing about all this."

"I guess that lets out Bill," Peg mused. "He might have been my first guess."

"If Alicia was telling me the truth."

"Do you think she might not have been?"

"I'm not sure. Certainly she was very eager to keep the man's identity a secret. Saying he was married might have been a way to throw me off track."

"I'll tell you the first thing that occurs to me," said Peg. "Barry Turk always struck me as someone who had a high opinion of his sexual prowess. If he found out that Alicia had something going on with someone else, I can see how he would have been very, very angry."

"You're thinking maybe Alicia killed him because she was afraid?"

"It's a possibility. Beth saw her go in the front door of the house. And yet Alicia was the first one to realize what had happened. How did she know?"

"She heard the shots," I said, although I wasn't sure that was true.

"Mother dogs will do almost anything to protect their puppies," Peg pointed out. "Humans are no different. It's instinct."

I frowned and changed the subject. "What about these accidents Alicia's been having? What do you think of that?"

"It seems to me that they sounded a lot worse in the

telling than they actually were," Aunt Peg said briskly. "Maybe she's playing on your sympathies again. Just because she claims to like Standard Poodles doesn't mean you should trust everything she says."

That reminded me of Faith. While I'd been talking on the phone, she'd grown bored and gone into her crate to lie down. Any idiot could see that meant that the cedar bed that lined the bottom was now sopping wet too.

"I have to go," I said. "Faith's waiting for her bath."

"Carry on," Peg said cheerfully. "And don't forget to clean her ears."

As if I could, with such an ever-helpful genie perched upon my shoulder. I woke Faith up, and added another item to the list of things to do.

Later that afternoon, when I had Faith lying on her grooming table and the dryer going full blast, the phone rang again. Davey was down the street playing with his good friend, Joey Brickman, so I was able to take my time about turning off the dryer and getting to the receiver.

"Hey," said Bertie when I picked up on the fourth ring. "I thought you weren't there. I was just waiting for the machine."

"I'm here. I'm blow-drying. What's up?"

"I talked with two of the women I told you about, Ann Leeds and Christine Franken. Ann shows French Bulldogs, and Christine has a couple of different toy breeds. Both of them spent plenty of time competing against Barry. Ann was the one who was actually going to file the complaint."

"Is she willing to talk to me?"

"She said sure, although now that Barry's out of the picture, she couldn't see how it would make any difference."

"What about Christine?"

"Same thing. She didn't think she knew anything that would help you, but she was willing to give it a try."

"Great." I reached for a piece of paper and pen, and copied down the addresses and phone numbers Bertie gave me. Christine lived in Pennsylvania, which meant it was likely I'd try and talk to her at a show, but Ann was in Bethel, only about forty minutes away.

"Thanks for the information," I said. "Do you mind one more question?"

"Shoot."

"Last spring, when I was looking into Monica Freedman's murder, you wouldn't give me the time of day. How come you're being so helpful now?"

"Last spring, I seem to recall, you thought of me as a suspect."

"I had good reasons."

"Yeah, well, I still wasn't too pleased about it. But now—" Bertie paused. "I guess I like you fine when you're not investigating me."

"Fair enough."

I hung up the phone and tucked the notes I'd taken away in a safe place. At this rate, Bertie and I might even become friends.

It didn't take much notice to get myself an appointment for an oil change at Premier Motors in Brewster. One phone call and I was on my way back up Route 684 the next morning. I'd specified I wanted Ralphie Otterbach to do the job, and the receptionist had jotted down my request without a quibble. Either I'd happened to hit upon his specialty, or good old Ralphie wasn't too busy.

Premier Motors was housed in what appeared to be a converted gas station on the outskirts of Brewster. My first impression was that the most premier thing about the operation was the sign. It was nicely lettered and freshly painted.

After that, however, it was all downhill. The lot out front held at least a dozen cars, most suffering from varying degrees of decay. Doors to two of the bays were open; the third was closed and several of the small panes of glass in its windows were cracked.

The bay next to the office was empty. I pulled in front of it and parked. The middle bay held a car up on a lift, which appeared to be unattended. I walked in the office and saw why. It was coffee break time.

"I'm telling you," Ralphie was saying, his thick forefinger poking the air to punctuate the statement, "this is going to be the Yankees' year."

"Like you don't say that every year," another man scoffed. He was wearing a putty-colored jump suit that looked as though it had never seen the inside of a washing machine. "So they got lucky once. With Steinbrenner in charge, I wouldn't bet on it happening again." He glanced over and saw me standing in the doorway. "Help you?"

"Yes, my name is Melanie Travis. I have an appointment for an oil change."

"That's mine," said Ralphie. "You can drive her right in there." He stared for a moment. "Do I know you?"

"We met at a couple of dog shows. I'm a friend of Beth's."

That was stretching things a bit, but Ralphie didn't seem to notice. As I left the office, he was being ribbed about his attendance at dog shows which, the other men assured him, were only for pansies and Poodles with bows in their ears. Good thing I'd left Faith at home. I could only imagine what they would have thought of her.

Ralphie walked through the connecting door into the first bay as I drove in over the lift and stopped. "This car looks new," he said. "How many miles you got on her?"

I checked the odometer. "Three thousand. It's not even due for its first checkup yet, but I've heard it's really important to get the oil changed frequently."

"Good thought." Ralphie assembled the tools he'd need to do the job. "This'll take about half an hour. We've got some magazines in the office, if you want to wait in there."

"Actually, I'd rather be out here." I lifted my hair off the back of my neck, felt slightly cooler for a few seconds, then let it fall. "It doesn't seem as hot."

"Suit yourself."

He reached under the car and adjusted the arms of the lift. Judging by the ease and speed with which he worked, it was a job he performed often. A moment later, Ralphie hit the lever and the Volvo rose into the air. Dragging an oil drain with him, he ducked underneath the car and went to work.

A wooden shelf ran along the wall behind me. I found a spot that didn't look too oil-stained and leaned back against it. "How's it look?" I asked.

"Great." His voice was slightly muffled. "You can't beat the Swedes when it comes to building cars, unless maybe you want to talk about the Germans. Shit, if they had this bolt on any tighter—" I heard him grunt, and surmised the bolt had given. Ralphie lapsed into silence and the oil began to drain.

Absently I traced my finger along the edge of the shelf. It came away coated with a thick layer of dust. "I guess Beth's pretty busy these days, now with Barry being gone and all."

"Beth's always busy." Ralphie gave another grunt. Whether it was a sound of disgust, or he was struggling with another bolt, I couldn't tell. "If you ask me, she works too hard."

"I guess she wants to get ahead."

"Ahead of what? Other dog people?" This time his tone left no doubt of his derision. "I know she likes what she does, but it sure doesn't seem like a real job to me."

"Did you ever meet her boss?"

"Barry Turk? Sure." He reached around, dragged a rag out of his back pocket, and swiped it across his face.

"Too bad about what happened, huh?"

"Yeah, I guess. Can't say as I miss him much, though. The man was a loser."

"Really?" I asked innocently. "I didn't know him very well."

"Consider yourself lucky. Turk was a pompous, arrogant son of a bitch. Just because Beth worked for him, he treated her like her owned her. I told Beth more than once that she was crazy to put up with that shit."

Scowling, Ralphie moved out from beneath the car and went off in search of an oil filter. I fanned my face with my hand and thought about what he had said. Barry had treated Beth as though he owned her? I could easily see how big, macho Ralphie would have resented that. I wondered how much he actually knew about their relationship and how much he merely suspected. Either way, it sounded as though I'd hit a nerve.

When he returned, I decided to probe in another direction. "Things must have gotten better after Alicia arrived. Everybody says she made a huge difference."

"Everybody doesn't know squat," Ralphie muttered. "Alicia was supposed to help out. That's what Beth told me. But mostly she just stood around looking decorative."

"When did you start going to the shows with Beth?"

"I guess I went to a couple over the winter."

Last winter was when Beth had had her affair with Barry. I found it interesting that right around the same time, her boyfriend had developed a sudden desire to go to dog shows with her.

"How come?"

Ralphie turned and stared. "What is this, twenty questions?"

"Just passing the time," I said easily.

"I told you you could've waited inside." He slipped under the Volvo and went back to work.

I gave him a minute, then said, "Talk to me. It takes my mind off the heat."

"What the hell?" Ralphie muttered. "It's not as though I'm going anywhere. I went to the shows with Beth because she asked me to. I think she had some idea that if I saw how serious and hardworking everyone was, I'd feel different about what she was doing."

"And did you?"

"Not really. It was bad enough watching those dogs get fussed over at home. But at the dog shows it looked even sillier, all that primping and prancing around. Beth worked her ass off, and in the end all those dogs ever won was a little scrap of colored ribbon. What's the sense in that?"

I understood what he was saying. As a relative neophyte in the sport of dogs, I was new enough to remember when I'd felt the same way. That was before I'd begun to understand the finer points of handling a dog, or how truly difficult it was to produce a puppy that exemplified the breed standard, plus had the health and good temperament to withstand the rigors of a show career. If you looked at only the surface of a dog show, you missed what they were really about—contests that served as the ultimate selection process for the best canine gene pools available.

"Heaven forbid Beth showed a dog and lost," Ralphie grumbled. "Some of those owners acted like she'd just drained their last quart of blood."

I'd seen that kind of behavior too. And while I couldn't seriously believe that anyone would kill a handler because their dog wasn't winning, I was curious enough to ask, "Like who?"

"Oh, you know. Just a bunch of dumb people. I didn't bother learning their names. If Beth was showing a dog, that meant it wasn't owned by one of the top clients. Not somebody like the Pullmans."

I moved around to the end of the car so I could see his face. "You were around when Barry had their Chow, Leo?"

"Sure. It was over the winter, right? I saw them a couple of times at the shows. The wife, what's her name?"

"Viv."

"Viv, yeah. She kind of stands out in a crowd, you know?"

I did. Compared to most of the people who frequented dog shows, Viv was younger, prettier, and more expensively dressed. I could easily see how she might have caught Ralphie's eye.

He lowered his arm and enjoyed a leisurely scratch. "I guess her husband must have plenty of money to hook a woman like that, because he sure doesn't look like much."

"Ron Pullman?" I said, surprised. "I think he's very good-looking."

"He's short," Ralphie said derisively. "And just about bald. On top of that, he's *old.*"

As if that were the ultimate insult. I pegged Ralphie's age at about twenty-two, which meant he had plenty of time ahead of him to regret that attitude. On the other hand, while Ron was a good deal older than Viv, he was neither short nor bald.

"That's not Ron. You must be thinking of Austin."

Ralphie's eyes glazed over, mirroring inner confusion, just like they do in cartoons. In an intelligence test, Faith could run rings around this man.

"What's the diff? They're not around anymore anyway." He was looking around the shelf, making sure he had everything he needed.

"That's because the Pullmans took the dog to another handler. You wouldn't happen to know why, would you?"

Ralphie shook his head. "Like I would care about something like that. Beth and me, we don't discuss her work. We got plenty of better things to do."

He wrapped up what he was doing and dropped his

tools on the bench. "Let me just write this up and I'll have you out of here in a jiff."

Five minutes later, I was back on the road. The bill had come to thirty-five dollars and I had a fifty-minute drive home. And what had I learned? Mostly that Ralphie hadn't liked Barry Turk. An educated guess could have saved me the trip.

I swung by home and picked up Faith, then stopped at Graceland Camp for Davey. He bounced into the car, flung his backpack over the backseat, and gave Faith a hug. She returned the sentiment by licking what looked like the remains of a cherry Popsicle off his face.

Before he even had a seat belt fastened, Davey was already telling me about his day. He likes to give a minute-by-minute description, and if he forgets something, he's apt to go all the way back to the beginning and start over.

Faith, meanwhile, was sitting on the seat beside him, her nose pressed to the narrow crack of open window I'd allowed her at the top. Given her preference, she'd have ridden with head out and ears flapping in the breeze. Aunt Peg had told me that was bad for a dog's eyes, however, and asked whether I'd consider letting my son ride that way. Since she tends to think of the Poodles as her children, the analogy seemed perfectly apt to me.

"Where are we going?" Davey asked when he stopped talking long enough to notice that we weren't on our way home.

"I thought we'd go visit Aunt Peg. She and I have some things to talk about, and you can play with her puppies."

I thought he'd be excited at the prospect of seeing Aunt Peg's litter again, but instead Davey zeroed in on the first part of what I'd said. "What are you going to talk about?" he asked. The gene for nosiness must run in my family.

"Just things."

"Like what?"

"Like Aunt Peg sending me on a wild-goose chase."

"You chased a goose?" Davey's eyes were round. Much to the town's dismay, our local park has a large population of Canada geese, and my son knows how big and how fierce the birds can be. "Did you catch it?"

"Not exactly."

"Too bad," said Davey. "Then I could have two pets." I nodded absently.

"Miss Grace has a guinea pig." He patted his lap, and Faith turned around and lay down, resting her long front legs crosswise over his. Davey had to crane his neck to see over her topknot. "It lives at camp during the summer."

"Mmm-hmm." I slowed to look for the turnoff. There are only a few roads that cut from back-country Stamford to back-country Greenwich. Miss them, and you can wander around for hours.

"In the winter Horace lives in one of the classrooms at Graceland school."

"Who's Horace?" I asked.

"The guinea pig!" His tone was filled with enough disgust to make me realize that his teenage years, while not exactly imminent, were definitely out there on the horizon.

"Miss Grace was looking for someone to bring Horace

home at the end of camp, and keep him until school begins. I told her I could do it."

"You . . . *what?*"

"I told her Horace could stay with us."

"No," I said firmly, then repeated the word for good measure. "No. You can tell Miss Grace tomorrow that she has to find somebody else."

"But I already told her I could!" Davey wailed. Faith flattened her ears against her head, a pained expression on her face. "She's going to lend us a cage and some food and everything!"

I turned and looked back at him over my shoulder. "Do we have to discuss this while I'm driving?"

"Yes." Davey sniffled loudly.

For her part, Faith looked ready to lick any tears away, should they appear. What a pair.

"Didn't it occur to you to ask me first?"

"Miss Grace said that if anyone had a nice mother, she'd be happy to help out. So I raised my hand."

"You raised your hand to say you had a nice mother?"

"Yes," Davey confirmed, all innocence.

One thing I've learned about parenting. Sometimes you believe what's true, and sometimes you just suspend disbelief and go with the moment.

That's how we got temporary custody of a guinea pig.

Fifteen

We found Aunt Peg at home, clipping faces and feet on her litter of six. Usually she did her grooming out in the kennel, but young puppies got special treatment. Peg had set up a portable grooming table in the middle of the kitchen floor and had her clipper plugged in to the outlet beside the sink.

"You could have called first," she said, disgruntled at the interruption. "What if I'd had guests?"

"You do," I said, ignoring her scowl. "Us."

As we'd walked in through the living room, I'd noticed a remote control sitting on top of the television. That was new. Peg didn't watch much TV herself. Now in the kitchen, there was a loaf of whole wheat bread on the counter. Since Peg preferred Twinkies with her morning coffee, I figured I could pretty much assume that someone else was responsible for the changes.

I boosted Davey over the gate and he sat down on the floor. To his delight, puppies immediately swarmed all over him. "We're going to have a guest," he announced. "He's a guinea pig named Horace."

Aunt Peg reached down and plucked up one of the puppies. Its face and the base of its tail were freshly clipped, but all four feet were still fuzzy. She placed the puppy in the middle of the rubber-matted table and reached for her clipper. "Why on earth would you want to get a guinea pig?"

"It's only temporary. Davey volunteered us to pig-sit for a few weeks at the end of the summer."

Aunt Peg didn't look appeased. When it comes to pets, she's totally chauvinistic about dogs. The frog we'd had the summer before had earned nothing but her contempt. She turned on the clipper and went to work. To my amazement, the puppy didn't seem to mind when she shaved the hair off its paws.

Faith, who'd been left outside the kitchen with the rest of Peg's house Poodles, leaned her head over the baby gate and whined softly under her breath. I reached over and scratched beneath her chin. "We'll be out in a few minutes," I told her. "Go play."

Before Davey and I got Faith, I'd thought it was funny the way people talked to their dogs, holding entire conversations as if they thought the dog might actually understand. Now I was guilty of the same thing myself. Of course the difference was, Faith *did* understand.

She cast a glance back over her shoulder at Simba and Chloe and Beau. Simba dropped her front end on the ground, which left her hindquarter up in the air, tail whipping back and forth like mad. Even I could figure out what that invitation meant. Eagerly Faith wagged her own tail in reply.

"Don't you pull her hair," Peg warned as the four Poodles went romping away.

I sank down on the floor beside Davey One puppy began to chew on my shoelaces. Another braced its front paws on my arm and batted at my hair.

"I guess you and Douglas must be getting along pretty well," I said.

Aunt Peg mumbled something under her breath. With the buzz of the clipper behind it, I couldn't quite catch the words, but her tone did its best to imply that the topic was none of my business.

Blithely, I ignored it. We'd covered similar ground many times in the past over my relationship with Sam. The way I saw things, it was Aunt Peg's turn to squirm.

"He seems like a nice man," I ventured.

"Of course he's a nice man," she snapped. "That's not the problem."

Problem? Had anyone mentioned there was a problem?

I gathered a puppy into my arms and prepared to enjoy myself. "What is?"

"What's what?" She'd finished clipping her puppy's feet. Now Peg was plucking hair from inside its ear canal—and being deliberately obtuse.

"The problem with Douglas."

"He's not a dog person." A real condemnation in Aunt Peg's book.

"You knew that when you met him."

"When I met Douglas, dogs were the farthest thing from my mind."

"So? Keep it that way. You two don't have to do everything together." I was thinking about the shows, but a loud bark and the rumble of running feet in the next room brought up another issue. "Or does he object to you having all these dogs in the house?"

"No, he's been very patient about that. They're Poodles, after all. Who could help but get along with them?"

Assuming that was a rhetorical question, I wisely kept my mouth shut.

"The problem is that Douglas thinks I'm too involved with the dogs. He says they take up too much of my time. What he doesn't understand is that before he came along, I liked having my time accounted for. Not only that, but I enjoy what I'm doing."

"So tell him."

"I did. At least I tried. But then he does things like make plans for Saturday afternoon when he knows perfectly well that I have a dog entered. Douglas said he had Jets tickets. As if I'd pass up a good judge to watch some silly baseball game."

"Mets," I mentioned.

"You see? How important can the team be if nobody even knows their name?" Peg finished the puppy she was working on and returned him to the floor. "Who's next?"

Not surprisingly, none of the puppies stepped forward to volunteer. She looked around and zeroed in on her next victim, a refined girl who was examining her reflection in the oven door.

"That always bothers them," said Peg. "They don't understand they're seeing their own reflection. They think I've got extra puppies stashed away in there."

"I think you're being too hard on Douglas," I said, unwilling to let her change the subject.

"That's easy for you to say. Sam's a Poodle breeder."

"Every relationship involves compromise."

"Pish," said Peg. The puppy she was working on was too young to know how to sit quietly on a grooming table. Instead, it wiggled like Jell-O. I'd have found all the movement distracting, but Peg just worked around it. "I didn't have to rearrange my life for Max. What gives Douglas the right to make demands?"

"Is that what he's doing? Demanding that you give up dogs?"

"Well . . . no." The admission was dragged from her unwillingly.

"I think he just wishes that the two of you could explore some other interests together."

"I don't have any other interests," Peg said stubbornly. "I never needed any."

"Well, now you do."

"Maybe not. What if this thing with Douglas is meant only to be short-term? After all, he's the first man I've dated since Max. Maybe he's my transitional man."

Aunt Peg had a TV in her grooming room in the kennel. Sometimes while she was blow-drying a dog, she'd been known to watch Oprah.

"Then again," I said just to be bratty, "maybe he's the man you're destined to spend the rest of your life with."

Peg frowned. "If he is, he'd better shape up."

I recognized that tone. It meant case closed. End of discussion.

On the floor around us, the action had quieted. Puppies' lives are simple at that age: eat, sleep, play. They have frenetic bursts of energy followed by sleep so deep that they drop where they're standing. Now Peg's litter was sacked out around the kitchen like mounds of boneless black fluff. Sam's boy—the one with the red shoelace around his neck—was snoring softly under his breath.

Davey stood up and walked to the gate. "Lift me over. I want to go play with Faith."

"Please lift me over?"

"That's what I said," Davey confirmed. I was never quite sure whether he was missing the point or pulling my leg.

I swung him up and over and he dashed away.

"I saw Ralphie Otterbach this morning," I told Peg.

She looked up with interest. "What did he have to say?"

"He wasn't happy about the fact that his girlfriend worked for Barry Turk."

"Did he know what Beth and Barry were up to?"

"I wondered that myself. I hate to say it, but I'm not sure."

"Maybe he bears watching," Peg mused.

"I was thinking the same thing."

Davey and I stopped and picked up a couple of videos and a pizza on the way home. All winter long, I'm in my work mode. Get up, go to school; come home, be a mother. Go to bed. Now, after four weeks off, I was really getting used to being on vacation. That didn't bode well for September, but in the meantime I was determined to make the most of my time off.

We sat on the living room couch, ate pepperoni-and-onion pizza, and watched a movie about a trio of lost pets finding their way home against incredible odds. Davey smirked while I blubbered shamelessly, but when I put him to bed later, I noticed he checked three times to make sure Faith was at the end of his bed, where she was supposed to be.

After he was asleep, I called Ann Leeds, one of the women whose name Bertie had given me. She was skeptical about her ability to be helpful but happy to try. We agreed on a time the next morning and she gave me directions to her house in Bethel. At the rate I was going, I'd be needing another oil change in no time.

I went up and checked on Davey, then came back down and finished off the last piece of pizza while watching Arnold Schwarzenegger bust a few heads. Action flicks are my secret vice. I got all pumped up, then went to bed alone. Sometimes being a woman of the nineties just isn't all it's cracked up to be.

Bethel is a small New England town in upper Fairfield County that has retained the quaint appeal of its early Connecticut roots. Traffic was light, and I enjoyed the early morning drive.

Since I was by myself, I opened the sunroof and turned the radio up until the speakers pulsated. Davey was at camp, and I'd left Faith at home, not wanting her to wait in the car while I was with Ann. This time of year, it was simply too hot to take a chance. I'd take a disgruntled Poodle over one with heatstroke any day.

The directions I'd gotten led me to a compact ranch-style house set at the end of a quiet residential street. Careful landscaping and four-foot fences concealed most of the backyard from view, and as I climbed out of the car, all was quiet.

Like many of the dog show exhibitors I'd met so far, Ann was a hobby breeder with one breed she cared about passionately and a need to keep the number of dogs she housed to a minimum. Judging by what I could see, she was trying to keep a low profile. Few breeders are as lucky as Aunt Peg, with acres of land and neighbors that are hidden from view. Bertie had told me that Ann Leeds had French Bulldogs, but I wouldn't have guessed there were dogs around from what I could see out front.

Of course all that changed the minute Ann opened the door and three Frenchies scrambled out onto the steps. To the uninitiated eye (mine) they looked like little barrels on roller blades as they shot past me and down the stairs.

"Manny! Ginger! Fleur!" Ann called after them. She was small in stature, but a mass of blond hair pulled up into a ponytail on the top of her head added some height. She wore a loose T-shirt over snug leggings and had dimples in either cheek when she smiled, which she did as she held out her hand. "Don't worry about the dogs. They'll come back in a minute."

The Frenchies had to have heard her call—as far as I could see, the biggest thing about them was their ears. Instead of responding, however, they were busy sniffing the tires on my car.

"Come on in," said Ann. "They love to investigate, but as soon as they see us leaving, they'll come right along."

She was right, and in no time we were settled in a sunroom in the back of the house with Manny, Ginger, and Fleur draped on the floor around us. Ann offered coffee, which I accepted, and then we got right down to business.

"I thought Barry Turk was pond scum," said Ann. "But I imagine that's not an uncommon opinion."

I nodded, sipped my coffee, and she continued.

"He never showed any Frenchies, thank God, so the only time I ever met up with him was in the group ring. While the judge was looking at somebody else, he'd kind of sidle over . . ." She stood up to demonstrate. "Maybe nudge you with his elbow, you know? Next thing, he's standing way too close. The first time I thought he was trying to get past me, so I tried to move out of the way."

"What did he do?"

"He whispered *in my ear!* I don't care to repeat the actual words. Let's just say the suggestion was pornographic. I was so surprised, I nearly dropped my leash. I was showing Fleur at the time."

Ann nodded toward a fawn bitch who'd fallen asleep with her head on my foot. "We'd had a group third under that judge the last time out, and it wasn't a strong group, so I was hopeful. But Barry got me so flustered that I totally blew it."

"Did he win?"

"Second," Ann said grimly. "With a class Bichon that was lucky to have won the breed. Fleur didn't place. At the time I was horribly upset. I felt as though it was my fault, that I should have been able to ignore him."

"Easier said than done, I'd imagine. Did it ever happen again?"

"Two more times. That's when I decided I was going to file a complaint."

"But you didn't."

"No." Ann sighed. "I started talking to other women who'd shown against Barry. He made me feel so dirty. I hated it. And I couldn't figure out why he'd singled me out. Then, of course, I found out that he hadn't."

"Bertie mentioned that she'd had the same kind of experience."

Ann nodded. "There were others too. I thought maybe there might be safety in numbers, that if we all signed the complaint together, something would get done. But it turned out I was the only one who was willing to go on record, and in the end I wound up convinced that the process would do more damage to me than him."

"Were you ever tempted to take matters into your own hands?"

"You mean like buying a gun and shooting him?" Ann made a sound that was half laugh, half snort. "I can't say I didn't fantasize about it. But that's all it was, a fantasy. Besides, if I had actually shot the bastard, I'd have aimed lower."

This time she did laugh, and I joined in. Fleur lifted her head in annoyance and flopped in the other direction. I reached down and ran a hand down the hard-packed muscle in her loin. Her coat was short and silky smooth.

"I'm just curious," I said. "Did you ever think about talking to Alicia about this?"

"No. Why would I?"

"Well, they were living together. Presumably she had some influence over him . . ."

Ann was shaking her head, but I plowed on regardless. "Not even in revenge? I can't imagine Alicia'd have been happy to find out Barry was thinking things like that about other women."

"Alicia might not have been happy, but I doubt she'd have been surprised. It's not like she didn't flirt pretty good herself."

That was news. "With Barry, you mean, when she was

still with Bill?" I asked, trying to sort things out. "Or after?"

"Both," Ann confirmed. "That's just the way Alicia is. Men love being buttered up like that, and believe me, she's good at it."

"Did you ever notice her with any one man in particular?"

"No, mostly they seem to be clients of Barry's. Or sometimes prospective clients. Being the cretin he was, Barry needed all the good PR he could get. And Alicia could work a dog show like a pro.

"You'd see her walking some man around a show ground, showing him the sights, and the next thing you know Barry had a new set of dogs in his string. Of course, sometimes it backfired and went the other way. Let's just say I don't think Alicia was friends with too many of the wives."

I could certainly follow the logic there.

"Listen," said Ann, her features hardening. "The best thing about all this is that Barry Turk's gone. I don't necessarily care how or why. Just the fact that he's never going to bother anyone again is enough for me."

↤✣ ✿ *Sixteen* ✿ ✣↦

Davey and I borrowed Aunt Peg's beach pass and spent that afternoon and the next one at the Greenwich beach. We swam in Long Island Sound, hiked on the trails, and ate all sorts of junk food from the snack bar. The only practical thought I entertained had to do with the frequent application of high SPF lotion, and I refused to think at all about dog shows, or sexual harassment, or babies who might shortly be born fatherless.

By the time the Elm City dog show rolled around that weekend, I was feeling refreshed and ready to go. I had the beginnings of a tan and a few blond highlights in my hair. When Davey sat beside me on the front seat of the Volvo and sang "The Itsy-Bitsy Spider" for most of the ride to the show ground, I even managed to join in for a chorus or two.

Though it was July, the club had chosen to hold their show at an indoor location. Keeping dogs safe in what may turn out to be extreme heat is always a consideration at summer shows. Luckily for Elm City, they'd drawn beautiful weather. The big doors on all four sides of the building were open wide. The space inside was large and airy with ample room for grooming, big rings, and a variety of doggy concessions.

Davey took one look at the dog toys displayed at the Cherrybrook booth and pulled me that way. "For Faith," he said earnestly, his gaze fixed on a Day-Glo, rubber boomerang. "Every time she has to stay home, you tell her she can come next time. It isn't fair."

I had to admit I agreed with him. In fact, I'd been planning to bring the Poodle to the show with us until a last-minute call from Peg had scotched the idea. "Is she freshly clipped and bathed?" she asked.

"No," I'd admitted reluctantly.

"Then she's in no shape to be seen." Moses had delivered tablets down from the mountaintop with the same tone of authority.

So now I knew. Next time I'd bathe and clip Faith in advance.

Looking over the choices at the concession stand, I picked up a sheepskin toy shaped like a dinosaur. "How about one of these? Faith chewed up her last one."

"Nah." At the age of almost six, stuffed animals are beneath my son's regard. "This one."

The boomerang was hard and shiny and looked quite capable of breaking windows when flung, rather than chewed, as the manufacturer had no doubt intended. "Let's think about it, okay? We'll stop back at the end of the day and pick up something then."

Sighing loudly, Davey allowed himself to be led away. Never one to miss an opportunity, he milked the situation for a stop at the food stand, which was why we arrived at Peg's setup carrying a plate of brownies.

Her eyes lit up at the sight of us. "No wonder you're my favorite niece," she said, helping herself before the plate had even touched down on top of Tory's crate. "Did you bring tea?"

No sense in pointing out that I was her only niece. I held out a white plastic cup.

"You should use paper cups," said Davey. "Those are bad for the environment. We learned that in economy."

"I think he means ecology," I said, opening out a folding chair and getting him settled with his bag of toys.

Aunt Peg lifted out the Lipton tea bag and set it aside. "Ecology, economy." She stared at Davey. "What grade are you in?"

"First," he told her proudly. Having completed kindergarten the year before, he'd be entering first grade in the fall.

"That's what I thought. When I was in first grade, we played with blocks and learned how to write our names."

"I can already write my name. Want to see?" Davey pulled out a pencil and piece of paper and went to work.

"Alicia Devane came by a few minutes ago," Aunt Peg told me. She eyed the plate of brownies for a moment, then selected another. "She asked if you were coming today. I think she wants to talk to you."

"About what?"

"She didn't say, but she certainly looked pleased about something. Pregnancy must agree with her."

"It didn't earlier. Maybe she's getting past the morning-sickness stage." And maybe the accidents she'd been having had stopped. Whatever the reason, I was glad to hear that Alicia was doing better.

"Do I smell brownies?" Terry Denunzio came up the aisle with a Shih Tzu tucked beneath his arm. He stopped and sniffed the air. "I knew there was a reason why we let Peg squeeze in beside us."

"Help yourself." I waved toward the plate.

"Homemade?"

"Only if the lady at the concession stand baked this morning."

"Never mind." Terry snagged the biggest and popped it into his mouth. "I'll suffer through."

"Did you see which way Alicia went?" I asked Peg.

"Alicia Devane?" said Terry. "I just saw her. She and Bill were watching German Shepherds with Austin Beamish."

"I wonder what they were doing with him."

"Oh, sweetie." Terry laughed. "Haven't you figured that out yet? Everybody knows everybody around here."

"Austin has a Shepherd special too," said Peg. "He's not as good as Midas, but he does his share of winning."

"Maybe I'll go have a look. Will you keep an eye on Davey?"

"Watch him?" said Terry. "Bribe me with another brownie, and I'll do the child up and show him."

Grinning, I held out the plate. "I was talking to Aunt Peg."

"Too bad." Terry sounded disappointed. Brownie in hand, he slid past me and headed toward the next setup. "Compared to some of the competition I've seen today, I probably could have won."

According to the schedule in the front of the catalogue,

German Shepherds were showing in ring twelve on the other side of the building. I also looked in the exhibitors' index and saw that Christine Franken, the other woman whose name Bertie had given me, had three Miniature Pinschers entered. Seeing her here at the show would sure beat driving to Pennsylvania. I decided to check the area around the Toy rings first.

It turned out Christine was easy to find. I simply stopped at the first Min Pin I saw and asked its owner if he knew her. "Sure," he said, pointing. "Right over there."

Min Pins are a smooth-haired breed, so they don't require much preparation for the ring. Christine Franken didn't have a grooming table set up, only a small bank of crates and a chair. She was thumbing through the latest issue of *Dog Scene* magazine, and looked up as I approached.

She was a striking woman in her mid-thirties. Short black hair set off a dramatic bone structure, and her lips were outlined in a vivid shade of red that few people could carry. On her, it looked good.

I held out my hand and introduced myself. "Alberta Kennedy said you'd be willing to talk to me about Barry Turk."

"I guess so." There was a small stool next to her chair, and Christine cleared the stuff that had been piled on top. "Here, sit down. You weren't a friend of his, were you?"

"No. I barely knew him. We certainly weren't friends."

"Well, that's a start. I thought the man was an out-and-out snake."

"You weren't alone. I've spoken with Ann Leeds."

"Yeah, she had her problems with him too. Good old Barry, he really got around."

"Ann told me she wanted to file a complaint, but that nobody else was willing to go along."

Christine stared down at the magazine in her lap. A two-page ad showed a Basset Hound named BlackJack winning Best in Show, but I didn't think that was what she was looking at. "I couldn't see the point," she said finally. "It's not as though it would have stopped him."

"You don't think so?"

"I know so. I've been showing a long time, I know how things work. I had my problems with Barry a while ago. I'd been showing my own dogs for years and doing some handling for my friends. I was good at it, good enough to think about setting myself up as a pro.

"God knows it's not an easy life, but I thought I had a shot. I even had my first big client. I guess that's when Barry decided to show me just how rough the competition could get."

"What happened?"

Christine shook her head. "You know that saying, If you can't stand the heat, get out of the kitchen? Well, I guess I just couldn't take the heat. After a while I began to dread going into the ring. Trust me, an attitude like that doesn't get you many wins."

"And yet here you are, still showing your dogs."

"*My* dogs, right. But not anybody else's," Christine said bitterly. "That dream ended five years ago, thanks to Barry Turk. It got so that I wasn't winning enough to satisfy my biggest client, and once he pulled out, I was pretty much out of business.

"After that Turk left me alone. I wasn't a threat anymore, you know? As far as I'm concerned, he got what he had coming to him."

"Any thoughts on who might have killed him?"

For the first time, Christine smiled. "I don't know, but when you find out, let me know. I'd like to shake the guy's hand."

By the time I made it over to the German Shepherd ring, Alicia and Bill were gone. Austin was still watching the judging, however, and he'd been joined by Ron and Viv Pullman.

"Hi, Melanie." Austin held out a welcoming hand as I approached. In true dog show fashion, he also kept one eye on the action in the ring. "Are you a Shepherd fan?"

"Not really—"

"Don't let that worry you," said Ron. "Austin isn't either. The only reason he likes the breed is that he's got one that's winning."

"Ron," Viv said quietly, laying a hand on her husband's arm. "Be nice."

Her hair tumbled to her shoulders in soft waves, the sort of style that looked entirely natural, but started with a hundred-dollar haircut. Her blouse was silk and the cream-colored linen pants she wore with it had not a single wrinkle. Still, there were lines of strain on either side of her mouth that I hadn't noticed before, and the set of her shoulders was tight.

"Yes, Ron, be nice." Austin's smile bared his teeth but didn't reach his eyes. "We wouldn't want Melanie to get the wrong impression."

Viv shot me an apologetic look.

Mostly because she looked so uncomfortable, I stepped

between Viv and Austin and changed the subject. "Which one is yours?" I asked.

Asking a dog person about their dog is like asking a mother about her baby. You'll learn more than you ever wanted to know.

"Gunter," said Austin pointing. "He's standing second in line."

I looked and saw a muscular, deep-bodied black-and-tan dog with sweeping hindquarter angulation and an alert expression. As the judge turned her gaze down the line of specials, Gunter's handler tossed a small piece of liver out onto the mat. The Shepherd followed the treat's flight with his eyes, but didn't move an inch.

"He's very handsome," I said. It's always a safe comment. Somewhat akin to assuring other mothers at the school play that their child is the one on the stage with the most talent.

"Thank you. I got him in California. He's rather young, but I think he's coming along nicely."

Evidently so did the judge. When she finished going over the class, she moved Gunter to the front of the line. Viv tensed slightly with excitement. Ron looked bored. Austin, who had the most at stake, kept his expression neutral.

"That's it," said Viv as the judge sent the line of dogs around the ring.

"Not yet," Austin said. "Not until she points."

The judge motioned to Gunter for Best of Breed.

Viv clapped her hands enthusiastically. Austin finally managed a grin. Ron was staring off toward Irish Wolfhounds in the next ring.

"Congratulations," I said. The response was so automatic, it took me a moment to realize that no one else had spoken up.

"Yes," Viv echoed quickly. "Well done!"

Ron swung his gaze back in our direction. "Did you win?"

Viv poked him in the shoulder, hard. "Of course he won, silly."

Of all the names I might have been tempted to call Ron Pullman at that moment, silly was not one of them.

Ron smiled tightly. "Best of luck in the group."

Austin turned toward me. "Did that sound sincere to you?"

"Yes," I lied.

"You're a diplomat," said Austin.

"My mother raised me well." Although she'd never had the slightest inkling that my good manners might be put to the test at a dog show. Garden club, maybe. She wasn't a dog person either.

I looked past Ron and Viv and gazed around the building. "I was looking for Alicia Devane. I don't suppose any of you know where she might be?"

"She was here a little while ago," said Austin.

"I saw her with Bill," said Viv. Her voice seemed unnaturally loud. Maybe the two men were getting on her nerves. They were certainly getting on mine.

"That's right," Austin agreed. "She was with Bill. They're probably over by the Sporting rings."

"Thanks," I said. "I'll check there."

It was a relief to have an excuse to get away. Hanging around Ron and Austin was like watching two boxers battle for the heavyweight title. Each was continually trying to land the knockout punch. I didn't envy Viv the job of trying to keep the peace.

I checked around the sporting dog rings, but didn't see Alicia anywhere. Figuring I'd wasted enough time, I was on my way back to Aunt Peg's setup, when I passed by the food concession and found Alicia at the head of the line.

Alicia paid for her food, then turned and saw me. She had a milk shake in one hand and a cardboard basket of french fries in the other, but still managed a three-fingered wave. "Come and sit with me. Do you have a minute?"

"Sure."

We found an empty table and sat down. The chairs were made of plastic and bolted to the floor. Alicia was once again wearing a loose summer dress. If I hadn't known she was pregnant, I wouldn't necessarily have guessed, but her movements were awkward as she swiveled the chair and settled herself heavily into the seat.

She looked at the table, then back at the food counter and sighed.

"Napkins?" I asked, already starting to rise.

She nodded. "And ketchup, if you don't mind. Lots of it?"

The ketchup came in little packets. I scooped up half a dozen and added napkins and a straw. When I returned with the supplies, Alicia was already gulping down her milk shake.

"Sorry," she said. "I had breakfast earlier, but these days it seems as though I'm always hungry."

"You're eating for two."

"I feel like I'm eating for twelve. The doctor says I

should aim to gain twenty to twenty-five pounds over the entire pregnancy. I've put on half that much already."

"You don't look it."

She smiled wanly. "Would you tell me if I did?"

I grinned in return. "Probably not."

"That's what I thought." She squeezed ketchup out onto her fries and dug in with gusto.

"I heard you were looking for me. Is something wrong? Have you had any more accidents?"

"No, nothing like that." A frown line appeared briefly in her forehead, then was gone. "I wanted to tell you that I changed my mind."

"About what?"

"About a lot of things, actually." She paused, taking much longer than necessary to swirl a fry through the mound of ketchup at the end of the basket. "I'm going back to Bill."

I sat and stared at her. Calmly, Alicia stared right back.

I couldn't say that her decision was entirely unexpected. Gut reaction, however, told me that it wasn't a good idea.

"Is he your baby's father?"

"That seems to be the common consensus, doesn't it?" Alicia shook her head. "I wish he were, but he's not."

"How does he feel about taking on someone else's baby?"

"He's okay with it. I told you he and I wanted children. In fact, he's even pretty happy about it."

So was Alicia, judging by her demeanor. Then I stopped and reconsidered. Happy wasn't the right word. It was more like smug. And here I was, about to burst her bubble.

"You know what people are going to say. Bill's made no secret of the fact that he wanted you back. Now that Barry's out of the way, he's getting exactly what he wanted."

Alicia waved a french fry in the air, but her expression was nearly as carefree as the gesture. "Let people talk. They always do."

"This time maybe there's some truth to what they're saying."

"Bill didn't kill Barry."

"You don't know that, Alicia. You've got to face facts. Somebody did murder Barry. And in all likelihood, it was someone you know."

"Not Bill," Alicia said stubbornly.

"He knows about guns."

"So do a lot of people. That doesn't mean anything."

"He hated the fact that Barry had taken you away from him."

"He was dealing with it."

"Really?" I arched a brow. "Well, I guess he doesn't have to anymore, does he?"

"Look," said Alicia. She leaned closer across the small table. "Maybe this isn't the best idea in the whole world. But it isn't the worst either. I'm pregnant. Bill will take care of me. What other choice do I have?"

"You could ask the baby's father for help."

Before I'd even finished speaking, she was already shaking her head. "No, not an option."

How could she be so blind? "Does Bill know that the only reason you're going back to him is that you're desperate? Has it occurred to you that maybe that's what he planned on all along? He had the means and he had the motive."

I paused, letting my words sink in. "And now he has you."

"You're wrong." Alicia's brown eyes flashed angrily as she braced her hands on the table and pushed herself up. "Bill wasn't the one who shot Barry. He and I are going to be fine. You'll see."

For her sake, I hoped so.

⌒❧ ❀ *Seventeen* ❀ ❧⌒

When I got back to Aunt Peg's setup, Davey was nowhere in sight. Knowing how much he likes to play hide-and-seek, I took this to be a bad sign. Peg had Tory on her feet on the grooming table and was concentrating on her scissoring. Once she starts trimming, almost nothing distracts her including, obviously, the departure of a clever five-year-old with sneakers on his feet. I wondered how recently my son had slipped away.

"Aunt Peg?"

"Hmm?" She lifted her head, blowing a breath upward to lift the hair from her eyes. One of the consequences of the new hairdo.

"Where's Davey?"

"He's with Viv." She straightened, then looked around the grooming area. "I guess they've gone off some-where."

"What's he doing with Viv?"

"She and Ron came by about ten minutes ago. Ron needed to talk to Crawford, who was on his way to the

Bichon ring. Off the two of them went. Nobody paid any attention to Viv."

Peg turned back to her trim. "I wonder how long it will be before Ron realizes she's not following along."

"Davey?" I asked, somewhat desperately.

"Oh, right. When everyone else left, Viv came over and volunteered to read him a story."

Davey's books were piled on his chair, and nobody was reading anything in the vicinity. I told myself to remain calm.

"Maybe they went for more brownies," Peg said hopefully. The paper plate on top of Tory's crate was empty save for a few crumbs.

I heard a delighted squeal and was just starting to turn, when forty pounds of running child hit the backs of my legs. It was a miracle we didn't both go down.

Following behind at a more graceful pace, came Viv.

"I went to the bathroom," Davey informed me. "Viv took me."

"Don't you mean Mrs. Pullman?"

His face screwed up in confusion. As Viv joined us, he pointed to her with some relief. "I went with her."

"I hope it's okay. I told him to call me Viv. Mrs. Pullman is my mother-in-law."

"Sure it's fine, if that's what you want. Thanks for taking care of him." I disentangled Davey's arms, opened his bag of toys, and got out his Matchbox cars. Instant distraction.

"No problem. It's not as though I was doing anything else." Viv frowned slightly, glancing over toward Crawford's setup. Terry was back now, using a blow dryer on a

Toy Poodle's bracelets, but Ron and Crawford still hadn't returned.

"Did Leo win today?"

Viv nodded. "So did our new puppy. But Chows showed first thing this morning, and the group isn't for another couple of hours yet. I hate it when that happens. Ron has too much time to get nervous in between."

"Ron gets nervous?"

"After all this time, you'd think he'd take the competition in stride, wouldn't you? But somehow, the more the dog wins, the worse it gets. He's very competitive. He can't stand to see Leo lose."

"Especially not to one of Austin's dogs," I guessed.

"You're right about that. Austin's a whole different kind of player, and on some levels, that really ticks Ron off. Leo was born in our family room. Ron raised him from a puppy. In some ways I'd swear that dog is like his child, or maybe an extension of his ego.

"Austin doesn't have to worry about bloodlines, or genetic testing, or middle-of-the-night whelpings. He just sees something he likes and he buys it. There's no risk involved with his method."

Aunt Peg had finished scissoring and was now putting up Tory's topknot. She managed to talk around the mound of rubber bands between her lips. "Except perhaps the risk that a breeder won't want to sell a really good one."

"To Austin? With his resources?" Viv's beige-tipped fingers drummed lightly on the top of the crate. "Unfortunately, nobody ever says no to him. We'd all be better off if someone did."

"Shhh!" said Terry in a loud stage whisper. "Stop talking about them. Here they come!"

Crawford strode through the grooming area, carrying the Bichon and a red ribbon. As the aisle was too narrow to walk abreast, Ron followed a step behind. The handler slanted Terry a look. "Gossiping again? I thought you were supposed to be working."

"I wasn't gossiping. I was eavesdropping. It hardly takes any effort at all."

Crawford eyed the freshly blown-out Toy Poodle. "Much like your grooming."

"I'm not done yet." Terry snatched up a pair of scissors. "What you see here is a masterpiece in the making."

"What I'd like to see is a class bitch with her topknot in."

"Slave driver." Terry pouted briefly, then brightened. "Lucky for you, I like that."

Shaking his head, Crawford put the Bichon away in its crate. As Ron and Viv strolled away, he went to check on his two Standard Poodles which were lying on top of their tables. He and Terry had worked on them earlier and both were just about ready.

Meanwhile behind me, Aunt Peg had begun to spray up. I knew what was coming. Without waiting to be asked, I went over and cupped Tory's muzzle in the palm of my hand.

"When you say you'll keep an eye on Davey," I said mildly, "that means you're supposed to know where he is."

"I did." Peg deftly feathered her comb through the long neck hair, stretching it until it stood upright, then spraying it into place. "He was with Viv, just like I told you."

There was no use arguing. Next time I'd try hanging a box of doughnuts around his neck. At least that would keep her attention.

Standard Poodles were scheduled to be judged at one o'clock with Minis and Toys following. On our way up to the ring, we ran into Bertie Kennedy. She was carrying a black Mini bitch and heading in the same direction.

"New client?" I asked, nodding toward the Mini.

"No, this is one of Beth's. She's stuck in the Pom ring. I told her I'd get this one up to ringside."

I took a closer look. "I think I did up that bitch last week."

"You probably did. With Barry gone, that operation's coming apart at the seams. Beth's taking any help she can get."

I wondered if I'd been insulted and decided it probably wasn't intentional. When it came to other women, Bertie wasn't inclined to be catty. Of course, with her looks, she didn't have to be.

As usual, she looked stunning. Her wide green eyes were softly lined with shadow, and her dress was a fluid column of soft teal silk. It was long enough so that she could stoop and bend without embarrassment, and short enough to show off plenty of leg.

I sighed softly. I thought I was doing well when I didn't have peanut butter or jelly smeared on me.

"Your brother called me," Bertie said.

"Are you going to go out with him?"

"Friday night. Didn't you know?"

"No, why would I?"

"He said we were doubling with you and your guy. Sam Driver, right?"

"Right. But this is the first I've heard of it."

"Wow," said Davey, tagging along at my side. "Can I come?"

"No." The answer was swift and automatic. Sometimes it felt as though my son spent more time with Sam than I did. I turned back to Bertie. "You're sure about that?"

"Positive. Mark your calendar." We passed the ring where Pomeranians were being judged, and Bertie veered away.

"Naughty, naughty," said Terry. He was two steps behind Davey and me, leading one of Crawford's Standards.

"What?"

"I know what you're thinking."

"That I'd like to strangle my brother?"

He shook his head. "You're thinking, why don't I look like that?"

"I am not."

His hands waved through the air, shaping a curvy, hourglass figure. "Trust me, Bertie is too much of a good thing."

"To you, maybe. You're gay."

"Oh, my God!" Terry cried. "I am? Don't tell my parents!"

I smiled, amused in spite of myself.

"I told you before, I could work wonders with your hair."

"I like my hair."

"Sure you do. You like it so much, you've worn it the same way since college."

No point in trying to refute that.

"Where's my comb?" said Aunt Peg. We'd almost reached the Poodle ring, where I could see that the Puppy Dog class was already being judged. "Who has my comb?"

"Right here," I said, hurrying to catch up.

"You can run," Terry called after me, "but you can't hide!"

"Goodness," said Peg as I handed over the wide-toothed comb for last-minute repairs. "What was that all about?"

"Just Terry being dramatic. He wants to cut my hair."

Aunt Peg reached for her can of hair spray. Applying any sort of additive to a dog's coat is illegal according to A.K.C. rules. The laws are rarely enforced, however, and few dogs appear in the ring in their natural state. Since she was spraying at ringside, however, she took the precaution of standing between Tory and the judge as she worked. No use in making a blatant infraction any more visible than it had to be.

Peg looked up, assessing my hair style as if she'd never noticed it before. "You have perfectly nice hair. Too bad it just lies there."

"Isn't it time for your class?"

Her head swung around quickly. "That's Open Dog," she sniffed. "Don't be mean to an old lady."

"Old? You?"

"Heaven forbid," said Crawford, coming out of the ring. He handed Terry the Open Dog who had just gone third in his class, and took the bitch. "If you're old, we'll all have to reconsider."

Puppy Bitch came and went. As at many shows, there

were no entries in the intervening classes, and Open Bitch was next. As Peg and Crawford both entered the ring, Davey and I moved up to the rail to watch.

"That looks like fun," said Davey.

"It is," I said. "Sort of."

It was also nerve-racking and painfully intense. After all the effort that went into preparing a Poodle to be shown, the actual time spent in the ring amounted to only a few minutes. First impressions count a lot. Mess up once, and you've often cost yourself the chance to win.

That's one reason many exhibitors hire professionals to show their dogs for them. In theory, the pros don't make mistakes. Watching Crawford handle his bitch was like watching Nureyev dance. He was a master at work.

"So who's going to win?" I asked Terry, who had come to stand beside us.

"You're asking *moi*? Do I look like a fortune-teller?"

I leaned back and pretended to consider. "Add a pair of hoop earrings, a feather boa, and you could probably pass."

"Pass?" He fluttered his eyelashes demurely. "Honey, I'm stunning in feathers."

The judge had finished her individual examinations. As she ran her gaze down the line, she didn't seem very interested in either Tory or Crawford's bitch. A moment later, she pulled out a leggy black handled by a pro from Pennsylvania and motioned her to the front. Tory was pulled third, Crawford's bitch, fifth.

"Too bad," I said.

Terry shrugged. "Crawford won't mind. He knew she wouldn't like what he was bringing her in Standards."

"Then why did he bring them?"

"She's doing the group."

I ran that through my thought processes twice. At the end, I wasn't any closer to understanding. If the judge didn't like his Standard Poodles enough to even give them their classes, what possible difference could it make that she was judging the Non-Sporting group? I gave up trying to figure it out, and asked.

"Leo has a real shot at going Best today," said Terry. "This judge has liked him before, and Crawford's hoping she'll like him again. It certainly doesn't hurt when group time rolls around that she's seen Crawford in her ring all day long, bringing her entries."

Now *that* I could understand. Judges are licensed by the American Kennel Club, but they're hired to judge by the individual kennel clubs that put on the shows. I'd thought about joining an all-breed club in the spring and I'd learned a lot about how they operate.

Kennel clubs serve a variety of functions, but holding dog shows is their chief source of revenue. Much careful planning is done to maximize each show's appeal to entry-paying exhibitors. Clubs vie for advantageous dates and sites, and they hire judges who they hope will attract the largest number of exhibitors.

A judge who doesn't "draw" is one who will eventually find himself with fewer and fewer assignments. Conversely, one who brings out the exhibitors will become very popular. No wonder, then, that judges tend to favor the handlers who bring them the largest number of entries.

"Who's doing Best?" I asked.

"Maggie Cowan. She hasn't had Leo before, but Crawford's heard she's said some nice things about him."

The dog show grapevine. Time-Warner should have a communications system this good.

"And supposedly she dumped Midas last month in New Jersey."

The light was not only beginning to dawn, it was shining like a beacon. No wonder Ron was nervous. A win over Austin's top dog would mean a lot. I began making plans to stay and see how it all turned out.

"Well, that was a waste of time," said Peg. Usually she's a very good sport, but today she looked positively disgruntled. The white ribbon in her hand attested to the fact that while I'd been talking to Terry, the judge had dropped her placement from third to fourth.

"Maybe you should hire a handler to show your bitch," Terry said.

Aunt Peg is a dedicated owner-handler. I expected a diatribe in reply, but instead she only laughed. "What for? Crawford did even worse than I did."

"Yes," I said. "But he'll get his eventually."

On the way back to the setup, Davey and I stopped off at the food concession and picked up lunch. There wasn't much of a choice. I vetoed the cheese-covered nachos my son had his eye on and went for hamburgers all around.

By the time we finished eating and Peg had Tory on the table for a quick brush-through and rewrap, the groups were already beginning. Herding was first. Holding Davey's hand, I wandered over to see how it would go.

Group judging is often a relatively speedy process.

Though each of the seven groups has a large number of breeds, the same person is often hired to judge both the group and the breeds within it. Since he selected the Best of Breed winners earlier in the day, going over them again is a perfunctory matter.

With the groups starting early in the afternoon, there was still a large crowd of spectators in the building. Most were clustered around the group ring, applauding vigorously for the dogs they liked. Davey and I found a spot to wedge ourselves in and had a look.

Austin's German Shepherd was an obvious crowd favorite, as were the rough Collie and Old English Sheepdog. The rarer breeds, which in this case seemed to mean those that had not been featured to a mass audience on TV, were greeted only with silence. I clapped enthusiastically for a nice Cardigan Welsh Corgi, but it was a lonely and thankless effort.

Fortunately the judge did his job, paying scant attention to popular opinion and rewarding the dogs he liked best. A Puli was first, followed by a Briard. Austin's Shepherd managed third, while the Corgi I'd picked out was fourth.

The Toy group was next. Even with a Poodle in it, the group has never been one of my favorites. As the little dogs began filing into the ring, Davey, who'd inherited his great-aunt's sweet tooth gene, began angling for ice cream. If I appeased him now, there was a good chance he'd stand still for the Non-Sporting group later. Besides, my son wasn't the only one who'd noticed the Häagen-Dazs stand over by the obedience rings.

We walked across the building and skirted around the grooming area. Most of the breed rings were now empty, but the obedience competition was still going strong.

Davey paused, enchanted, as a beautifully trained Border Collie flew over an obstacle, picked up a dumbbell its handler had tossed, then spun around and leapt back over the jump.

"Cool!" he cried. "Can we teach Faith to do that?"

"Sure, when she's finished in the breed ring, and we cut off her hair." One problem at a time. "Standard Poodles make great obedience dogs because they're so smart."

"I bet Faith could learn to do anything."

I bet she could too. Whether or not I could teach her was another matter entirely.

"Look," said Davey. "There's Viv."

I looked where he was pointing, but didn't immediately see her. Nor could I imagine what she'd be doing on this side of the building. "I don't think so. Come on, let's get that ice cream."

"No," said Davey with all the determination a five-year-old could muster. "It is Viv. She's yelling at that man."

So I had another look. And what do you know, Davey was right. Viv was standing over in the shadows on the far side of the obedience ring.

Even more interesting, the man she was arguing with was Austin Beamish.

⌖✿ *Eighteen* ✿⌖

It wasn't any of my business.

That didn't stop me from staring.

"What about my ice cream?" asked Davey.

The ice cream stand was at the end of the ring. I fished two dollar bills out of my wallet and sent Davey running on ahead.

The Border Collie had finished its turn and been replaced by a Shetland Sheepdog. Watching as the dog heeled off-lead, I strolled casually in Viv and Austin's direction.

Obedience competitors, like their counterpart in breed, are very committed to what they're doing. The sign by the gate identified the class as Open B, which meant that those involved had plenty at stake. No one standing ringside seemed to be paying any attention to Austin and Viv but me.

Viv wasn't yelling anymore, but even from a distance she looked angry. Austin was speaking in a low voice.

When he reached out and placed a hand on her arm, she quickly shook him off.

I'd hesitated for a moment, not wanting to interrupt. Now I started forward again, some vague, unformed thought in my mind that maybe Viv needed rescuing.

As I drew near, she looked past Austin and saw me. Immediately Viv took a step back as Austin turned to see what she was looking at. I pasted a smile on my face that probably looked as phony as it felt.

"Davey wanted ice cream," I said, hoping that explained, more or less, what I was doing there. "Thank you again for your help earlier."

"Help?" asked Austin, looking baffled.

"Viv's help. With Davey. He can be quite a handful."

"No, he wasn't." Viv shook her head. "He was fine."

"Excuse me, I believe the Sporting group is about to begin." Austin turned and strode away.

"Is everything okay?" I asked Viv.

"Sure." She looked as though she wanted to leave too. Maybe I'd been wrong about the rescuing part.

"Are you and Austin having a problem?"

"It was nothing."

"It didn't look that way."

"You know what Austin's like. He can be pretty intense."

Poor Viv, surrounded on all sides by competitive men.

Out of the corner of my eye, I was keeping track of Davey's progress. He'd worked his way to the front of the line and was making his selection. Any minute now, he'd be back.

Viv looked as though she were wishing desperately that I would change the subject, so I decided to oblige her. "You know, there's something I've been wondering about. Maybe you could clarify things for me."

"What's that?"

"Your Chow, Leo. Barry Turk used to show him, didn't he?"

"That's right."

"I heard that Ron took the dog away from Barry last spring, and I was wondering what went wrong. Did they have a disagreement over something?"

"Not at all," Viv said firmly. "Putting Leo with Crawford was my idea. Ron had nothing to do with it. I thought Crawford could do better with the dog, and obviously he has."

"Hey, Mom! Look what I got!" Davey skidded to a stop beside us, waving a double chocolate ice cream bar. And not a napkin in sight.

"That looks great." Viv smiled down at him.

"Want a bite?"

"No, thanks. I'd better be getting back to the group ring. Ron's probably wondering where I've gone."

"We'll see you back there," I said. "We can all cheer for Leo together."

The line at the ice cream stand had grown. While I waited my turn, I pondered what I'd just heard. Peg had once mentioned that Ron had been involved with Chows for nearly twenty years. That had to have been longer than he'd known Viv, unless their relationship had started when she was in grade school.

Watching the Pullmans at the shows, I'd gotten the distinct impression that as far as the dogs went, Ron was in charge. So why had Viv claimed to be responsible for a decision as important as who would handle their top winning dog?

Ice cream in hand (or on shirt, depending which one of us you looked at), Davey and I made our way back to the big center ring, where the groups were being judged. In our absence, Toys had come and gone and Midas had coasted to an easy victory in the Sporting group.

I found Aunt Peg standing with Bill and Alicia as the Non-Sporting group entered the ring. Peg took one look at my chocolate-bedecked son and placed him directly in front of her, where she could keep an eye on his sticky hands.

"You had ice cream?" she said, censure clear in her voice. "And you didn't bring me any?"

"We'll go back again," I offered. Now that Alicia had told me she was moving back in with Bill, I wasn't sure how much I wanted to reveal to either one of them, but I did want to ask Peg about what Viv had said. "Come on, let's go."

"Not now. After Non-Sporting."

The dogs formed a line along one side of the ring, with the biggest in front and the smaller ones to the rear. The idea was to give each dog the opportunity to gait at the speed that suited it best. The Standard Poodle was in front, followed by the Dalmatian. Crawford and Leo were four or five places back. The Chow was larger than the Mini Poodle and the Finnish Spitz, but didn't move as fast.

"Wow, there's Terry," cried Davey, leaning into the ring. Terry was near the end of the line with a Tibetan

Spaniel. As my son waved enthusiastically, I grabbed the back of his T-shirt and hauled him back.

"He waved to me! Did you see him?"

Terry had indeed waved. While the rest of the handlers were busy fussing over their dogs so that they would look their best when the judge made her first pass down the line, Terry was gabbing to the exhibitor beside him. He appeared only marginally aware of the dog on the end of his lead. Luckily the little Tibetan Spaniel was stacking itself.

I've been coming to dog shows for a year, but the subtle implications of the behavior I see in the ring still sometimes eludes me. "Why isn't he paying more attention?" I whispered to Aunt Peg.

"Because he's not supposed to win," Peg whispered back. No one at ringside talks in a normal tone of voice. It's too easy to be overheard. Even when what you're saying seems to be innocuous, it's safer to keep your guard up. The judge was passing in front of us now, pausing to have a look at the Keeshond that was set up just on the other side of the rail.

Peg waited until the judge had moved on before continuing. "Leo is Crawford's top specials dog. Obviously he's the one Crawford is hoping to win with. No handler with a top winning dog would agree to take another special in the same group. After all, he can show only one at a time. I'd guess that the Tibetan Spaniel is a class dog of Crawford's that got lucky and won his breed. Crawford doesn't want him giving Leo any competition."

"Then why show him at all?"

All Best of Breed and Best of Variety winners are eligible to show in the group, but they aren't required to if they didn't want to. Group winners, however, are required to compete for Best in Show.

"Maybe his owners are here and wanted to see him in the group ring," Peg said in an undertone. "Besides, don't forget that the woman who's in there judging now is the same one who did these breeds earlier. She liked that Tibetan Spaniel enough to give it the Breed.

"Crawford certainly wouldn't want to insult her good judgment by not showing the dog. On the other hand, I'm sure he's told Terry to make sure the dog isn't a threat. Crawford wants to make it perfectly clear to the judge which of his two entries he intends to win with."

"Jeez." I felt frown lines wrinkling my forehead. "I'm never going to get the hang of all this."

"Sure you will. Another ten or fifteen years of showing and you'll be an old pro."

What a pleasant prospect that was.

The Chow prevailed easily, setting himself up for a confrontation with Midas, among others, in the Best in Show ring. While the Hound group was being judged, Peg, Davey, and I went back for another round of ice cream. On the way, I told her about what I'd seen and heard earlier.

"What on earth would Viv and Austin have to argue about?" she asked.

"I wondered the same thing. Viv said it was nothing."

"Maybe it was." She didn't necessarily sound convinced.

"What about the business with Viv and Leo?" I prodded. "Doesn't that seem odd?"

Sometimes when dog-related things don't make sense to me, Peg is able to put another spin on the situation and everything sorts itself out. This time, however, her reaction was the same as mine.

"I'll say it does. I can't imagine Ron letting her make a decision like that."

"Maybe he didn't, and she's covering for him. Maybe Ron and Barry had a huge fight, and now with Barry dead, he'd just as soon nobody knew about it."

"My, you have a devious mind." Peg grinned happily. She likes it when her relatives demonstrate unexpected ability. "I was thinking along less sinister lines myself. Ron's been breeding Chows for years, you know. His first wife, Mona, was very involved with the dogs and the dog shows."

As we reached the Häagen-Dazs cart, I reminded Davey that we had apples back at the setup.

"Ice cream," he said stubbornly.

"You just had ice cream."

Aunt Peg ended the argument by placing an order for two more ice cream bars. "He's a growing boy," she said. "Let him eat."

"I do let him eat. He can have all the fruit he wants."

"Oh, pish." Peg paid the man and distributed the booty.

Once again, it was left to me to remember napkins. "Tell me about Mona," I said as we started back.

"I don't think Mona's the issue, really. It's just that she seemed to be an equal partner in Ron's breeding program in a way that Viv isn't. Maybe there's a bit of lingering jealousy there. Or perhaps Viv is just trying to make herself seem more involved than she really is. After all, nobody can dispute the fact that the decision turned out to be a good one."

"I like the big-fight theory better," I decided.

"Me too," Peg admitted. "Do you suppose Ron knows anything about guns?"

"These days, it seems as if almost everyone does."

"I know about guns," Davey said proudly. He pointed his ice cream bar toward us and moved his finger as though pulling a trigger. "Bang!"

"Great," I muttered. "What else do you know?"

"Guns are very dangerous. They can kill people. Just like drugs."

Aunt Peg lifted a brow.

"Just Say No," I explained. "Hunting Ridge is a very progressive school."

"I should say so," said Peg, not sounding entirely pleased about the things her five-year-old nephew was learning.

I couldn't say as I blamed her. I'm sure I'm not the only mother who finds herself torn between wanting to protect her child's innocence, and understanding the need to prepare him to deal with the real world.

When we got back to the ring, the Terrier group was just ending. The Irish Terrier collected the blue ribbon and joined the line up for Best in Show. By now the crowds had thinned and I was able to pick out Ron and Viv, who were standing with Terry at one end of the ring. Across on the other side, Austin was with a group of people I didn't know. It seemed just as well that the two men had the length of the ring separating them.

As the Best in Show judging began, Aunt Peg watched the proceedings with great attention. Unfamiliar with most of the participants, I was less absorbed. Could Ron have murdered Barry? I wondered. What could they have been fighting over that was that important? And if he'd already voiced his unhappiness by moving Leo to another handler, why come back three months later with a gun? The whole thing made no sense at all.

A burst of applause brought me out of my reverie. Peg and Davey were both clapping like mad—Peg, no doubt, because the dog she favored was at the head of the line, and Davey because he hates to be left out. As I looked into the ring, the judge turned and pointed at Leo and Crawford.

Even from thirty feet away, I could hear Terry squeal with delight. And that gave me an idea.

If anyone knew why the Pullmans' Chow had left Turk's kennel and gone to Crawford, it was Crawford himself. Getting him to talk, however, was about as easy as teaching a Bulldog to retrieve. In the hustle and bustle of a dog show, I would never be able to pin him down.

A visit to his home might be another matter. Especially if I already had a nice, innocuous reason for being there. Terry'd offered twice to cut my hair. This seemed like an excellent time to take him up on his offer.

Here's a tip for anyone who wants to pay a visit to a professional handler and is hoping to generate goodwill: go in the middle of the week. Thursday and Friday are spent preparing for the weekend shows, and Monday is the day to recover and get everything put back together. Tuesday and Wednesday are about as close as handlers ever get to a day off. Their dogs still have to be fed and exercised, but the bulk of the work can be set aside for later.

I spoke with Terry Monday night and he told me to

come Wednesday morning. He didn't mention whether or not Crawford would be there, and I didn't ask. I'd wing it, I decided, and hope for the best. Bedford, where Crawford's kennel was located, was only a short hop over the state line into Westchester County. Even if I didn't get to ask any questions, with luck, the haircut would make the trip worthwhile.

Thunderstorms were forecast for late afternoon, but when I dropped Davey off at camp, the day had yet to cloud over. The sky was a vivid shade of blue with only the merest wisps of airy white clouds scudding across the horizon. Faith was on the front seat of the Volvo beside me. Terry had said that Crawford wouldn't mind if I brought her along.

Of all the kennels I've ever visited, Crawford Langley's is the nicest. It's set way back from the road on a parcel of land that's bigger than my whole block in Flower Estates. The house is a white colonial, large and well maintained.

The kennel building is behind the house and looks as though it was designed to match. Runs spread out from either side: covered, to the left; uncovered, to the right. In addition, several acres of land have been fenced off into a series of large paddocks.

As I parked beneath the spreading branches of a beautiful old maple tree, two Standard Poodles were busy entertaining themselves by chasing each other along the chain-link fence in their adjoining paddocks. Fence running, it's called, and it's a wonderful source of exercise. Immediately Faith stood up and pricked her ears.

"You want to join them, don't you?"

Her paws did a little dance on the seat. Faith didn't

need to know how to talk. Her method of communication made her feelings perfectly clear.

I slipped the looped end of the lead over her head and hopped her out of the car. Being a Standard Poodle, Faith's manners are impeccable. But as I led her to the house, she was still casting envious glances back at the two playing Poodles.

Terry answered the door wearing cutoff denim shorts and a loose tank top. His feet were encased in a battered pair of Top-Siders and he hadn't bothered to shave. Don Johnson has to try to look this good. On Terry, it just seemed to come naturally.

"Welcome," he said. "Come on in."

Faith whined softly under her breath. Terry glanced at her, then out into the field, then up at me. "It's your choice. She can come inside with us, or I can set her up out there in the empty paddock."

Faith leapt up in the air and placed her front paws on Terry's chest. "Paddock it is," he said.

At least they'd pretended to consult me.

Five minutes later, Faith was happily fence running with the other Standard Poodles. Terry had checked to make sure that the water bucket in the paddock was full. I'd looked at the angle of the sun and decided that one end of the paddock would remain shaded for at least another hour. We left Faith making new friends and went inside.

"Come on in the kitchen." Terry led the way through the back door. "Crawford is such a neat freak. If we're going to make a mess, we may as well do it someplace he never goes."

"I heard that," said Crawford. He was pouring himself

a cup of coffee from the pot on the counter. Like Terry, he was dressed casually. Even so, his khakis were creased and his hair was neatly combed. "Are you implying I can't cook?"

"I wouldn't dream of it." Terry pulled out a chair from a bleached wood table beside a window and invited me to sit. "You heat up Lean Cuisine better than almost anyone I know."

Crawford ignored him, directing his next question to me. "The boy wonder tells me you're letting him cut your hair. Are you sure that's a good idea?"

"I've heard he's very good," I said, hoping I hadn't heard wrong.

"Honey, I'm not just good. I'm faaabulous." Terry opened a drawer, whipped out a sheet, and fastened it around my shoulders. "By the time I'm done, you'll look like Whoopi Goldberg."

I started to rise. Terry's firm hand on my shoulder pushed me back down. "Just kidding."

A comb, a spray bottle of water, and a pair of scissors appeared in his hands. All at once, I felt like one of Crawford's Poodles, standing on a grooming table and waiting to be done up. I wondered if there weren't easier ways to gather information.

On the other side of the table, Crawford pulled out a chair and sat down. Sections from the morning's *New York Times* were scattered over the tabletop. Crawford took a pair of glasses out of his pocket, picked up the front page, and began to read.

"Relax," he said. "Terry's actually pretty talented."

That made me feel better. Marginally. "Does he do your hair?"

"No."

I started to get up again. Terry, busy spritzing, pushed me back down. "You have to sit still. Otherwise I won't be responsible for the consequences."

Consequences? That sounded serious. I forced a smile. "Not too short, okay?"

"Did the Pope tell Michelangelo how to paint the Sistine Chapel?"

"Actually"—Crawford looked up from his paper—"I believe he did."

Seated between the two of them, I felt like the straight man in a Three Stooges comedy. I just hoped I had enough hair left at the end of all this for someone to call me Curly.

Scissors flashed in the corner of my eye as Terry made the first cut. "Congratulations on Leo's Best in Show on Sunday," I said to Crawford. "The Pullmans must have been thrilled."

"I'll say—" Terry began.

"They were very pleased." Crawford deftly cut him off. "The dog showed beautifully."

"You've done very well with him."

He nodded.

"Especially since you've had him only a matter of months."

Crawford flipped the top corner of the paper down and stared at me over the top of his reading glasses. "Melanie," he said sternly. "You are not nearly as subtle as you think you are."

I wasn't?

"If you're here to have your hair cut, I'm Liberace. Knowing you, you probably want to talk about Barry's murder. So why don't you just get to it."

"Okay." That wasn't an invitation I was about to turn down. "What do you know about Barry Turk and sexual harassment?"

The question seemed to surprise him. Crawford set down the paper and took a moment to think about it. "I heard rumors," he said finally. "Didn't know if they were true, didn't particularly want to know."

"Apparently he's been bothering women handlers for years. One, Christine Franken, gave up handling because of what he did."

"Really?" asked Terry.

"I wouldn't know," said Crawford. "I do remember when Christine was starting out. One month she was showing for Austin Beamish. Next month she wasn't. It's not an unusual story. Lots of people who think they're going to make it as a pro don't."

"She says Barry set out to put her out of business."

"Barry wasn't out to make any friends, that's true. This is a competitive sport. Every time you walk into the ring, it's either the other guy or you."

"Speaking of which, why did Ron and Viv take the dog away from Barry last spring and bring him here?"

"I don't know."

I stared at him, hard. "You don't know, or you don't want to say?"

"Both." Crawford pushed aside the newspaper and stood. "Anything I'd tell you would be pure speculation. I don't care to do that."

He picked up his coffee cup and left the room. When I turned to watch him go, Terry gently repositioned my head. He was bending close, lifting the hair with the comb, and feathering in layers.

"Three words," he said softly. *"Cherchez la femme."*

ಕ❋ *Nineteen* ❋ಎ

Look for the woman? What woman? Viv? She'd told me she'd been responsible for Leo's switch in handlers. Maybe I should have believed her.

Obviously enjoying himself, Terry was humming under his breath.

"Viv Pullman," I said. "You're talking about Viv, right?"

"No."

No? What other woman was there?

He finished the side he'd been working on and began to pin up the other. Without the benefit of a mirror, I had no idea what he'd done. I reached a hand up to my shoulder. The hair that had been there was gone.

"Sit still." Terry slapped my hand away. "Or you'll end up looking like one of Bitsy Farnsworth's Shih Tzus."

Bitsy Farnsworth was an owner-handler, and not a very talented one at that. Dogs she'd groomed tended to look like they had recently passed through a wind tunnel. I took the threat seriously and settled back in my chair.

If not Viv, then who? What other woman could have been responsible for Leo's move? What other women were there?

There was Beth certainly, Barry's assistant. Had Ron been dissatisfied with the way she'd cared for the dog? If so, a few pointed comments to Barry should have been sufficient to clear up that problem.

What about Alicia? She was there too, although not in any capacity that would have given her much contact with Leo. As Terry happily spritzed and snipped, I mulled that over. It wasn't until I stopped focusing on the dog and started focusing on the people that I remembered what Ann Leeds had said about Alicia buttering up potential clients.

And about the fact that Alicia wasn't friends with many of the wives.

Alicia, who was now pregnant with a baby she claimed belonged to neither Barry nor her ex-husband. Just how well had Alicia gotten along with Barry's biggest client?

"Alicia," I said aloud. "Alicia and Ron."

Terry smiled, wielding his scissors like a pro. "I didn't say it."

"Is it true?"

He glanced toward the kitchen door, and I knew what he was thinking. Crawford wouldn't be happy if he thought Terry was blabbing his clients' secrets. Besides, he'd already said enough.

I lifted a hand. "How's it coming?"

"Almost done."

Only a moment passed before Terry put down his scissors. He pulled back, studying me critically. I was pleased to note that for all the snipping I'd heard, there didn't seem to be that much hair on the floor around me.

He stared for so long that I began to get nervous. "How does it look?"

"Fabulous! It's like magic. Your eyes look huge. Have you ever thought about lining your lids with brown eye shadow?"

"Yeah, right." I was busy fishing through my purse. There was a small mirror in my compact.

"No, really. Come." Terry pulled off the sheet and set it aside, then led me to a powder room in the hallway off the kitchen. He reached out and flipped on the light. "Look."

He seemed so pleased that for a moment I was almost afraid to. I glanced up, down, anywhere but directly at the mirror.

"Would you look?" Terry cried.

So I did.

"Wow," I said softly.

He hadn't done a lot, just added some layers around my face and a sweep of bangs that did, somehow, seem to highlight my eyes. My hair was shorter than it had been, but it wasn't short. I turned to the left, then the right. It swung when I moved, then settled back into place.

Terry stood behind me, grinning like a kid on Christmas. "Am I good, or what?"

"You're great," I assured him. "And totally wasted on dogs."

"Of course." He preened happily. "What can I say? Life threw me a curve. I found it was more important to be where Crawford was."

"It was important for him too." I took Terry's hand, suddenly serious. "There's been such a difference in Crawford. Last winter, people were wondering if he might retire. Now he's on top again. He seems . . . just happier, I guess."

Terry looked pleased. "Crawford thought he was getting old. Hopefully, I've shown him he was wrong."

I stood up on my toes and kissed him lightly on the cheek. "You did a great job."

A throat cleared softly behind me. "I'd be surprised to think that I might be interrupting something," said Crawford. "But on the off chance, would you two like some privacy?"

"No." The thought made me giggle. "I was just leaving."

"I see he didn't scalp you."

"No, he did a terrific job."

"That's what I just heard you say."

Terry and I shared a smile.

"Don't praise him too much," said Crawford. "I wouldn't want it to go to his head."

I pulled out my wallet. "What do I owe you?"

"I'm shocked!" cried Terry. "Shocked! To think that you'd give money to an artiste!"

I dug out a couple of bills. "You have to take it. Otherwise, I'll never be able to come back and ask you to do it again."

"Oh." Terry snatched the money and stuffed it in his pocket. "Since you put it that way, okay."

I turned to Crawford. "And while we're on the subject of money . . ."

He frowned, guessing what was coming. "One last question. That's it."

One was better than nothing. "Alicia says that Ron still owes Barry money. You say you wouldn't have taken him on as a client if the bill weren't paid. Who's right?"

"Could be we're both right."

"That doesn't make sense."

"It depends on how you look at things. Leo wasn't the only dog that Barry showed for Ron. The Pullmans bred plenty of good Chows. They probably finished several dozen over the years. With those kinds of numbers, it's not like Ron made it to every show to see every single dog go in the ring."

Terry nodded as though he'd figured out where Crawford was going. I still hadn't a clue. "So?"

"Let's just say Barry Turk wasn't above cutting a few corners. Suppose a dog goes out with a handler to get its championship. Six months later, it's finished and home. The owners paid bills for thirty or forty shows. Who's to say whether or not the dog actually went in the ring that many times?"

Crawford headed for the door. I followed along behind. "You mean Barry was billing Ron for shows he never went to?"

"Oh, I'm sure Barry went to the shows. But sometimes things happen. Maybe a handler's running late, or there's a scheduling conflict—a handler has two dogs that have to be in different rings at the same time. It's not unheard of for a dog to be entered, go to a show, and never make it out of its crate."

"How did Ron find out what was going on?"

"I don't know all the particulars," said Crawford. "I

imagine he showed up somewhere that Barry wasn't expecting him. Or maybe he checked his receipts against the show results in the *Gazette*. Anyway, he contested several bills, and I couldn't say as I blamed him. Barry, of course, denied everything."

"Was there a lot of money involved?"

"Not enough to be worth killing over, if that's what you're thinking. Disputes like this aren't uncommon. They usually get worked out with an adjustment on the next couple of bills. Nobody would have known a thing about it if the Pullmans hadn't decided to move Leo and Barry hadn't raised a fuss. End of story. Okay?"

Considering I'd been allotted one question, I figured I'd done pretty well. I thanked Crawford for the information and Terry for the haircut, and left.

Faith and her new friends had all run themselves into a state of happy exhaustion. My Poodle was lying down in the shade when I came out, but she jumped up as soon as she saw me. I let her out of the paddock and put her in the car.

We picked up Davey at camp and I spent the rest of the afternoon waiting for him to notice my new haircut. No dice. Try putting a pear instead of an apple into his lunch box and he'll talk about it for weeks.

Finally, over a dinner of shish kebabs that we'd grilled out back, I said, "Does anything look different about me?"

Davey took so long considering his answer, Faith got up from her spot beside the table to see what he was staring at. Then she barked. I was betting she knew.

Not my son. "No," he said, and went back to building a mountain of rice with his fork.

I gave up.

The next morning I called Winmore Kennels and Beth picked up. Yes, Alicia was still there, Beth told me. She was busy packing up all her stuff. Would I like to talk to her?

I said no thanks and went out and got in the car. Lately it seemed as though I was spending all my spare time on the road. But what I had to ask Alicia was important, and I'd just as soon see her face when she answered.

In the month since my last visit, fortunes at Winmore had declined visibly. Whereas once the kennel had seemed much too small for the number of dogs it housed, now more runs were empty than full. The impatiens that had brightened the yard were wilting, unwatered, in the August sun. Though Alicia was still in residence, her heart had already moved on.

When I arrived, she was just coming out the front door carrying a large, unwieldy box. Carefully she maneuvered her way down the front steps. I parked the Volvo behind a half-filled Ford Explorer and hurried over to help.

"Here, let me take that."

Alicia gave up the box with a murmur. It fell into my arms, and was considerably heavier than it looked. No wonder her face was so red. I shoved it inside the Explorer's open back door. Alicia was already heading back into the house. She hadn't looked surprised to see me. I imagined Beth must have told her I was coming.

"Your hair looks good," she said.

"Thanks, Terry did it."

Alicia nodded. "He did me a couple of months ago. Back when I was first pregnant and had morning sickness like crazy. I think he was trying to cheer me up."

I followed her up the front steps. "Are you sure you ought to be working like this?"

At four months, Alicia was now visibly pregnant. Not only had her torso thickened, but her arms and legs seemed plumper too. Even her face had taken on a smooth, rounded quality. The only thing that was missing was a beatific maternal glow. Alicia Devane was scowling mightily and sweating like a football player.

"Do I have a choice?" she asked. "The stuff's got to get moved."

"Where's Bill?"

"He had some work to do. He lent me his car." She nodded toward the Explorer. "He'll help me unload at the other end."

"How about taking a break?"

She thought for a moment, then nodded. "I guess I could use one. You want some lemonade?"

"Sounds great."

In the kitchen, she poured two tall glasses. I sat down at the table, but Alicia continued to work as she drank, taking china out of the cupboard, wrapping it in newspaper, and putting it in a box on the floor.

Though the back door was open, the air in the room was hot and still. A small fan on the counter seemed to be turning at half speed. If it was cooling things off any, I couldn't feel the difference.

"Maybe you could hire movers to do that," I suggested.

"No money."

"Bill?"

"I left on my own." Her expression tightened. "I'll return the same way."

I took a sip of lemonade. It was good: homemade, and just tart enough to be really refreshing. "We need to talk."

Alicia turned and looked at me. "That sounds serious." When I didn't answer, she walked over, pulled out a chair, and sat down. "What have you found out about Barry now?"

"Actually this was more about you."

"Oh?"

"And Ron Pullman."

"I see." Alicia reached for her lemonade and took a long drink.

"Is Ron your baby's father, Alicia?"

"Since you're here, I imagine you already know the answer to that."

"When did the affair start?"

"Does it matter?"

"Not really. When did it end?"

Alicia lifted a brow. "Who says it has?"

I choked on a sip of lemonade. "You mean you're still sleeping with him?"

"Actually, no. Not since spring." Alicia gave a soft laugh, though she didn't sound amused. "I just didn't want you to think you knew everything."

"There's plenty I don't know."

"Like who fired the shots that killed Barry."

"For starters. And about Leo."

"The Chow? He's a dog. What else is there to know?"

"He was Barry's specials dog. What happened?"

"Viv Pullman happened," Alicia snorted. "That's what."

"She found out about you and Ron?"

"No." Alicia shook her head. "She couldn't have. We were very careful about that."

"Viv told me that she was the one who made the decision to move Leo over to Crawford." I was thinking aloud now, trying to make the pieces fall into place. "Why did she do that if she didn't know about what was going on?"

"Maybe she had her suspicions. More likely, she was just playing it safe. She and Ron have been married what, two, three years? I guess the honeymoon was ending. Ron's like a big old tomcat, he always has his eye out. Believe me, if he were my husband, I'd worry too. He was married to Mona when he met Viv, you know."

"No, I didn't know."

"Well, he was. But that didn't stop him from falling for Viv. She was smart, though. Don't ever let yourself be fooled by that sweet southern drawl. Viv's no Daisy Mae. She knew a good thing when she saw it. Ron's got looks, money, connections . . ."

Presumably all the things that had also attracted Alicia, if the expression on her face was anything to go by.

"Viv made sure he knew she was interested and then she held out for marriage. In the end, she got just what she wanted. Viv may be in love with Ron, but I doubt that means she trusts him. Let's face it, if he were the faithful type, he'd still be with Mona, right?"

I nodded.

"Like I said, Viv's smart. Once she got hold of Ron, she wasn't about to lose him. She sent Leo over to Crawford's because she knew perfectly well that nobody over there was going to tempt him.

"And Ron's no dummy either. When she told him she wanted the dog moved, he read between those lines pretty damn quick. He had to make a choice, and he did."

"Even though you were carrying his baby."

"Neither of us knew that at the time. I doubt that it would have made a difference if we had. Ron's in love with Viv. He may stray a little, but that's all there is to it."

Maybe it was point of view, maybe it was semantics, but my idea of being in love had nothing to do with having affairs on the side.

"Besides," said Alicia. "It's not as if Viv would let him go without a fight. She worked long and hard to become Mrs. Ron Pullman, and you better believe she intends to stay that way."

"When did you tell Ron that the baby was his?" I asked.

"After Barry died. I figured he had a right to know."

Amazing, wasn't it, the way Ron's right to know had neatly coincided with Alicia's loss of support? "What did he say?"

"At first he denied being the baby's father. Then he offered me money for an abortion." Alicia's finger traced idle patterns in the condensation on the outside of her lemonade glass. "Not that I would have done it, but it was too late anyway."

"What about after the baby is born?"

"I'll be with Bill then. Everything will be fine."

Ah, yes, Bill. Another spurned lover. I like to think of myself as a liberal person, but compared to Alicia, I was beginning to feel positively old-fashioned.

"And Bill's okay with all of this?"

"Of course," said Alicia. "I told you that."

"What you told me was he doesn't mind being a father to someone else's baby. Are you sure he doesn't mind that you don't love him?"

"What makes you so sure I don't?"

"Call it a good guess."

"Then you're a better guesser than Bill is," said Alicia. "Like most men, he hears only what he wants to hear. I told him that my leaving was a huge mistake. I apologized, okay? But I certainly didn't have to grovel."

I stared at her in disbelief, wondering if she had any idea how callous and self-serving she sounded. All at once it occurred to me that Bill wasn't the only one whom Alicia had fooled. I'd thought she'd made her choices based on a desire to do what was best for her baby. Now I realized that the baby was only a side issue. Alicia was looking to do what was best for Alicia.

"Look," she said. "I appreciate the fact that you tried, but maybe asking you to help wasn't such a good idea. Back then, I thought I needed to know who killed Barry. But now . . ." She did her best to look both sad and brave. "Now I think it's best if I just put the whole thing behind me. I have to move on."

Figuratively and literally, I thought as Alicia went back to her packing. "It seems to me that you were happy to have me asking questions until I started asking about you."

"Don't be absurd." She turned and stared. "Life goes on, okay? All I'm doing is going with it. The police will track Barry's murderer down. That's what they're paid for."

And if they didn't succeed, it wouldn't matter, because now Alicia had Bill to take care of her. A month earlier she'd been floundering, but now the situation had changed. Alicia had found a new means of support, and the last thing she wanted was me asking questions that might hit too close to home and muck things up for her.

I stood up, carried my lemonade glass over to the sink, and poured what was left down the drain. Then I walked out the door without looking back.

When I got home, I called Aunt Peg and told her about everything that had happened, including the fact that I was no longer searching for Barry's killer.

"But you can't stop now!" she wailed. "We still don't know who did it."

"Alicia seems to think that the police will figure it out."

"Do the police know about Ralphie Otterbach and Ann Leeds?" she demanded. "Have they figured out who the father of Alicia's baby is?"

"I don't know." The back half of Faith was standing beside my chair. The front was in my lap. I slid my fingers under her wraps and scratched her ears. "Why don't you call them up and ask them?"

"Don't be fresh," said Peg. "I'm thinking."

That was not necessarily a good sign.

"What if Ron killed Barry in a jealous fit because they were both sleeping with Alicia?" she asked.

"What right did he have to be jealous? According to Alicia, he was happy in his marriage. All he wanted from her was an affair."

"What if Barry found out about the affair and threatened to spill the beans to Viv? Maybe Ron killed him to shut him up."

The possibility seemed remote, but I had to give her an A for effort. "Except that Barry wasn't killed until several months after the affair ended. By then Leo had been moved, which means that Viv was already suspicious."

"Then maybe she did it."

"Why?"

The silence on the other end of the line lasted just long enough to make me think that I'd finally succeeded in stumping her.

"Viv does know how to handle a gun," I mentioned, playing devil's advocate. "She told me she used to go hunting with her brothers when she was little."

"You see?" said Peg. "Maybe she *was* jealous. Maybe she thought the affair was still going on and intended to put an end to it."

"By killing *Barry?*"

"Quit interrupting. How do you ever expect me to make a decent point if you keep jumping in? Think about this. Barry was shot at night, from a distance. Anyone who'd been at the show that day would know that he and Alicia were going to arrive home together. Maybe she was the intended victim and the killer made a mistake."

I had to admit it was an interesting theory. Of course, what did I care? As of that morning, it wasn't my problem.

When I didn't answer immediately, Aunt Peg knew she'd scored a point. "Just think about it," she said.

As if I had a choice.

⌒❋ Twenty ❋⌒

In the meantime I had plenty of other things going on in my life, like the prospect of a double date on Friday night. I'd finally heard from my brother in the middle of the week. Frank wasn't at all apologetic about making plans without consulting me.

"What if I'd been busy?" I asked.

"Are you?"

"That's beside the point. What if Sam were still away?"

"I take it he's not," said Frank, the patience of a saint clear in his voice.

"Well, no."

"And I bet you even have a sitter."

Thanks to Bertie's advance warning, I did. Not that I was about to admit it. Frank and I may be adults, but we still bicker like children.

"Little Kitchen, seven o'clock," he said, naming a popular Chinese restaurant in New Canaan. "Bertie and I will meet you two there."

Sam arrived just after six. I had Brie and crackers on

a serving tray, cold beer in the refrigerator, and visions of Sam and me spending time catching up on the things we'd missed in each other's lives recently. Unfortunately, I'd managed to forget all about Davey, who was just as pleased to see Sam as I was.

"Let's play Nintendo!" he cried before Sam even had the door shut behind him. Faith was dancing around the hall on her hind legs, waiting to be greeted. And there I was, suddenly feeling like I was last in line.

Sam looked terrific in dark, pleated pants and a linen shirt. His wide smile seemed to encompass all of us.

"One game," he said to Davey. "I'll be there in a minute. Go get set up."

Davey ran off to the living room. Sam ruffled his hands quickly through the hair on Faith's shoulders, then sent her scooting after Davey. That left just the two of us, with enough privacy for a nice, long kiss.

"I've missed you," Sam murmured.

"No wonder."

His hands slid down, squeezing just above my hip, where he knows I'm incredibly ticklish. I yelped and pulled back out of his arms.

"Something's different," he said. "Did you wash your hair?"

Sam's a great guy, but he isn't perfect.

"I had it cut. Doesn't it look shorter?"

"I guess so. I like it."

End of discussion. Women friends want to know who did the cut for you and when you had it done. They'll ask about upkeep, and whether or not you're pleased with how it turned out. Not men. Sometimes I think you're lucky if a man even notices that you have hair on your head.

Sam went off to play Nintendo with Davey, and I ended up serving the cheese and crackers in the living room, where the two of them picked at the food between taking turns trying to beat the system. By the time their game ended, the baby-sitter had arrived. Joanie is a neighborhood teenager who's great with children. The only drawback is that her eyes tend to pop out of her head whenever she sees Sam.

He and I didn't have a moment to ourselves until we were in his Blazer on the way to the restaurant, about a twenty-minute drive. I thought Sam might talk about his trip to California. Instead, he wanted to know what I'd learned in the last ten days about Barry Turk's murder.

Sam likes solving puzzles as much as I do, so instead of telling him that I was no longer involved, I simply laid out the facts as I knew them. Maybe his fresh perspective would turn up something I'd overlooked.

"It seems like you've got a lot of new information," he said. "I'm just not sure where it's all leading."

"Me either," I agreed. "Plenty of people had good reasons to be angry at Barry Turk. Beth, who'd been jilted and demoted. Ann and Christine, who'd been harassed. Ralphie, whose girlfriend was sleeping with the boss. Not to mention Ron Pullman, who's had to listen to Barry bad-mouthing him all up and down the East Coast, and Bill Devane, whose wife ran off with him. For someone without much talent or visible charm, Barry certainly cut a wide swath."

"Don't forget about Alicia. She doesn't seem to have lacked for motives either."

"Yes and no. She inherited Barry's assets, but a business that's now in trouble and a house that's heavily mortgaged don't add up to much. And while she might have been angry at him for having an affair with Beth, Alicia claims not to have known about that until later."

"She was probably too busy with Ron Pullman to notice," Sam said with a frown.

"Nevertheless, once again Alicia has managed to land on her feet. I get the feeling she's good at that. Bill seems happy to take her back. I just hope it's occurred to him to wonder how long she'll stay."

"Do you think there's a chance Ron might leave Viv for her?"

"Not really. Only because if there were, I bet Alicia would be pursuing the idea like crazy. She's not, which makes me think that she believes what she told me— that Ron and Viv's marriage is pretty solid."

Sam snorted softly under his breath. I was glad to hear that his assessment of the relationship was the same as mine.

"I wonder what Viv and Austin had to argue about," he said.

"Maybe she was telling him to stay away from Ron. When those two men get together, it's like watching a pair of Kerry Blues spar."

Sam slanted me a look.

I sent the same look right back. "You know what I mean."

Sparring is an exercise used in the terrier rings to encourage the dogs to show to advantage. With their naturally scrappy temperaments, terriers are accustomed to defending their turf. Occasionally the judge will ask two or three to step to the center of the ring and face off.

The dogs are on lead and carefully controlled. They stand at attention, tails up, ears pricked. Many will growl, almost none will show weakness by backing down. Kerry Blues are among the largest of the terrier breeds. When they're sparring, the sound effects can often be heard two rings away.

"Aunt Peg has a theory that Viv Pullman could have been the one who fired the shots, possibly thinking that she was shooting at Alicia."

Sam thought about that for a moment, then shook his head. "No, I don't think so."

I smiled at his naiveté. "Viv's too much of a lady, right?"

"Actually, I wouldn't know her well enough to say. But whoever murdered Barry wanted something desperately, and I don't see that person as being Viv. She already had what she wanted."

"Unless she's not as confident as Alicia thinks. Maybe Viv *was* afraid that Alicia would succeed in taking Ron away."

As we'd been talking, Sam had been driving down Main Street in New Canaan, scouting for a parking space. There weren't any, so he made a left into the town hall driveway and parked in the lot behind the big brick building. Punctuality isn't my brother's strong suit, so when we got back out to the sidewalk, I was surprised to see Frank and Bertie walking toward us from the other direction.

The block where Little Kitchen is located has half a dozen restaurants, so at seven o'clock on a Friday night, foot traffic is heavy. As Frank and Bertie strolled toward us, more than one man turned and had a second look at the tall redhead. She was wearing a black jump suit made out of slithery material, and when she walked, there was plenty of jiggling and bobbing to gawk at. Beside her, Frank was beaming like the happiest man on earth.

Sam, I was pleased to note, was not staring. He was, however, grinning. "First date?" he asked under his breath.

I nodded. "Frank looks like he just won the lottery, doesn't he?"

"Happier. Much happier."

Frank had made a reservation, and we were seated at a round table by a large window overlooking the sidewalk. I could tell that my brother was nervous. He pulled out Bertie's chair for her, then forgot to push it back in. When tea came, he poured for everyone, then misjudged the weight of the pot and set it down on the glass-topped table with a loud crack.

Bertie jumped in her chair.

"Sorry," Frank mumbled. "Here, have some noodles."

Bertie eyed the deep-fried Chinese noodles he put in front of her, but didn't take any. No doubt a figure like hers wasn't maintained by digging into high-calorie snacks. She reached for her cup and took a sip of tea.

Sam was studying his menu. I was pretending to study mine, but inside I was chortling happily. My brother had the same pained look on his face he'd had in sixth grade when he'd discovered that middle school gym involved stripping down in the boy's locker room.

The waiter came to take our order. Frank asked for

Goo Goo Mai Pan. The waiter didn't bat an eye. Bertie, however, was beginning to smile.

When the waiter left, she said, "Are you always this nervous around women?"

"No," Frank blurted out, red around the ears. "Are you always this gorgeous?"

"Yes." She reached out and patted his arm comfortingly. "Get over it."

Amazingly, by the time our main courses had arrived, Frank looked like he almost had. Bertie had fumbled with her chopsticks when the appetizers were served and happily accepted a lesson from my brother on their management. Since I've never known her to be anything but competent, I suspected Bertie was putting him on, but Frank didn't seem to notice.

As we ate, the talk turned to dogs and dog shows. My brother, who'd been to only one show in his life, didn't have much to contribute. Instead, he kept himself occupied by sitting and staring at Bertie. When she got tired of that, she made her feelings known by abruptly changing the subject.

"So," she said to me, "have you figured out who murdered Barry Turk yet?"

I shook my head. Mouth filled with curried beef, it was easier than trying to explain that since my last meeting with Alicia, I was no longer trying.

"Who's Barry Turk?" asked Frank.

"He was a professional handler," Bertie told him. "Mostly Poodles, but he had some other breeds too. Nobody liked him much, and it turned out that somebody hated him enough to shoot him in the back."

Frank stared at me in amazement. "And you're trying to figure out who did it?"

"I was," I said, hoping to downplay my involvement. The last thing I needed was Frank feeling he needed to play the role of protective brother.

"Did you ever get in touch with Ann and Christine?" asked Bertie.

"I spoke with both of them. Their stories were pretty much just what you said they'd be."

"What's shocking to me," said Sam, "is that Turk would have been allowed to get away with such offensive behavior for as long as he did."

"What behavior?" asked Frank, looking around the table. "What did he do?"

As we finished our meal, we brought my brother up to speed on the facts surrounding Barry Turk's murder. "What a slimeball," he said at the end. "Why didn't anybody stop him?"

"Somebody did." Bertie smiled slightly.

"Ann wanted to," I said. "But when nobody else was willing to go on record, it was only her word against his."

"You have to understand how the system works," said Bertie. "It's no different at dog shows than it is anywhere else. Barry'd been around for a long time, and he had friends where it counted. With that kind of support, it wouldn't have mattered whether he was right or wrong.

"The most he'd have gotten was a slap on the wrist. Ann's an owner-handler. Dog shows are her hobby. But this is what I do for a living. If I got branded as a trouble-maker, I'd put myself right out of business."

"You were strong enough to deal with it," I pointed

out. "According to what Christine told me, Barry ended up putting her out of business anyway."

"That may be the story she's telling now. It isn't the way I remember things."

"No? Christine said her problems with Barry cost her her biggest client."

"That's one version." Bertie used her chopsticks to snare a shrimp on her plate. "Christine's big client was Austin Beamish, and he wasn't only her client, if you know what I mean."

"They were involved with each other," said Sam.

"Right." Bertie favored him with a dazzling smile. I couldn't even imagine what it would be like to have such an arsenal of enticing expressions at my command. "Austin had only a couple of dogs back then, and they weren't as good as the ones he has now. But for a handler who was just starting out, they made a nice string."

"Christine said Austin took his dogs away because she wasn't winning enough."

"Austin can be pretty ruthless," said Bertie. "He wants what he wants, and if he doesn't get it, watch out. But right around the same time he moved his dogs to another handler, his social relationship with Christine ended as well. Gossip at the time said that part came first, not the other way around."

"That doesn't excuse the way Turk acted," said Sam. "If nobody's willing to stand up to him, there's nothing to prevent the next jerk who comes along from doing the same thing."

As the waiter left us a plate of fortune cookies, I voiced

my agreement. Still, I could understand why Bertie had acted the way she had. She was working hard to build a career. In the insular world of dog showing and breeding, it wouldn't help to ruffle any important feathers.

Smiling at Bertie, Frank refused to take sides. Instead, he played peacemaker and changed the subject by asking if anyone had seen any good movies lately.

I'd never seen him so besotted. Actually, I found it rather endearing. Shallow perhaps, considering the fact that his infatuation was clearly based on Bertie's looks, but still somehow sweet. Besides, I figured Bertie could take care of herself. She'd probably been dealing with this kind of attention for years.

We settled the bill, then walked outside into the warm August night and went our separate ways. Now that my brother had stopped bumbling and stumbling, I could tell he was dying to get Bertie alone. That was fine with me. My brother wasn't the only one with romance on his mind.

Back at home, Davey was already in bed asleep. Faith padded out onto the upstairs landing to say hello, then trotted back to Davey's room. I paid Joanie for the evening, and she left to walk home. That left just the two of us. My kind of odds.

"Come here," said Sam, patting the couch beside him. "Have I had a chance to tell you how great you look tonight?"

I sank down beside him. Sam drew me close and buried his hands in my hair. "No, you haven't. I thought maybe I didn't measure up to the competition."

Sam chuckled softly. "Fishing for compliments, are we?"

"You bet."

His lips grazed the side of my cheek. "You are the most beautiful . . . smartest . . . sexiest . . ."—each word was punctuated by a kiss—"woman I've ever met."

"Works for me," I said, leaning back on the couch and pulling him down on top of me. His weight settled down the length of my body and I wiggled in satisfaction. "Ah, I see it works for you too."

Eventually we made it up to the bedroom. But once there, we still didn't get much sleep. It seemed as though I had barely closed my eyes, when Davey and Faith came bouncing in to wake us up.

Having Sam spend the night is a relatively new thing for us. For Davey's sake, I'd waffled over making that commitment for months. Then, in the spring when it finally happened, I found my reservations had been for nothing. My son was delighted with the new arrangement, and I was left to wonder why we hadn't done it sooner.

Ah, parenthood. It's not for the faint of heart.

We made pancakes and scrambled eggs for breakfast, then all piled in the car and drove to Sam's house in Redding. On nights that he's away, he makes use of a pet-sitting service for his Poodles, but I knew he wanted to get back home and make sure everything was okay.

His house is made of cedar and glass and perched high on the side of a hill. In winter, the driveway's a terror to negotiate, but once you reach the summit, the views are spectacular. Sam works at home designing computer software, so he'd chosen the setting with care.

Sam's five Standard Poodles were fine, although after his night away, they did their best to convince us that they'd been starved for attention and affection. Once that deficit was remedied, they welcomed Faith into their pack like a long-lost member of the family. Sam's yard was several times the size of mine, and Davey joined the troupe of Poodles in racing from tree to tree.

In the afternoon, Davey mounted an exploration of the woods around the house. By evening, he and Sam were setting up a tent outside the back door and making plans for the three of us to camp out. Sleeping for the first time under the stars, Davey was enthralled. With Faith snuggled on top of his sleeping bag, he fell asleep quickly and never even noticed when Sam and I slipped away for a little while to find some privacy.

The rest of the weekend passed in a quiet blur of good times. Sam and I try to spend as much time together as we can, but we're working around the demands of a two-career schedule that often leaves little time for maneuvering. Having an entire weekend to ourselves felt like an unexpected gift, and it was over much too quickly.

We were all sorry when Sunday night came. Back home Monday morning, Davey sat at the kitchen table and dawdled over a breakfast of Cheerios and sliced bananas. Faith was in her usual spot beside him, looking for handouts. I was rummaging through the refrigerator, hoping to find a container of yogurt whose date hadn't yet expired, when the phone rang.

It was Alicia Devane. "Melanie, thank God I got you," she said, her voice high and breathless. "Can you come right now?"

"Come where? What's wrong?"

"I'm at Bill's house in Patterson. The ambulance is on its way."

"What ambulance? Alicia, what's going on?"

"It's Bill." Her voice broke on a sob. "I think he's dead."

❧❀ *Twenty-one* ❀❧

He couldn't be dead. It wasn't possible.

I started with that thought and was still clinging to it an hour later when I reached Bill's farm. The details Alicia had provided on the phone had been sketchy at best. Considering how upset she was, I hadn't wasted any time talking. Instead, I'd hustled Davey off to camp, then raced up to Patterson.

It didn't occur to me until I was almost there that Alicia might not be at Bill's. If he had been taken to a hospital, I was sure she would have gone with him. Rounding the last corner, I slowed the car to look for Bill's driveway. I needn't have bothered.

Yellow crime-scene tape had been strung from fence to tree along one side of the road, marking the approach clearly. A cruiser and two other cars were parked by the side of the road. Several policemen were engaged in examining the area. Another stood ready to wave me by.

I stopped at the end of Bill's driveway and rolled down my window. "I'm here to see Alicia Devane."

The officer stared at me briefly. "Is she expecting you?"

"Yes, she asked me to come." There seemed to be little doubt now, but I asked anyway. "Is Bill . . . dead?"

"Yes, ma'am, he is." He pointed up the driveway. "I believe you'll find Mrs. Devane in the house."

Conscious of his eyes following me, I drove slowly down the long driveway and parked at the end. Muffled barking sounded from the direction of the barn, probably Bill's two Labs. The front door to the house was open. Through the screen I could see Alicia sitting on the couch. I knocked lightly and let myself in.

She didn't rise. Indeed, she didn't even look up. Her hands were clasped together around a handkerchief in her lap. "Bill's gone," she said quietly.

"I know." I walked over and sat down beside her. Though her eyes were red, Alicia wasn't crying. Instead, her features seemed almost immobile, frozen. I wondered if she was in shock. "Do you want to talk about it?"

"No. Yes." She shook her head.

I waited and let her make up her mind. The house felt empty and eerily quiet. A cup of cold coffee sat on the table beside her. I wondered if one of the officers had made it for her, and why they'd left her sitting there all by herself.

"Is there anything I can do?" I asked. "Anyone you want me to call?"

"No." Her voice was barely louder that a whisper, and the effort to speak seemed to take all her energy. "The police asked me the same thing. I told them I just wanted to be left alone. I'm sorry, I . . ." Her hands fluttered helplessly. "I didn't know what else to do. You said before that you'd come if I needed you."

"I'm glad you called me." I slipped my arms around her shoulders. For a moment Alicia held herself stiffly away, then all at once her body seemed to melt, sliding boneless into my embrace. Still, she didn't cry.

"I was here," she said when a few minutes had passed. "I must have been upstairs in the bedroom when it happened."

She sat up, looking around the room as though she'd never seen it before. "I heard the dogs barking, but that didn't seem unusual. I'd just gotten up and Bill wasn't in the house. I figured he'd walked out to the end of the driveway to get the newspaper. He does that every morning."

I nodded.

"Biff and Tucker were barking like crazy, but I didn't pay much attention. I thought they were chasing a rabbit or something. Bill doesn't like them to make too much noise, he's afraid it'll bother the neighbors, so I figured he'd quiet them down and I went in to take a shower."

She stopped, looking around the room again. Her gaze was vacant and skittered from one place to another.

"Can I get you something?" I asked.

"Maybe a drink? There's some orange juice in the fridge."

"Sure." I leapt up, glad to have something useful to do. "Be right back."

I found two tall glasses in the cabinet and poured us each some juice. When I returned to the living room, Alicia was sitting where I'd left her, dabbing at her eyes with the handkerchief.

"That's fresh-squeezed," she said, her voice catching. "I guess it's stupid that something like that would make me cry. Bill got the juice 'specially at a little vegetable stand up the road. He said it would be good for the baby."

Silently I handed her the glass.

"He was such a nice man. Everybody liked him. That's why I just can't understand how anybody could have wanted to kill him."

"You still haven't told me what happened," I said gently.

"Oh." Alicia shook her head, looking flustered. "I'm sorry. I guess I told the story so many times to the police, I thought you already knew."

"Were you the one who found him?"

She nodded. "When I came downstairs after my shower, the dogs were still barking. That's when I knew that something was wrong. I put on some shoes and went out to have a look.

"Biff and Tucker were all the way down at the end of the driveway. That was odd too, because Bill never lets them go anywhere near the road. I didn't see him, and when I called out his name, he didn't answer."

Alicia closed her eyes briefly and drew in a long sigh. "I was walking down the driveway, and then all at once I just knew something terrible had happened. I started to run, but I was too late." She gulped heavily. "It felt like . . ."

I knew what she was thinking. For the second time in six weeks, Alicia had been witness to the death of someone she was close to. "It felt like the night you saw Barry get shot?"

She nodded silently, shadows clouding her features. "Bill was lying by the side of the road. Biff and Tucker were standing over him. The police said it was a hit-and-run."

"Do they think it was an accident?"

"No." Her fingers twisted, mangling the handkerchief. "They said there weren't any skid marks. The driver never even tried to stop. Bill was probably standing next to the mailbox when he was hit. He wasn't even in the road."

Oh, Lord. A second murder.

"I don't understand what's happening," said Alicia. "Where am I going to go now? What am I going to do?"

"What about your family?"

She shook her head. "I have an aunt in Toledo and a sister in Santa Fe. We're not very close."

She'd mentioned that before, I remembered. On the day she'd come to my house and told me about the accidents she'd been having. Bad luck, she'd said at the time.

"Alicia, did you tell the police about all the other things that happened to you? The fire? The broken step, the day your car broke down?"

"Yes. They wrote it all down, but I don't think they took it too seriously. I knew what they were thinking. A broken step, a burst hose? Things like that happen to everybody."

Maybe, but two murders didn't. And Alicia had been right in the middle of both of them. One by one, her options were disappearing. I couldn't imagine her staying in this house all by herself.

"Why don't you come home with me?" I offered impulsively. "At least for a day or two, until you figure out what you want to do next."

Alicia looked up. Surprise, then relief, showed on her

face. "You mean it? I wouldn't want to put you to any trouble."

"You won't," I said firmly, pushing aside the question of where, exactly, in my two-bedroom house I was going to put her. "I'd like you to come."

Alicia went upstairs and packed a small suitcase. It wasn't until we got outside that we both remembered the two Labrador Retrievers in the barn. Alicia opened the door and Biff and Tucker came flying out. They ran to the house and scratched at the door we'd just locked behind us.

"They're looking for Bill," Alicia said. "They don't understand what happened either."

We put the Labs in the back of the car and left my name and address with one of the officers at the end of the driveway. Neither of us felt like talking on the way back to Stamford. The only sound in the car came from Biff, who was crying softly under his breath.

Back at home, I put Faith and the two Labs out in the fenced backyard and told them to cope. Then I went up and moved Davey's stuff around to make room for Alicia. Now that my son had developed a taste for camping, I figured he could sleep on my floor in his sleeping bag for a few nights.

With the addition of three guests, my small house felt as though it were bursting at the seams. I picked Davey up from camp along with his best friend, Joey Brickman, and took both boys to the beach for the afternoon.

Alicia had a number of phone calls to make. Funeral arrangements had to be taken care of, and various members of Bill's family needed to be told what had happened. I wanted her to have as much privacy as possible.

When Davey and I got home around five, Alicia was napping. I'd explained things to Davey, and he wasn't taking being kicked out of his room lightly. "What about my cars?" he asked. "And my desk? All my toys are in there."

"You'll manage."

I stood him in the middle of the kitchen floor and stripped him down to the skin. At five, he wasn't yet old enough to be modest in front of his mother, and undressing him here had the distinct advantage of dropping most of the sand he'd brought back with him in one easily cleanable spot. "When Alicia wakes up, you can go in and get a few things. In the meantime, there's a change of clothes on my bed. And be quiet, okay?"

Davey scooted upstairs with Faith trailing along after him. Biff and Tucker stayed with me. They were lying down in the kitchen, their two large bodies taking up most of the floor. The fact that I kept having to step over them didn't incite them to move, or even, actually, to look up. It was clear these boys weren't Poodles.

I shook out Davey's bathing suit and towel and put them in the dryer. Heading to the sink to refill the dogs' water bowl, I noticed that Alicia had left a note on the counter.

Peg called, it said. *She's coming to dinner.*

That was a fine state of affairs, especially since I didn't have enough food in the house to make dinner for three, much less four. A call to a local rib joint remedied the first part of the problem. I followed it with a call to Aunt Peg to tell her to pick up dinner on her way.

"I can't believe it," she said when she picked up the phone. "Bill Devane is murdered, you have the closest thing to a witness right there in your house, and I have to hear the news from Crawford Langley?"

"Crawford called you?" Peg's connections shot up several notches in my estimation. Crawford Langley never called me.

"Actually he called to tell me that the Standard bitch he's been showing broke her toe. She's entered next weekend and there was a major spot on, so the major's broken. But that's beside the point. Of course when he told me about Bill, I immediately called you. Imagine my surprise when Alicia picked up the phone. You could have knocked me over with a feather."

Hah. Aunt Peg was made of stern stuff. A two-by-four, maybe. But a feather? Never.

"So you told her you were coming to dinner."

"Of course I did. I'm not about to miss an opportunity like this. Don't cook anything elaborate."

"I'm not," I said, and told her about the order I'd placed.

Peg sighed audibly, but when I bribed her with homemade brownies for dessert, she agreed to make the stop. Alicia walked into the kitchen as I was hanging up the phone.

"Your son's darling," she said.

"Did he wake you up?"

"No, I was just kind of drifting and I heard him talking to Faith. Davey was telling her not to make any noise." Alicia smiled wanly. "It was just as well I got up. To tell the truth, I was lying in bed feeling very sorry for myself."

"You have every right to feel sorry for yourself."

"Maybe. But it doesn't help anything, you know?" She pulled out a kitchen chair and sat down. "I was feeling hopeless, and then I saw Davey and I thought, maybe if I'm lucky, my son will be just like that someday."

"Yeah." I smiled, feeling pretty lucky myself.

"Hey, Mom!"

Davey came skidding around the corner at top speed. He'd entered the kitchen that way many times. This was the first time, however, that there'd been a hundred and thirty pounds of Labrador Retriever draped across the floor.

He hit Tucker broadside and went flying. Somebody, boy or dog, grunted with the impact. Davey rolled across the floor and bounced up. At five, kids can still do that. Awakened by my son's spectacular entrance, Biff opened his eyes and flapped his tail up and down.

"So," said Davey, "when's dinner?"

"It's only five-fifteen."

"But I'm hungry now."

I gave him a string cheese and a bowl of grapes. Then I got out the ingredients for brownies and went to work. They're one of the few things I can make from scratch. Luckily there's a great recipe right on the chocolate box.

As I melted and stirred and blended, Davey chattered nonstop. He told Alicia all about his camp, his friends, and his afternoon at the beach. Sometimes she answered him, but mostly she just sat quietly and listened.

At the first sign that he was bothering her, I'd have shooed him away. But instead, the opposite seemed to be true. In his own energetic way, my son provided a wonderful distraction.

When Faith ran to the front door, I left Davey licking

the bowl of brownie batter and went to let Aunt Peg in. She thrust the fragrant bag of ribs into my arms, scratched Faith under the chin, and marched to the kitchen to offer her condolences.

An afternoon at the beach goes a long way toward wearing my son out. His energy began to flag over dinner, and by the time he finished his first brownie, his eyelids were drooping. Telling myself that a swim in the Sound was almost the same as a bath, I let him get away with only brushing his teeth before bundling him into his sleeping bag.

While Davey had been among us, nobody had brought up the subject of Bill's murder. Now that he was gone, it didn't take Peg long.

"What will you do now?" she asked Alicia.

"I don't know. I have to think . . . I guess I have to make plans."

I shot Peg a warning look. "Not tonight you don't. Just relax."

Alicia stood. "I'm a little tired. If you don't mind, I think I'll go to bed too."

Peg glanced at her watch. "But it's barely—"

I kicked her under the table. Hard.

"Barely dark out," she said, recovering quickly. "Are you sure you'll be able to sleep?"

"I'll be fine," said Alicia. She left the room.

Peg got up and poured herself another cup of tea. "Shame on you. What if I had brittle bones?"

"Shame on you," I replied. "Her husband died this morning. I can't believe you wanted to grill her for information."

"Ex-husband," Aunt Peg corrected me, choosing

another brownie and sliding it onto her plate. "She wasn't in love with the man, she told you that herself. Going back to Bill was a matter of convenience. Under the circumstances, it seemed perfectly natural to ask about her future plans."

"Two men are dead," I said grimly. "And for what? I just don't see what anybody had to gain."

"Alicia, maybe."

"What?"

"I was just thinking," said Peg. "It's obvious that she's the common thread."

"Yes, but why? Who would want to hurt her?"

"What about Viv? She certainly has good reason."

I shook my head quickly. "If Viv wanted to punish Alicia for sleeping with her husband, she'd have killed Alicia, not the people around her."

"True," Peg allowed, frowning. "Well then, what about Ron? Alicia had Barry to take care of her, and now he's gone. Then she thought she had Bill, and he's gone too. Alicia's carrying Ron's baby. Maybe he's trying to clear the way so that she'll go to him."

Interesting thought. What about Ron?

☙❊ *Twenty-two* ❊☚

I asked Alicia that question the next morning after I took Davey to camp.

Unexpectedly, when I got back I found her brushing through Faith's coat. I keep my portable grooming table in the basement along with the rest of Faith's grooming supplies. The light down there isn't very good, however, and when I need to work on Faith, I set things up in the kitchen. We'd talked about that the day before. I'd also admitted that my care of Faith's growing coat was nowhere near as steadfast as it should have been. Still, I hadn't expected Alicia to volunteer for the job.

Faith was lying calmly on her side as Alicia line brushed her mane coat. Biff and Tucker were outside in the yard. "Hey," I said. "You don't have to do that."

"I don't mind." She reached for a spray bottle and spritzed a section of flyaway hair. "I like being useful. Besides, I find brushing relaxing."

"You do?" I found it annoying.

"Sure. It's all hands and no brains. Very soothing."

If you had the time. My problem was that I always seemed to find myself trying to fit coat care into a schedule that was already too full.

"You know," said Alicia. "If you kept her in oil, you wouldn't have to bother brushing. That's what we did with most of the Poodles at the kennel."

Oil is the term used for very heavy conditioners that are applied to the hair after a bath and not rinsed out. The slick, greasy coating protects the hair from damage and allows it to grow without matting. The downside is that the dog always looks dirty, and that subsequent baths, where the oil needs to be washed out and replaced with a fresh coating, take forever. For groups of dogs living in kennels, it's an efficient method of dealing with hair; but for my one dog, I wanted no part of it.

"Yuk," I said eloquently.

Alicia smiled. "It was just a thought."

Faith glanced in my direction. Since I'm the one who usually brushes her, I knew she was wondering what I was doing standing on the other side of the room. "Do you want me to finish that?"

"No, sit. I'm almost done with this side anyway. Aside from a few tangles, it's been a breeze. For her age, this coat's in really good shape."

"Thanks." I perched on a stool by the counter. "Try telling that to my Aunt Peg."

"Not me. I wouldn't presume to tell anything to Margaret Turnbull."

My brow rose.

"She doesn't intimidate you?" Alicia asked.

"No." At least not anymore, I added silently.

"Then you're probably in the minority. One glance at

that disapproving look of hers can scare the starch right out of me. Even Barry used to power-down when she was around."

"Is that why you didn't tell her to mind her own business last night?"

"Not really. She was curious. Hell, who wouldn't be? I'm wondering what comes next myself." She picked up a slicker brush and ran it quickly through Faith's bracelets.

Faith knew what that meant. One side was done and it was time to turn over. When I'd first seen Aunt Peg's Standard Poodles do that, I'd reacted with amazement. Now Faith knew the routine so well, she could all but brush herself. Casual observers tended to credit me with great feats of training. In reality, Faith had pretty much figured things out on her own.

"Last night, after you went to bed, Peg and I were talking. Two men have been murdered, and the most obvious thing they had in common was you."

Alicia looked up. "I know. I've thought about that too."

"Two of the three men you were involved with are gone. That leaves only Ron."

"Surely you don't think that Ron had any reason to kill Bill?"

"The reason could have been you, Alicia. You and your baby."

Faith reacted to our rising voices by lifting her head. Automatically, Alicia placed a hand on her neck, soothing her back down. "That's not possible."

Sam had told me that Viv couldn't have committed murder. Now Alicia was saying the same thing about Ron. Everyone wants to believe that the people they know aren't capable of killing another person. The problem was, someone *had* killed, and they'd done it twice.

"Think about it," said Alicia. "Ron didn't have to kill anyone to get to me. If he'd asked, I'd have gone with him in a minute. But Ron has Viv. That's who he really wants."

"Maybe," I said, thinking aloud. "But Ron already *has* Viv. Maybe he wants more. Maybe he wants both of you. Ron strikes me as pretty arrogant. It's like Bertie said about Austin the other night. Both those men are very determined when it comes to getting what they want."

Alicia was shaking her head. "Arrogance, I'll grant you. Determination too. But not the rest of it. As far as Ron was concerned, I was just a fling. Maybe subconsciously I was wishing for something more, but I always knew it wasn't going to happen."

"If you don't go to Ron," I said, "what will you do?"

"That's the sixty-four-dollar question isn't it? All I can say is, I wish I knew."

As the day passed, Alicia made some decisions, at least for the short term. She completed the arrangements for Bill's funeral, which was to be held on Thursday. Then she called Beth and told her that she'd be moving back into Barry's house the next day.

I heard only Alicia's side of the conversation, but Beth seemed to take the news pretty well. Apparently she'd had hopes of making enough money handling to buy the house, but obviously that hadn't happened yet. In the meantime, the place still belonged to Alicia, and there wasn't much Beth could do about any decisions that were made.

Davey decided that he enjoyed sleeping on the floor so much that it more than made up for not having his own room. He was sorry to see Alicia and the Labrador Retrievers go, and he offered to come along and help with the moving. I've had Davey's help before. It doesn't always hasten a job along. Instead, I called Joey Brickman's mom and arranged for him to go to their house after camp, freeing up most of the next day.

As Alicia hadn't been at Bill's long enough to unpack, our stop in Patterson the next morning was a short one. Between my station wagon and her Toyota, which she'd left in the barn, we managed to fit almost everything of hers into one car or the other. As I carried out the last load, Alicia lingered upstairs in the master bedroom.

Outside, Biff and Tucker were waiting patiently on the backseat of her car, doors open on either side so they'd stay cool. Upon our arrival, the two Labs had leapt from the car excitedly, racing around the familiar yard and waiting for Bill to appear. Now, an hour later, they seemed resigned to his absence.

While I waited for Alicia to come out, I wandered over to the vegetable garden Bill had planted near the barn. The area was small, but obviously well tended. Plants were lined up in meticulous rows, and I didn't see a bug or a weed anywhere. The tomatoes were large and heavy, vines sagging beneath their weight.

Sometimes it's the little, unexpected details that blindside you and make you see the injustice of life. For Alicia, it had been fresh-squeezed orange juice. For me, it was vines filled with plump, red tomatoes and the two Labrador Retrievers waiting patiently for the return of a master they'd never see again.

A door slammed behind me, and I turned as Alicia walked over and looked into the garden. "Bill would hate the thought of all his hard work going to waste," she said. "Come on, let's take them with us."

She went into the barn and emerged a moment later with a pair of burlap sacks. Twenty minutes later, we'd picked every tomato in the garden. When we were done, I felt a little better. It wasn't much, but it was something.

From Patterson, it was only a short drive to Poughkeepsie. When we pulled in and parked, Beth stuck her head out of the kennel and waved, then went back to what she was doing. Alicia got out of her car and went into the house. That left me standing in the driveway between the two buildings and feeling very much like a fifth wheel.

I sauntered over to the kennel and opened the door. Beth was sitting at Barry's desk, doing paperwork. A shaft of sunlight poured through the window behind her, adding to the heat in the already stuffy room. She glanced up but didn't stop writing.

"Alicia and I have some stuff to unload," I said. "Do you feel like helping?"

Beth's hand stilled. "I guess."

"It's not much. With three of us working, it shouldn't take very long."

She pushed back her chair and stood. When we walked outside, Alicia hadn't yet returned.

"I thought you said there were going to be three of us," Beth said, looking at the cars. There was no mistaking the edge to her tone.

I opened the back door of the Camry and Biff and Tucker came spilling out. "There will be. Just give her a minute."

"What about the dogs? House or kennel?"

"I don't know." Biff was sniffing the bushes by the side of the driveway. Tucker was eyeing a loose Beagle down the block. I hooked my fingers through his collar before he got any ideas. "Why don't we put them in the kennel for now? Is there room?"

"If that's a joke, I'm not laughing." Beth got Biff and led the way back into the building.

"I wasn't trying to be funny. I guess your numbers are down?"

"Almost nonexistent. At the moment I have three clients' dogs and four local boarders. Thank God it's summer, or we'd be just about empty. I've spent the last week calling around, trying to line up an assistant's job somewhere else, but so far it's not happening."

We walked through the office and out the other door into a cool, dark room filled with crates and pens. Most weren't in use. At the end of the row was a large double pen.

"How about here?" Beth said. "Then they can be together." We released both Labs into the pen and she closed and locked the gate behind them.

"What are your chances of lining up any more clients?" I asked as we walked back outside.

Beth shook her head. "At this point, I'm pretty much out of business. If Alicia were charging me the rent this place is worth, I would have had to move out already. Even a couple of small clients wouldn't be enough. What I need is some really serious exhibitors, the kind who finish three or four dogs a year and always have new puppies coming along."

"Like the Pullmans?" I asked, remembering the Chow puppy of theirs Crawford had been showing at Elm City.

"They'd do great." Beth frowned, glancing in the direction of the house. "Not that there's any chance of them coming back here. Too bad."

I opened the back of the Volvo and hauled out a box. "So Barry handled other dogs for the Pullmans before Leo?"

"Sure." Beth reached for a box as well. "We had a bunch. Ron and Barry got along pretty well. Ron always thought of himself as Mr. Important Client, and Barry always treated him that way, so the relationship worked."

We grinned at each other and walked up to the house. Alicia had left the front door unlocked. I used a rock to prop the screen door open, then carried my box just inside the living room and left it. Beth followed suit. There was still no sign of Alicia. I wondered where she'd gone off to.

"Does Ron finish a lot of dogs?" I asked as Beth and I walked back out.

"Tons. He likes going for all those top breeder awards, so if he isn't going to show a puppy, lots of times he sells it to people who will. Back when he and Barry were getting along, he'd send us new clients with puppies of his all the time. It was great for business. In the last couple of years, we finished Chows for Alison Chu, Robert Sturgess, and Austin Beamish."

"Austin?" I repeated, surprised to hear his name. "What was he doing with one of Ron Pullman's Chows?"

Beth shrugged. We'd come to the car and she reached inside to pull out another box. "Austin's the type of guy who buys a lot of dogs. I seem to remember something about Viv recommending this one to him. It wasn't a great one, but Barry finished it pretty easily."

"Sorry about that!" Alicia strode out the open door and down the walk. "Bathroom break."

"That's okay." I pulled out a box that didn't feel too heavy and handed it to her. "There's still plenty to do."

With all us working together, it didn't take long to finish unloading the two cars. Beth and Alicia barely spoke to each other. I gathered neither was pleased with the way things had turned out. Not that I could blame them.

Alicia had thought she'd be living with Bill in comfort and security. Beth had thought she was gaining her independence. In Alicia's short absence, she'd moved her things out of the kennel and into the house. Now they would have to reestablish who was in charge. I doubted the process would be easy or comfortable.

When we'd finished getting everything out of the cars, Alicia offered to fix lunch. Beth's expression set stormily. Even if I hadn't had to get back for Davey, that was enough to make me decline. The sooner I got out of their way, the sooner these two could start working things out.

Alicia walked me to the door and gave me a quick hug. "Thanks for everything," she said. "I don't know what I would have done without you."

"It was no problem. You have my number. Call if you need anything else."

"I will. And, Melanie?"

I paused on the step.

"You will be coming to Bill's funeral, won't you?"

Until that moment, I hadn't thought about it.

"It's in Patterson on Thursday afternoon," Alicia said when I didn't answer right away. "I'd really like it if you'd come."

"Okay." I made a mental note to make arrangements for Davey. "In the meantime—"

"I know." Alicia smiled. "I'll be careful."

"Seriously. Think about what's happened. I'm glad Beth's going to be here with you. Until the police figure out what's going on, you're better off not going anywhere alone."

Her expression turned sober. "I have been thinking about it. And I know now that I was wrong to tell you that I didn't need to know who killed Barry. I must have been crazy to think I could just put it behind me and go on."

Her tone was earnest, her expression imploring. I've seen Basset Hound puppies that were easier to resist. "You will help me, won't you?"

I didn't answer out loud, but I did nod. Then I got in the car and kicked myself all the way home.

∞* *Twenty-three* *∞

The large number of people at Bill's funeral was testament to how popular a member of the dog show community he'd been. It also helped that the event took place mid-week. Holding it on a weekend would have cut down on attendance dramatically.

I left Davey at Joey Brickman's house and drove to Patterson with Aunt Peg. Since neither of us had called ahead for directions, we got lost twice on the way to the church. Luckily, Aunt Peg drives so fast that we still managed to arrive in plenty of time. We sat in the back for the service, then joined the procession of cars to the cemetery.

Dressed in a black suit whose long jacket bulged a bit with her pregnancy, Alicia looked like she was holding up well. As the minister intoned a few more words, she stood at the grave site, flanked on either side by people I didn't recognize. Presumably they were members of Bill's family.

Looking around the rest of the assemblage, I saw plenty

of familiar faces. Crawford and Terry were there, as were Viv and Ron Pullman. Austin Beamish was standing with a group of judges and exhibitors. Midas's handler, Tom Rossi, was there as well.

Beth Wycowski had come, and brought Ralphie Otterbach with her. He looked uncomfortable in a brown cotton suit and had already unfastened the top two buttons of his shirt. He shuffled his feet restlessly as the minister spoke.

Also nearby, Bertie Kennedy was composed and dry-eyed. I wasn't sure how well she'd known Bill Devane, but I knew she had to realize that this was a good place to be seen. She was standing amid a group of women that also included Christine Franken.

"Big turnout," I said under my breath to Aunt Peg.

"Bill was very well liked. I'm glad to see he's being sent off in style."

I looked around and sighed. When I'd started trying to figure out who'd killed Barry Turk, the field seemed wide open. The man had so many enemies that nearly everyone seemed eager to be rid of him. Bill Devane, on the other hand, had apparently been enormously popular. His murder did nothing but confuse me. The two deaths had to have been connected. But how?

When the service at the grave site was finished, we drove back to the house in Patterson, where a buffet lunch had been set out to feed the gathering. As soon as we arrived, I went to look for Alicia. I found her in the kitchen. She'd kicked off her heels and was walking around in stocking feet.

"Anything I can do to help?"

"No thanks. So many people have offered, I barely have to lift a finger."

Despite her words, Alicia's cheeks were pale and sadness haunted her eyes. Lifting a finger looked to be about the most she might manage.

"You're sure you're okay?"

"Okay?" She laughed softly. "I'm not even close to okay." She gazed slowly around the room. "Bill and I spent more time here than in any other room in the house. He loved to cook and I loved to eat. In some ways, we made a good pair."

Alicia brushed a hand past her eyes. "Why don't you go out and mingle? Let me sit in the kitchen and have a good cry. That's what funerals are for, aren't they?"

The door swung open behind me and Christine Franken stuck her head in. "Need any help?"

"Everything's under control," I said, exiting through the door and taking Christine with me. "Alicia just wants a few minutes to herself."

Together we walked back into the crowded living room. Christine headed to a table along one wall where a bar had been set up, and I followed along behind.

"Wine?" she asked, going straight to a bottle of Chablis. "Sure."

She poured us each a glass and took a long swallow from hers. "What a shame this is," she said. "Bill was such a decent guy. You don't see a lot of that in the dog show world."

I sipped my wine more slowly. "If that's the way you feel, then why do you do it?"

"I like the dogs. I like the winning. I don't have to like the people." Christine gazed past me, her eyes narrowing.

As she lifted her glass to her lips once more, I turned to see who she'd been looking at. Austin was standing by the fireplace, talking to Crawford and Terry.

"Austin was the big client that Barry cost you, wasn't he?"

"Right-o." Christine reached for the bottle and poured herself a refill. "I couldn't see it at the time, but he wasn't a great loss."

"Maybe now that Barry's gone, you can start handling for other people again."

"Like Austin?" Christine grinned mirthlessly. "I don't think so. Trust me, that ship has already sailed. Whatever I thought we had going ended the day he dumped me for Vivian DuCoyne."

Aunt Peg had introduced me to scores of people at dog shows in the last year. I wondered if she'd been one of them. "I don't think I know her."

"You probably do, just not under that name. She's Viv Pullman now. But back then, she and Ron weren't married yet."

"And she was involved with Austin?"

"No. Viv and Ron were already engaged at the time, and she wasn't interested. That didn't stop Austin, though. His ego is so large, he figured he could win Viv away. The jerk. So he ended up with nobody, which is just what he deserved."

Her voice had risen. Several heads turned in our direction.

Christine lifted a hand to fan her throat. "Is it hot in here, or is it me?"

Even with the windows open, the press of bodies in the room had raised the temperature, and Christine was suddenly looking very much like she could use some fresh air. "It's a little warm," I agreed. "Why don't we go outside?"

"Good idea."

The yard behind the house was large and shady. The grass was freshly mowed and the smell of clippings hung in the air. A wooden bench sat beside an empty bird feeder. Christine sank down onto it and closed her eyes.

"Ahh," she said. "Much better."

I left her there and went back inside to check on Alicia. Several women were standing in the kitchen, but she was not among them. Picking up a platter to deliver to the buffet table, I walked through to the living room and spotted Alicia chatting with Viv Pullman.

All right, so I'm nosy. If I hadn't had that platter in my hands, I'd have been over there like a shot. Unfortunately, just as I was putting the food down, Aunt Peg grabbed me.

"There you are, I've been looking all over. Have you seen this?" She held up a copy of *Dog Scene* magazine.

"No. Why?"

"It's next week's issue. Hot off the presses. It goes in the mail this afternoon."

Out of the corner of my eye, I was keeping tabs on Viv and Alicia. "So?"

"There's an obituary in here for Bill Devane. Of course, it's very complimentary. And the picture they used is ten years old at least. I don't know who the editors think they're fooling. Melanie, would you please look at me when I'm talking to you?"

My gaze swung back around. "What?"

"Dear girl, what are you looking at?"

"Viv and Alicia," I whispered. "Over there. What do you suppose they're talking about?"

"Maybe this." Peg held up the magazine and shook it. "That's what I've been trying to show you."

"Bill's obituary?"

"No, here. On the gossip page. There's an item alluding to Ron and Alicia's affair. It doesn't mention any names, but it's clear as day who they're referring to. Listen to the ending. *'Revenge is a powerful motivator. And when it comes gift-wrapped in southern-fried charm, watch out.'"*

"Good Lord." I snatched the paper from her hands. "Let me see that."

"I thought you might be interested," Peg said smugly as I skimmed through the column.

The piece was short but eye-catching. As Peg had said, the writer hadn't named names. Even so, the majority of the dog showing fraternity would have no trouble figuring out who he was talking about. And Viv came off looking like the woman scorned.

"None of this is true," I said, outraged. "They've made it sound as though Alicia stole Ron away from Viv."

"It doesn't have to be true. That's why it's running on the gossip page. Besides, Alicia did steal Ron away, at least for a little while."

"And killing Bill was Viv's revenge? That's crazy. Viv's a smart woman. She would have to know she was much better off with Bill alive than dead. He would have taken care of Alicia. Now she has no one."

"No one but the father of her baby," said Peg.

As one, we turned to look. While we'd been reading the magazine, Viv had disappeared. Now Alicia was talking to Bertie.

"You said this was next week's issue," I said. "Where did you get it?"

"Terry had it. He was the one who showed me the item. I don't know where it came from before that."

The crowd in the room was beginning to thin. I didn't see Terry or Crawford among the guests that remained. Still holding the magazine, I hurried out the front door. A line of cars had been parked along the length of the driveway. Crawford and Terry were heading toward a gold Lexus near the road. I ran to catch up.

"Wait!"

Both men turned and paused.

"The item about Viv," I said to Terry, breathing hard. "The one you showed Aunt Peg. Who planted it?"

Terry cocked his hip and braced a hand on it. "Now, how would I know that?"

I glanced over at Crawford. He smiled slightly. "You give me too much credit, Melanie. I don't know everything."

"You could find out," I said.

"Maybe." Crawford shrugged and continued walking. "If I wanted to."

"Terry?"

"Don't get me in trouble, hon."

"Please?"

"Deliver me from whining women." Terry took the magazine from me. "Thank God I'm not straight."

"Please, Terry?"

"Oh, all right," he whispered. "I'll see what I can do."

I spent the next day waiting to hear from Terry. When he didn't call, I didn't dare get in touch with him. Already

I was presuming on his goodwill. Applying more pressure certainly wasn't going to help my case any.

When the phone finally did ring the next evening, it was Aunt Peg. "I need a favor," she said. "Are you coming to the Danbury dog show tomorrow?"

"Possibly," I said, hedging. Sam was working. He had a rush project he had to finish, so Davey and I were free. Knowing Aunt Peg, however, I wanted to hear more before committing myself. "What's up?"

"Douglas is going to be there, it's his first dog show since mid-July. You know how distracted I get when I'm showing a dog. I was hoping you could keep an eye on him and make sure he enjoys himself."

All things considered, that didn't sound like too hard an assignment. Besides, going to the show would give me a chance to talk to a few people.

"Do you know if Crawford will be showing Leo?"

"I imagine so, the dog's entered every weekend. Why?"

"Now that Bill's gone, I'm curious to know what Ron plans to do next. Maybe I'll find a chance to pull him aside and ask him."

"Not tomorrow, you won't. He mentioned yesterday that he was going away over the weekend. Viv's staying home to hold down the fort, but I wouldn't expect to see her at the show either."

Too bad, I thought. But I could still use the opportunity to try and pin down Terry.

"Here's an idea," said Peg. "Why don't you bring Faith along so I can see how her hair is coming?"

Checking up on me, that's what she was doing. This was Aunt Peg's subtle way of making sure that I didn't slack off on Faith's coat care. I glanced down at my watch and considered the possibility of factoring bath and blow-drying time into the evening's activities. It would be a tight squeeze. Then again, I was the one who'd been feeling guilty every time Davey and I went off to a show and left the Standard Poodle behind. This idea might end up working out to suit all of us.

"All right," I said. "We'll see you there."

The Danbury dog show was held outdoors in a large, lovely field at the base of a small mountain. The rings were well laid out, and there was plenty of space set aside for parking, even for spectators like Davey and myself, who didn't arrive until mid-morning. Since I'd brought along my portable grooming table for Faith to sit on, I pulled over to the handlers' tent and unloaded. Standard Poodles were scheduled for noon, but most were already out on their tables being worked on.

"It's about time!" Peg said as we approached. "I was beginning to think you weren't coming."

"Mom slept late," Davey confided. "You can yell at her."

In the eyes of my son the early riser, anything after six A.M. was considered late.

"Never mind. What matters is that you're here now. Go park the car then make yourself useful. Douglas said something about Scottish Deerhounds and went off wandering. Maybe you can find him."

"Will do." I hopped Faith up onto her table. Wagging her tail happily, she touched noses with Tory as I opened Davey's chair and placed his bag of toys in the seat. "Are you staying here or coming with me?"

"Faith and I are staying with Aunt Peg." Davey was

eyeing Peg's tack box hungrily. At least I'd managed to get oatmeal into him for breakfast.

I parked the Volvo, then headed over to the main tent with its double row of parallel rings. Scottish Deerhounds are one of the largest breeds of dogs. Though there weren't many entered, I could pick them out from across the field. Douglas was standing in the shade beneath the tent. Catalogue in hand, he was concentrating so intently on the proceedings in the ring that he didn't even notice my approach. Aunt Peg might make a dog fancier out of him yet.

"See anything you like?" I asked.

"Oh, Melanie, hello." Douglas leaned down and kissed my cheek. "Look at these dogs. They're magnificent, aren't they?"

"They're certainly big." Several feet away a Deerhound stood awaiting its turn in the ring. Its back was higher than my waist, and I was sure it outweighed me.

"Big? Of course they're big. They were bred in the Scottish Highlands to hunt wild stags. They needed to be that size to get the job done. Did you know this breed has been around since the Middle Ages? They've served for centuries as guards and companions of the Scottish lairds."

"You're very well informed. Is this a new interest?"

"I've been studying up a bit." Douglas smiled sheepishly. "I guess it shows."

"You know more than I do."

"No, I don't. But I hate feeling ignorant about something. I knew that if I were going to enjoy myself at dog shows, I needed to understand where all these different breeds came from, and why they developed the way they did. I bought several books and I've started reading."

I stared at him incredulously. "You mean you know that much about every breed?"

"Heavens, no." Douglas looked startled by the thought. "I'm just beginning my education, after all. I started with the breeds that looked interesting. To me that means the big ones, the ones that have been useful in some capacity. Once you understand how these dogs came to look the way they do, it's really quite fascinating. The Rhodesian Ridgebacks will be along shortly. Did you know they were originally bred to hunt *lions?*"

"No," I said, grinning. His enthusiasm was infectious. Sometimes I get so caught up in the small world of Poodles that I tend to forget about all the other great breeds there are. It was nice to be reminded once in a while that there were other things in the world beside topknots, bracelets, and big hair.

"You think I'm silly," said Douglas.

"No," I said quickly. "I think you're charming. And I hope my aunt is making half as much effort to learn about your interests."

"We're working on it. Peg doesn't take to compromise easily."

"You've noticed, have you?"

We laughed together, then watched the rest of the hound breeds. Douglas kept up a running commentary on the breeds he'd read about. It was a refreshing change from the usual ringside chatter, heavy on fact and history, and totally unconcerned with current fads and who was beating whom.

Toy breeds were being judged two rings down. When

Maltese were called to ringside, I kept an eye out for Terry and Crawford. It didn't take long for them to appear.

"Would you excuse me for a minute?" I said to Douglas. "There's someone I need to talk to."

"By all means," he said, eyes still trained on the action in the ring. Just like an old hand, I thought happily.

"Isn't that nice?" Terry said, seeing my smile as I approached. "A happy person. At a dog show, no less. I think you may be an oxymoron."

"You're too young to be such a cynic."

"But getting older by the minute. Here, spread this towel for me, would you?"

He handed me a thick terry-cloth rectangle in a wicked shade of neon green. The words *Bedford Kennels* were stitched along one end in script. In the ring, Crawford was showing his class dog. Terry had the Maltese special in his arms.

I spread the towel out on the ground beside the barrier and he carefully set the Maltese down upon it. The tiny dog was immaculate, its coat ice-white and silky smooth. Two small black bows held up the hair above its eyes. Terry took out a brush and fussed needlessly.

"About that item in *Dog Scene*," I said. "Did you have any luck finding out where it came from?"

Terry shrugged as he knelt down beside his tiny charge. "The whole point of that gossip page is that it's anonymous. If people had to own up to what they were saying, there wouldn't be anything to print."

"What they said about Viv wasn't true."

"It didn't have to be. In fact, even though you read it that way, the item didn't even have to be about Viv. It never mentioned her name."

I stared down at him. "You're not going to tell me, are you?"

"I would if I could, hon. Honest. I tried, but all I got was a dead end. I called the editor. Pat's a friend, if you know what I mean. I thought he'd help out. Instead, he gave me some nonsense about editorial policy."

Terry shook his head sadly. "I want you to know I've lent that man my best pumps, and his feet were much bigger than he said they were. Ask me if those shoes will ever be the same."

Sarcasm was desperately called for. I told myself that Terry was trying his best, and I held my tongue.

"So I asked Pat, then who sets the policy? And he said, that would be the owners." Terry rolled his eyes. "Pat can be a little dense when he wants to be. So I tried again. And who would they be, I asked?"

I glanced in the ring. Crawford's entry had just gone Reserve, and he was heading in our direction. "And?"

"And he said the owners of *Dog Scene* were Greyhound Publishing and Austin Beamish."

❧❖ *Twenty-four* ❖❧

Austin Beamish?

Funny, I thought, the way his name kept popping up.

"Thanks, Terry," I said distractedly.

"Don't mention it, hon."

Lost in thought, I wandered back to Aunt Peg's setup. Faith was lying contentedly on the table where I'd left her. Davey was coloring in his fire truck coloring book. Peg was putting up Tory's topknot.

"Where's Douglas?" she asked.

"Douglas?" I'd forgotten all about him.

"Melanie, what on earth is the matter with you?"

"I'm thinking."

Peg frowned. "Well, apparently it doesn't suit you."

"Did you know that Austin Beamish is one of the owners of *Dog Scene* magazine?"

"No." Peg picked up a slender knitting needle and deftly parted Tory's long topknot hair. "I'd imagine that a man with his money has lots of investments. Does it matter?"

"I don't know. It just seems like every time I turn around, somebody else mentions Austin's name. Did you know that he bought a Chow from Ron Pullman and had Barry Turk finish it for him?"

"No, but Austin's had all sorts of dogs. Was it a good one?"

"Not according to Beth. He bought the dog because Viv recommended it to him."

"Odd," Peg muttered, mouth filled with rubber bands.

Belatedly I was beginning to realize that much of the time Austin's name came up, Viv's did too.

"Christine Franken told me that Austin dumped her because he was interested in Viv," I said.

"Viv's married."

"She was only engaged when they met."

"That must have been several years ago."

"It was. But Bertie says that Austin's a very persistent man."

Aunt Peg laid down her comb and stared at me. "What are you trying to say?"

"I don't know exactly. But I remember a comment you made a couple of weeks ago about Austin and Ron. You said that for two men who didn't like each other, they certainly seemed to spend a lot of time together. Maybe we were missing the point. I always thought Viv was trying to keep those two apart. Maybe it was she who unwittingly brought them together."

Aunt Peg considered that for a moment. "You could be right," she allowed finally. "But that still doesn't explain who shot Barry Turk."

"Austin did."

"Why?"

I'd been afraid she'd ask that.

Peg reached out, took my hand, and placed it under Tory's chin to hold her head steady. While I thought, she finished putting in the topknot.

"All right, listen to this. Austin wants Viv. Viv wants Ron."

"End of story."

"No," I said, shaking my head. "Because although Ron wants Viv, he also wants Alicia. And now she's pregnant with his baby."

"Which everyone thinks is Barry's."

"Maybe not everyone. Maybe Austin knew differently."

"How?"

I sighed windily. "I'm not a mind reader. Just go with me on this, okay?"

"All right, keep talking." Topknot done, Peg removed my hand and set it aside just like the rest of her equipment. She popped the rubber band holding Tory's ear wrap and unbound the long hair within.

I perched on the edge of Faith's grooming table, nestled her head in my lap, and continued to think aloud. "Austin wants Viv to leave Ron and come to him. She's not interested. For a while there's nothing he can do about that but pine from afar. Then Ron screws up big-time and Austin sees his chance."

"So he kills Barry to force Alicia to turn to Ron for support," said Aunt Peg, finally getting into the spirit of things.

"Except she doesn't. She turns to Bill instead. Austin hasn't counted on the fact that Bill is happy to take her back. Bill doesn't even care that the baby isn't his."

"So he has to kill Bill too." Peg didn't look entirely convinced. "So what about the item in the gossip column? What was the point of that?"

"Let me think," I said. There had to be a way to fit it into my theory.

"You're making this up as you go along!"

"Well . . . yes. But you can't say it doesn't make sense."

"Maybe to someone with a very warped mind."

"Can you imagine a murderer who doesn't have a warped mind?"

Aunt Peg finished unwrapping Tory's ears. She stood the Standard Poodle up on the grooming table and began to scissor. I kept working on trying to make sense of things.

"Do you remember when I told you about those accidents Alicia kept having?" I asked.

"Vaguely. There was a broken step, wasn't there? And a car that didn't run? I remember that it didn't seem like much at the time."

"There was also a small fire. And you're right, it wasn't much. Not enough to seriously injure someone, but maybe just enough to really scare them. Especially a woman who was alone and pregnant."

"You think Austin engineered those things to force Alicia out of that house?"

"Possibly. And maybe he planted the item in *Dog Scene* to make Viv look bad."

"But—"

I held up a hand and didn't let her interrupt. "Ron has now become Alicia's only means of support. If nobody knew about the situation, the three of them could have worked things out quietly, leaving the Pullmans' marriage to go on the same as before. But once everything's out in the open, it practically forces Ron to choose. Will he go to the mother of his child, or suffer the embarrassment of staying with a woman who's rumored to be a murderer?"

"I don't know," Peg said, frowning. "It all sounds quite Machiavellian to me."

It did to me too, but that didn't mean there wasn't some truth to it. Things were finally beginning to fall into place. I was sure I was on the right track. "I need to talk to Viv."

"The Pullmans aren't here today," said Peg. "I told you that before."

"Here we are," said Douglas, striding back to the setup. "And in plenty of time too. I know how hard you've been working, so I brought you a snack."

Peg eyed the plate of fresh vegetables he held as if she were afraid one of the carrots might leap up and bite her.

"She doesn't have time to eat right now." I took the plate and set it on Tory's crate. I couldn't imagine how he'd managed to find carrots, celery, and broccoli at a dog show. Maybe he'd brought the vegetables from home. "The Poodle judging starts in fifteen minutes and she still has to spray up."

"Later, then," Douglas said easily. "What can I do to help?"

"How would you feel about watching Davey for a little while?"

"Young Davey?" Douglas's face lit up. "I'm quite good with children."

Peg gave me a suspicious look. "Where are you going?"

"I told you, I want to talk to Viv. From here, I can get to Katonah in less than half an hour."

"You'll miss the Poodle judging."

"You can tell me what happened later." I stood Faith up and she danced on the tabletop, eager to be included. "By the way, have you seen Austin today?"

Peg shook her head.

"Nor have I," Douglas mentioned.

"That's odd," said Aunt Peg. "He's almost always around somewhere when Midas is being shown. Do you want to leave Faith in Tory's crate?"

I glanced at the Standard Poodle. She was wagging her tail happily. "No, I'll take her with me. Viv won't mind."

Crawford gave me directions to the Pullmans' house and told me I couldn't miss it. When I got there, I saw what he meant. The entrance to Pullman Manor—Lord, what a name—was marked by a pair of lantern-topped gateposts at the end of a long driveway. The house was a large white colonial, deliberately ostentatious, with a row of wide columns supporting an overly ornate portico.

The driveway forked as it reached the house. One branch led around the back, where there appeared to be several outbuildings, including a kennel. The other branch of the driveway formed a circular turnaround in front of the door. I pulled up to the house and parked.

It was too hot to leave Faith in the car. I held the door open and she leapt out joyously. We walked up the front steps together. The doorbell had a deep melodic tone that seemed to echo through the house. Nobody answered the first ring, so I tried it again, then waited another minute.

"What do you think?" I asked Faith. "Nobody home?"

The Poodle cocked her head to one side. She was looking at a window on one end of the wide porch. I wondered if she'd seen something there. Because it was easier than getting in the car and driving back to the show, I rang the bell again. This time the door opened.

Viv was casually dressed in a pair of tight white jeans and a chambray shirt with tails unbuttoned and knotted at her waist. She didn't seem surprised to see me standing on her front step. Perhaps it was she Faith had seen in the window.

"Hi," I said. "Sorry to stop by without calling first. Do you mind if I come in?" I don't usually chatter on, but Viv's tight expression compelled me to fill the silence.

She held the door partway shut and stood, blocking the small opening. "It's not a good time."

"I think we need to talk."

Something that almost looked like panic flickered in her eyes. "Not now."

Viv started to close the door. I braced my palm against the solid panel and pushed back, catching her by surprise. Apparently nothing in her southern upbringing had prepared her for rude guests who didn't know how to take no for an answer.

"Are you okay?"

Her gaze skittered away, up, down, and sideways. She didn't answer.

"Are you alone?"

Beside me, Faith stiffened. Her feet tightened and arched. Whatever was wrong, the Poodle sensed it too. Hairs on the back of my neck prickled. Suddenly I wanted to be anywhere but there.

"Why don't we go for a drive?" I suggested. My voice came out sounding high and unnaturally bright. "My car's right here. Come on."

Abruptly the door drew back. Austin appeared in the opening, standing just behind Viv. "That won't be possible," he said. "Viv's busy right now."

Though he was smiling, Faith growled softly. The sound rumbled deep in her throat. I agreed with her assessment. Whatever was happening here, I didn't want any part of it.

The only problem was neither, apparently, did Viv. She looked at me imploringly. I thought of Ann Leeds, who'd hoped to find safety in numbers but had been disappointed by the women she'd turned to for support. Now Viv was turning to me. I probably should have stopped to consider, but I didn't. I shoved the door aside and walked inside the house. Faith, like the well-behaved Poodle she was, trotted at my heels.

"I suppose there's time for a short visit," Austin said, frowning. "Perhaps your Poodle would rather wait outside."

"I can't leave her out there," I said. "She'll run away." I was lying, but I figured he wouldn't know that. After all, his own dog hadn't even recognized him.

"Really?" Austin glanced at Faith dismissively. "I thought they were supposed to be smarter than that. I've never had a Poodle myself. I couldn't stand the thought of dressing a dog up in that silly hairdo."

He held out his hand, fingers extended, for Faith to sniff. She did so briefly, then turned her head away. No doubt she was sensing the same undercurrents I was.

"Viv?" I asked. "Are you all right?"

"Of course she's all right," said Austin. "I'm here, aren't I?"

In my mind, that was precisely the problem. "Maybe she could tell me so herself."

"I'm fine," said Viv. "Everything's fine. Really."

She didn't look like she believed that any more than I did.

"I thought you'd be at the show today, Austin. Isn't Tom Rossi showing Midas?"

"He'll win whether I'm there or not. He always does. Today I had something more important to do." Austin glanced in Viv's direction. Pointedly, she looked away.

"Really, what was that?"

"Viv and I had a few things we needed to settle. You're the first to know. She and Ron are splitting up." He paused, looking at me shrewdly. "Or perhaps you'd already guessed."

For a moment I was so startled by his announcement that I couldn't think of a thing to say. Austin mistook my silence for denial. "Oh, come, Melanie," he chided. "I know you've been asking questions about me."

No I hadn't, more's the pity. What I'd been doing was asking questions about Barry Turk's murder. And Bill Devane's.

"That must have been a recent decision." I glanced over at Viv. Her eyes were wide with fear. She looked like an animal who'd been caught in a trap and was contemplating gnawing off its own foot.

"It isn't . . . I mean I'm not . . ." She stumbled over the words. Austin reached out a hand and Viv shrank back as though the thought of his touch repelled her. Her voice lowered to a whisper. "Melanie, it was him. He's the one who did it."

"There, there," Austin said soothingly. "You're just overwrought. Once I get you away from here, everything will be fine, you'll see." He turned and looked at me calmly. "You'll have to excuse Viv. She seems to be a little confused."

"I am not!" Her voice was louder and edged with emotion. "He's the one who's crazy. He killed Bill and Barry. Ask him, he'll tell you!"

One look at Austin's face, and I realized that any questions I might have posed would have been superfluous. It was one thing to suspect, quite another to confront the truth head-on. Worse still, in that instant of recognition that passed between us, he knew that I knew. I felt my stomach plummet.

Before I could react, Austin quickly moved to block the door. "I'm afraid this changes things," he said quietly.

Faith pressed herself against my legs. Her tail was down, her ears flattened against her head. I knew exactly how she felt. Now what?

Austin stared at me as though he was wondering the same thing. Clearly I hadn't been part of his agenda. We were even then, because finding myself in this predicament certainly hadn't been part of mine.

Behind his back, Viv began to edge her way across the hall toward an arched doorway that led into an expansive living room. Maybe she had a plan, I thought hopefully. Maybe I could help by providing a distraction.

"You've wanted Viv for a long time, haven't you?" I asked.

Austin didn't answer, but he did incline his head

slightly, inviting me to continue. I tried out the same theory that I'd run past Aunt Peg.

"Viv didn't want you. She wanted Ron."

"That was her mistake. But I knew she'd come to see that she was wrong. Ron was bound to slip up sooner or later."

"And then he did. With Alicia." I saw the pained expression that crossed Viv's face, but kept talking anyway. "He had an affair with her and she got pregnant."

"He didn't deserve Viv. What sort of fool goes out for hamburger when he has steak at home?"

"You thought Viv would leave Ron then, but Alicia let everyone believe that Barry was the baby's father, and there was no way for Viv to know otherwise."

"Of course there was a way!" Austin snapped. "I told her what had happened. She didn't believe me."

Oh, yes, she had. Either that or she'd had suspicions of her own, because she'd yanked Leo out of Turk's kennel and sent him to Crawford, hoping to remove Ron from the path of temptation.

I glanced at Viv. By now she was nearly into the living room. Austin started to turn too. "You wanted Viv," I said loudly. "Ron was the one in your way. Why didn't you kill him? Why go after Barry Turk?"

"That was obvious. Turk was inconsequential, a nobody. Besides, there was no way anyone would connect his death to me. Turk had so many enemies, the police had more suspects than they could count." His voice was chillingly calm. For all the concern he showed, we might have been discussing the weather.

Anger, white and hot, seared through me "What about Bill Devane? Was he a nobody too?"

"You probably won't believe me," said Austin, "but I didn't mean for that to happen. I went to his house to try and reason with him. To convince him that it wasn't in his best interests to take Alicia back. But he wouldn't listen me. He said he knew what he was doing."

Viv slipped around the corner and disappeared.

"But your plan wouldn't work unless Alicia went to Ron. You hadn't succeeded in breaking up the Pullmans' marriage, but you were pretty sure that she could."

"I knew she could," said Austin. "Viv is rather charmingly old-fashioned. There was no way she was going to tolerate another woman in her marriage, especially not one carrying her husband's bastard. All I had to do was push Alicia to the breaking point, then let her do the same to Viv."

"*All* you had to do . . . ?" My voice rose and Faith tensed beside me.

Suddenly Viv reappeared in the doorway. Her arms were extended in front of her, her hands clasped tightly around the grip of a small silver handgun. One finger hovered near the trigger as she pointed the weapon at Austin.

"Now, Viv," Austin said gently. "This is not good."

"Oh, stuff it, Austin." Viv's tone was tough, but her hands trembled. "It's over. Whatever you thought you were up to here, it's not going to happen."

I looked back and forth between them. A gun? That was Viv's bright idea? Any more improvements like this, and I'd probably see my life flash before my eyes.

Austin took a step toward Viv.

She took a corresponding step back. "Don't come any closer, Austin. I mean it. I know how to use this."

"Of course you do." Austin extended a hand. Viv glanced at it warily. "But that doesn't mean you will, does it?"

Before he'd even finished speaking, Austin was already bounding toward her. Viv's retreat a moment earlier had told him all he needed to know. She might fire the gun, but she wouldn't do so without hesitation; and he intended to force the issue before she could react.

For that single crucial second, Viv froze. Austin grabbed her hands and wrested the pistol away. "That's better," he said. "Now I need to think."

"Take your time," I muttered unhappily. As if things hadn't been bad enough. Austin had already killed twice. Anyone should have been able to figure out that arming him was not the way to go.

I reached down and threaded my fingers through banded hair in Faith's topknot, tugging on it hard enough to get her attention. I'd never yanked on her hair before, and she looked up at me reproachfully. I hadn't the slightest idea if Faith would protect me. I certainly hoped she wouldn't need to. But I wanted her to be ready, just in case.

Austin hadn't given her presence a second thought. His dogs were commodities, not friends and companions. It probably hadn't occurred to him that Faith would help me if she could. Though he kept the gun trained on me, he hadn't even glanced at her. As far as he was concerned, she was only a Poodle in a silly hairdo. Maybe we could surprise him.

"It will have to look like an accident," he said after a moment. "Everyone knows you've been snooping around. You came over here and tried to break in. Already nervous because of what happened to Bill and Barry, Viv shot you by mistake."

She gasped sharply.

"Viv won't go with you," I said. Beneath my hand, Faith began to quiver.

"Yes, she will," Austin said with the confidence of a man who is used to getting what he wants. "She'll come to understand that this was how it had to be." He gestured with the gun. "Go through there, down that hall. We'll do it in the kitchen, near the back door."

I glanced where he'd indicated. The hall was narrow and unlit. At its entrance stood a marble pedestal that displayed a bronze statue of two Chows playing. Dog art. Many fanciers' homes were filled with it.

"Come on," Austin said impatiently. "Viv, you go first. Then Melanie."

Viv had that dazed look on her face again. Her brief rebellion quelled, she didn't question Austin's instructions. She began to walk, and when he motioned with the gun again, I followed. There wasn't time to think or analyze. There wasn't even time to pray. When I hung back, Austin fell in right behind me.

Reaching the pedestal, I swept the bronze off the top. It was heavier than I'd expected and felt powerful in my hand. A welcome rush of adrenaline made me believe I might even be able to pull this off. I spun around, swinging the statue in front of me like a weapon.

I'd hoped to hit his arm, but Austin saw me coming and jumped back. Instead, the bronze slammed into the barrel of the pistol and sent it flying. The gun skittered across the Italian tile floor. Immediately Austin went after it. I went after him.

He was quicker than me and a step ahead. I'd have never reached him in time, but as it turned out, I didn't have to. Faith flew past me and launched herself into the air. Austin was off balance, reaching for the pistol when all forty-five pounds of her hit him in the back. He grunted and went down heavily.

Before he could recover, the gun was in my hands.

Austin rolled over and looked up. Standing above him, Faith showed him all her teeth. Clean, white, and strong, with a perfect scissors bite.

"What the hell?" he muttered, hand going to his head.

Faith growled menacingly. Who cared if it was all for show? It looked pretty good to me.

"The Poodle with the silly hairdo sends her regards," I said.

❧✲ *Twenty-five* ✲❧

I held the gun on Austin while Viv called the police. After that she went out to the garage, came back with a coil of rope, and trussed him expertly. There was a look of grim satisfaction on her face when she was done.

"How long have you known?" I asked.

"That Austin thought he was in love with me, for years. I figured if I didn't give him any encouragement, he'd eventually give up. He isn't, you know. In love with me, I mean. He hardly even knows me. He's just obsessed with something he can't have."

I nodded. "When did you figure out about Barry and Bill?"

"Too late obviously." Viv sighed. "When Barry died, I never even suspected. I guess that was the plan, wasn't it? But then Bill was dead too, and that piece came out in *Dog Scene*. I knew that was Austin's magazine, and I also knew how much he likes to control things."

She spared him a withering glance. "That item wouldn't have appeared without his approval. That's what made me begin to wonder. Even so, until he showed up here today, I didn't really believe it. He told me he loved me. How can you kill somebody in the name of love?"

I didn't have an answer for that, and Austin, who might have, wasn't saying anything.

As soon as Viv's hands were free, I gave her back the gun. It was the first time I'd ever held one, and I couldn't wait to get rid of it.

The local police responded quickly to Viv's call. I imagine that's one of the perks of living in a place called Pullman Manor. We explained the situation in detail. The two officers didn't look entirely convinced by our version of events, but they did agree to take Austin in and hold him until their superiors could speak with their counterparts in Poughkeepsie and Patterson. I knew that Austin would have access to the best lawyers money could buy. I could only hope that with Viv and me filling in some missing pieces, the police would be able to build a strong enough case.

I left Viv speaking on the phone to Ron and drove back to the dog show to pick up Davey. I was hoping to slip in and out, but Aunt Peg was having none of that. Terry and Crawford came over and listened while I explained what had happened.

The recital was quick and concise. I skimmed over most of the unpleasant parts, and punched up Faith's role in my rescue. My audience nodded in satisfaction; there wasn't a Poodle doubter in the group.

Crawford asked a number of questions, and Peg had some of her own. Terry, however, was strangely silent.

When he finally spoke, he was more upset than I'd ever seen him.

"It was all my fault," he said.

"What do you mean?" Crawford asked sharply.

"I was the one who told Austin that Ron was the father of Alicia's baby. I didn't know that it mattered. It was at the end of June, we were at the Staten Island show. He asked and I told him."

I thought of the weeks it had taken me to pry that information out of Alicia. "How did you know?"

"Alicia'd been at the show the day before, and she wasn't feeling well. They call it morning sickness, but she was green all day. We were sitting around waiting for groups to start, and not much was going on, so I offered to do her hair. I thought it might cheer her up, you know?"

I nodded. Terry's credo: When in doubt, do hair.

"So of course we got to talking. I can't put my hands on somebody's head without opening my mouth. Kidding around, I said, 'Hon, you'd better hope that baby doesn't have Barry's nose.' Alicia just laughed and laughed, then said, 'Believe me, there's no chance of that.' It wasn't as though I couldn't figure out what that meant. I have eyes, don't I?"

Terry paused, looking stricken. "But I never knew that Austin . . ."

"None of us knew," I said firmly. Crawford and Aunt Peg nodded their agreement. "If he hadn't found out from you, I'm sure there'd have been another way."

The Non-Sporting group was announced over the loud-speaker and Crawford and Terry went to get Leo. I thanked Douglas for taking care of Davey and packed up my son's toys. On our way out of the tent, we passed Beth and Ralphie, loading up their van to go home. Even though I knew she'd want to know who killed Barry, I wasn't up to explaining again. Besides, I was sure she'd read about it in *Dog Scene* soon enough.

"Good show?" I asked automatically.

Beth shrugged. "Is there such a thing?"

"It's no way to make a living," Ralphie said. He loaded in the last crate and slammed the side door shut. "At least she's finally beginning to figure that out."

I reached around him, opened the door, and closed it again. It slid smoothly in its tracks. Ralphie looked at me and grinned. "Damn thing used to stick all the time until Beth told me about it. Am I good, or what?"

"You're good, Ralphie."

When we got home, I fixed Davey his dinner and let him eat it in front of the TV while I went into the kitchen and called Alicia. By the time I got her, she'd already heard the news. Amazingly Viv had called to offer some sort of an apology. Shortly after that, the police had been by to ask some questions. It was looking as though there would be enough physical evidence at the scene of Bill's murder to link Austin's car to the crime.

Alicia also mentioned that when Bill's will was read, she'd been named the sole beneficiary. She'd inherited the small farm they'd lived in together and was planning to stay there at least until after the baby was born. Beth was still interested in buying Barry's kennel, probably for boarding rather than showing. She and Alicia were working out the details.

Davey and I ate tomatoes until we never wanted to see another one, then donated the rest of Bill's bumper crop to a local soup kitchen. I was sure he'd have been pleased to know they went to a good cause.

The following week, Sam stopped by Aunt Peg's and picked up his new puppy. Tar was freshly bathed and clipped and looked like a woolly black lamb in his puppy trim. Sam and Peg are already talking about the shows next spring that he'll be eligible for.

School starts in a couple of weeks, and in the meantime we have custody of a guinea pig. Davey has a birthday coming up next month, and Faith's still growing hair. It's pretty much business as usual except that Aunt Peg's taken to wearing a Mets T-shirt and throwing around terms like RBIs and earned run average.

"Will wonders never cease?" I asked her.

"Not if I can help it," Peg said, grinning.

I'm taking that as a promise.

Please turn the page for
an exciting sneak peek of
Laurien Berenson's newest
Melanie Travis mystery
WATCHDOG
now on sale wherever
hardcover mysteries are sold!

Never lend money to relatives. It isn't one of the Ten Commandments, but it ought to be.

So when my brother, Frank, came to me with his hand out, I didn't have to think twice about what to say. I turned him down flat. Unfortunately, with Frank it's never that easy.

"Trust me, Mel," he said. "It's the opportunity of a lifetime."

The opportunity of *his* lifetime, maybe. Mine? I doubted it.

For more than a quarter century, ever since he was old enough to walk and talk, I'd watched my little brother maneuver himself into and out of tight spots. He was bright, charming, and impetuous. What he'd never been was practical.

That was my job apparently. I was the diligent big sister who, more often than not, had to stay behind and pick up the pieces when Frank dropped whatever he was doing and went barreling on to his next grand scheme.

"At least let me tell you what it's about," he said. "You can't turn me down without giving me a fair shot."

"Sure I can. Watch me. N-O."

"I'm not listening." Frank raised his hands and put them over his ears. "I can't hear you." With a maturity level like that, you can see why he would come to me rather than going to a bank.

I glared at him for a moment, but the effort was half-hearted. It was 8:30 on a weekday morning. In the normal way of things, I wouldn't have expected my brother to be out of bed yet, much less across town and standing in my kitchen. He must have really thought this was important.

"You've got ten minutes," I told him. "No more. Davey's bus already picked him up and I was just on my way out the door. You're not making me late for school."

Davey was my son, six years old and filled with all the joy and wonder and mischief of his age. In short he was a great kid, at least in his mother's eyes. He'd started first grade a month earlier and was delighted to be riding to school on the bus.

The year before, we'd commuted to Hunting Ridge Elementary together. I'd been employed there for the last six years as a special education teacher. Over the summer, however, I'd taken a new job at Howard Academy, a private school near downtown Greenwich. Four weeks into the school year, I was still trying to make a good impression.

"Relax." Frank glanced at the clock over the sink. "You've got plenty of time."

My brother is an expert at relaxing, probably because he gets so much practice. I was tempted to drum my fingers on the countertop.

People meeting us for the first time often comment that we look alike. Though we have many of the same features—straight brown hair, hazel eyes, and the strong jawline often associated with stubbornness—I've never been able to see the similarity. Maybe I don't want to see it.

While I waited for Frank to get to the point, I walked to the back door and looked out. The small yard behind the house was enclosed, and Faith, Davey's and my Standard Poodle, was having a last bit of exercise before I left for the day. When I opened the door, she raced across the short distance between us and bounded up the steps.

"That is one strange looking animal," Frank said as Faith came sliding into the kitchen, did a quick turn on the linoleum floor, then jumped up and waved her front paws in the air waiting for the biscuit she knew I'd be holding.

I flipped the peanut butter tidbit into the air and watched Faith catch it on the fly. "Nine minutes. You know, most people hoping to borrow money from me wouldn't start by insulting my dog."

"With that hairdo? The comment wasn't an insult, it was a statement of fact."

All right, so Faith's appearance was a little odd. It wasn't my fault. At least, not entirely. She'd been a present from my Aunt Peg, a devoted Standard Poodle breeder whose Cedar Crest Kennel has produced a number of top winning Poodles over the years. Like her ancestors before her, Faith was a show dog.

Accordingly, her hair was being maintained in the continental clip, a modern descendant of an old German hunting trim, and one of only two clips adult Poodles were allowed to wear in the ring. Faith's dense black coat was long and scissored into a rounded shape on the front half of her body. At the same time, most of her hindquarter had been clipped down to the skin. There were pompons over each of her hip bones and just above her feet on all four legs. A bigger pompon wagged at the end of her tail.

Because the topknot on her head was nearly a foot long and needed to be kept out of the way when she wasn't in the ring, I'd sectioned the hair into a series of ponytails, which were held in place by brightly colored rubber bands. The long, thick fringe on her ears was protected by matching plastic wraps, which were doubled under and banded in place.

Standards are the biggest of the three varieties of Poodles. Faith is twenty-four inches at the shoulder, which means that she and Davey stand nearly eye to eye. Maybe that explains why they get along so well; or maybe it was just that kids and Standard Poodles are a great combination.

Faith also has wonderfully expressive dark brown eyes. Sometimes I could swear she knows exactly what I'm thinking. Like now, as she gazed at Frank with her head tipped to one side. No doubt she was wondering what he was doing there and why I hadn't left for school yet. I reached down and gave her chin a scratch.

"Fine by me," I said to Frank. "You want to discuss the dog's trim, it's your eight minutes."

"Nine," he said, probably hoping to impress me with his counting skills. "I've still got nine."

I waved a hand. It wasn't worth arguing.

Frank waited until I was still, then made his grand announcement. "I'm starting up my own business, Mel. This is your chance to get in on the ground floor."

Probably just where I'd remain, too.

"What kind of business are you going into?"

It wasn't an idle question. In the half decade since college, my brother has held a variety of jobs—everything from bartender to sales clerk to general handyman. If he had chosen a career path, I had yet to see the signs.

"I'm opening up a coffee bar. You know how popular they are. Everyone's looking for a neighborhood hangout, and I've managed to secure a great location."

From the sound of things, Frank was going to need every minute of the time I allotted him. I went back to the table and sat down. Faith hopped up and draped her front legs across my lap, then angled her head upward so her muzzle rested just below my shoulder.

As she settled in, I could feel the creases being pressed across the front of my skirt. Luckily I buy most of my clothes at Eddie Bauer and L.L. Bean, so they can take a few knocks. I burrowed my fingers through the Poodle's thick coat and rubbed behind her ear.

"Where is it?"

"Right here in north Stamford. Remember Haney's General Store out on Old Long Ridge Road?"

I nodded, picturing a small clapboard building with a wide porch and room for four or five cars to park out front. In the early fifties when the farms and open acreage of north Stamford were being developed into affordable housing to accommodate the post-war family boom, Mr. Haney had opened his small general store. It served as a convenience for harried mothers who hadn't wanted to run all the way into town for a carton of eggs or a bottle of milk. In those days, he'd done a thriving business.

But as the city of Stamford continued to grow by leaps and bounds, supermarkets and strip malls had sprung up within easy reach of almost every shopper. Mr. Haney grew older and the wares that he stocked weren't replenished nearly as often. It had been at least two years since I'd been to his store, and even then the building had begun to look run-down.

Signs covering the front windows advertising the weekly specials couldn't disguise the fact that the glass needed a good cleaning. The red paint on the front door had faded to a musty pink. To top it off, the gallon of milk I'd purchased had been sour. I hadn't been back since.

"Is he still in business?" I asked.

"Not anymore. That's what I'm trying to tell you. As of last month, Mr. Haney retired and moved to Florida. I'm the new owner."

"Owner?" That got my attention. "Frank, how could you afford to buy a building?"

"Maybe partial proprietor is a better term. I don't exactly own the place."

No surprise there.

"I have a long-term lease, and I'm doing renovations. Haney's General Store is going to become Grounds For Appeal. By Christmas we'll be ready for the grand opening."

"Grounds For Appeal?" I frowned. "It sounds like a cut rate law office."

"That's not set in stone yet," Frank said quickly. "I'm still working out some of the details. You could help. Like I said, things are just beginning to get moving. Now would be the perfect time for you to invest."

"Why?"

"Why?" The question seemed to puzzle him. "Well, to be perfectly honest, because I could use some cash."

As if I couldn't have guessed. "Actually, Frank, I was wondering why you think this would be a good idea for me."

"Because once the coffee bar gets up and running, I'm going to be making a ton of money. What kind of a brother would I be if I didn't offer my only sister to have the chance to get in on it?"

"Solvent?" I ventured. I checked my watch. If I wasn't out the door in five minutes max, I was going to miss the first bell. "Look, I don't really have time to discuss this right now. And as you know perfectly well, I don't have any extra money. At least not the kind you're looking for."

"You've got Bob."

Bob was my ex-husband and Davey's father. After a four-year absence from our lives, he'd shown up unexpectedly in the spring looking to get reacquainted with his son. At the same time, he'd reinstated the child support payments he was supposed to have been making all along.

Thanks to his contributions, Davey and I were a good deal better off than we had been. We'd been able to have the house painted and take a modest vacation over the summer. We were not, however, in any position to be looking for investments.

"Bob went home to Texas, Frank. He has a new wife there."

"He also has an oil well."

"That's his money, not mine."

"You could ask him for some."

"I could," I said, nudging Faith off my lap so I could stand. "But I'm not going to. Whatever you've gotten yourself into this time, you're just going to have to take care of it without my help."

"Okay, if that's the way you want to be. Most people would jump at the chance to get into a deal with Marcus Rattigan, but if you're not interested, I guess that's your business."

I was halfway to the door but I stopped and turned. "Marcus Rattigan? What do you have to do with him?"

"He's the guy who bought the building. Didn't I mention that?"

He knew perfectly well he hadn't.

Marcus Rattigan was a local entrepreneur whose influence in the construction and development business was well documented in Fairfield County. Over the last decade more than a dozen apartment complexes had sprung up in surrounding towns, their signs sporting the familiar blue and gold logo of his Anaconda Properties.

Rattigan was known for buying up tracts of land, then bending local zoning laws to the breaking point in order to accommodate the greatest possible housing density. He supplied my newspaper with a steady stream of front page stories, and town officials in most municipalities kept a wary eye on the proceedings while fervently wishing him elsewhere.

"Marcus Rattigan bought Haney's General Store? Why would he be interested in a little place like that?"

"Dunno," said Frank. "But he snapped the place up when Haney sold out. The way things have grown up in north Stamford, the store is surrounded by houses now. It's a nonconforming property in a two-acre zone. He can't build on the lot or enlarge the building that's there. I guess that's why he was happy to let me have the lease."

"He knows you're planning to turn the place into a coffee bar?"

"Sure he knows. I certainly couldn't do it without his approval. He and I are partners on the deal."

"Partners. You and Marcus Rattigan?" It was all a little much to take in.

"Sure. Fifty-fifty. He supplied the building. I supply the know-how."

Interesting. As far as I knew, my brother didn't have any know-how.

"He even co-signed my loan at the bank."

"He did?"

"Yup. Happy to do it, he said. Seeing as we were going to be partners and all."

I stared at Frank suspiciously. "If you have a bank loan, what do you need me for?"

"As it happens, I'm running a little low on funds. You know how it is with construction. Estimates never seem to cover the final cost. In the beginning—"

"The beginning? How long ago did you get involved in this project?"

"It's been about six weeks."

"And I'm just hearing about it now?"

Frank shot me a look. As siblings went, we weren't close. Though he only lived one town away, we'd never spent much time together. Our temperaments were just too dissimilar for us to really enjoy each other's company. In fact, now that I thought about it, bad news was much more apt to bring us together than good.

"It seemed like the right time," said Frank. "You know, with the opportunity for you and all. It's not like I need the moon. I figure five thousand should do it."

"Five thousand *dollars?*" I'd always suspected he was daft. Now I knew. There was no way I had that kind of money lying around, and if I did, I certainly wouldn't have trusted Frank with it. "Where on earth would you think I'd get five thousand dollars?"

"All right, so you don't ask Bob. You've been living in this house for what, eight, nine years? You must have some equity—"

"No." I cut him off swiftly. "This is Davey's and my home. I'm not going to risk losing it when you decide to go off and tilt at another windmill. You said Rattigan's your partner. Why don't you go to him?"

"I can't. No way. Marcus put me in charge and I told him I could handle it. How would it look if the first time there was a problem I went running back to him?"

Not great. Even I had to admit that. "Look, Frank, I'm sorry. I just don't have the kind of money you need."

My brother took one last meaningful look around the room, but didn't argue. Instead he pushed back his chair and stood. "Okay, I figured I'd ask. It was worth a shot."

I picked up my jacket and pulled it on. "What will you do now?"

"I don't know. I'll have to think about it." After a moment his expression brightened. "You're not the only family I have, you know. Maybe I'll talk to Aunt Peg."

That would go over well, I thought, but didn't voice the opinion aloud. As things turned out, I should have given him the money. It would have been easier than his next request.

Two weeks passed without another word from Frank. To tell the truth, I'd pretty much forgotten about his latest venture. My brother's not above bailing out when times get tough. For all I knew, he might have gone back to reading the want ads.

Between the new job, taking care of Davey, and a dog show for Faith coming up on the weekend, there was plenty to keep me busy. I had twenty students from a variety of grades in the tutoring program, so my schedule was full. Just to keep things interesting, it also varied from day to day.

On Wednesdays I got out of school around the same time Davey did, so I swung by Hunting Ridge on my way home and picked him up. When I reached the elementary school, the buses were loading. Davey was waiting for me at the curb near the front door. His best friend, Joey Brickman, was with him.

The two of them were swinging their backpacks and shoving each other playfully. Any minute they were bound to fall off the curb and into traffic. I'm a mother, so that's the way my mind works.

I slid the Volvo into an empty spot and tooted the horn lightly. Davey looked up and waved when he saw me. Both boys shouldered their packs and scrambled in my direction. Joey was pug nosed, freckle faced, and built like a linebacker-to-be. When he threw himself into the backseat, the car shuddered from the impact.

Davey was smaller and more slightly built, but what he lacked in heft, he made up for in speed. He moved with his father's grace, and also had the same heavily lashed, chocolate brown eyes. Today they wore a serious expression as he climbed into the car and shut the door.

"Seat belts," I said, although the boys hardly needed a reminder. They were already reaching around to get the straps in place before I'd even put the car in gear. "Everything okay? You two have a good day at school?"

"It was awesome!" cried Joey. "I lost a tooth. Wanna see?"

I looked in the rearview mirror, thinking he'd show me the tooth. Instead Joey was angling his head upward, mouth agape, pudgy finger pointing at an empty space.

"Pretty impressive. Aren't you a little young to be losing teeth?"

"That's what the teacher said," Joey said proudly. "I'm the first in the whole class."

I glanced back at Davey, who had yet to say a word. "How about you, champ? How was your day?"

"Fine."

"Just fine? That's all?"

"It isn't fair." Davey pushed out his lower lip in a pout. "I wiggled all my teeth and none of them are even loose. I want the tooth fairy to come to our house, too."

"It's so cool!" said Joey. "She's going to take my tooth and leave me money instead."

Davey crossed his arms over his chest and stared out the car window.

"Don't worry," I said. "Your turn will come."

"But I want my turn now."

That's my boy. He has many wonderful attributes, but patience isn't one of them.

I switched on my blinker and turned up our road. Our house is a small, snug Cape; one of many that all look pretty much the same in a neighborhood that was built in the fifties. The homes have small yards, mature plantings, and streets that are quiet enough for children to ride their bikes. Considering the price of real estate in Fairfield County, I could have done a lot worse.

Joey's family lives at the end of the street. His father's a lawyer in Greenwich and his mother stays home with his two-year-old sister, Carly. Alice Brickman and I have been friends since the boys were small.

I pulled into the driveway, and Davey and Joey spilled out of the car. Faith, whose internal clock is more accurate than my Timex, was waiting just inside the front door. I could hear her excited yips as I fit the key to the lock. When the door swung open, she was dancing on her hind legs to greet us.

Problems forgotten, Davey gathered Faith into his arms and gave her a hug. His face disappeared into the thick ruff of her mane coat. Standing upright, the Poodle was taller than he was. Hopping together, they managed an awkward dance of greeting around the front hall.

"Sheesh," said Joey. "She's only a dog."

"She is not." Davey shook his head, and Faith's ear wraps flapped around him. "She's the best dog in the whole world."

Joey was not impressed. "Big deal. What have you got to eat?"

The three of them headed for the kitchen. Davey knew how to unlock the back door and let Faith out into the fenced yard. The milk, glasses, and shortbread cookies were on shelves low enough for them to reach. Confident that they could fend for themselves, at least for a few minutes, I headed upstairs to change my clothes.

A few weeks earlier, at Aunt Peg's suggestion, I'd started roadworking Faith. It's not easy being beautiful, even if you're a dog, and especially if you're a Standard Poodle whose grandfather won the group at Westminster and whose breeder has plans for you to finish your championship. Sixty years old and more autocratic than ever, Aunt Peg has a way of always getting what she wants. Certainly I've never figured out how to turn her down. Which was why Faith and I were now running two miles around the neighborhood several times a week.

The steady, rhythmic jog was developing Faith's muscle and building up her hindquarter. As a nice bonus, it had also knocked a couple of pounds off of me. So far, my biggest problem had been finding the time to fit jogging into my schedule.

Luckily, Alice seems to think that having two six-year-old boys entertain each other is easier than having one at home by himself, and she'd volunteered to watch Davey while I ran. As soon as I was suited up in sweatpants, T-shirt, and trusty sneakers, I walked both boys down to her house and dropped them off.

Though I've heard of something called a runner's high, I had yet to experience it. For me, jogging was hard work. Not so Faith, who completed the entire distance with head up and tail wagging. I guess that's the difference between four legs and two. We stopped and picked up

Davey on the way back, then walked the length of the street to cool down.

Davey was chattering on about a new board game Joey had just gotten, and I was thinking of a nice hot shower, when we let ourselves in the door. My answering machine is on the kitchen counter, and its message light was blinking. I pressed the button, then picked up Faith's bowl and refilled it with fresh water while I waited for the tape to rewind.

"Mel!" Frank's voice sounded tinny, but I could hear the urgency in his tone. "I'm at the coffee bar. You know, Haney's old place? Where the hell are you? I need you to get over here right away."

The Amanda Hazard Series
By Connie Feddersen